Dancing in the Rain

SHELLEY HRDLITSCHKA

ORCA BOOK PUBLISHERS

Library and Archives Canada Cataloguing in Publication

Hrdlitschka, Shelley, 1956–, author
Dancing in the rain / Shelley Hrdlitschka.

Issued in print and electronic formats.
ISBN 978-1-4598-1065-5 (paperback).—ISBN 978-1-4598-1066-2 (pdf).—
ISBN 978-1-4598-1067-9 (epub)

I. Title.
PS8565.R44D36 2016   jC813'.54   C2016-900463-5
                    C2016-900464-3

First published in the United States, 2016
Library of Congress Control Number: 2016933652

Summary: In this novel for teens, sixteen-year-old Brenna tries to make sense of her life after her beloved adoptive mother dies.

Orca Book Publishers is dedicated to preserving the environment and has printed this book on Forest Stewardship Council® certified paper.

Orca Book Publishers gratefully acknowledges the support for its publishing programs provided by the following agencies: the Government of Canada through the Canada Book Fund and the Canada Council for the Arts, and the Province of British Columbia through the BC Arts Council and the Book Publishing Tax Credit.

Cover images by Dreamstime.com and iStock.com
Design by Teresa Bubela
Author photo by Leslie Thomas

ORCA BOOK PUBLISHERS
www.orcabook.com

Printed and bound in Canada.

19 18 17 16 • 4 3 2 1

For Sharon Brain
Playmate
Theater date
Mentor
Beloved friend

one

I only miss you when I'm breathing.

(JASON DERULO, "BREATHING")

Brenna tugs a wad of tissue from her pocket and passes a couple of pieces to her father. She takes some for herself and hands the rest to her sister, Naysa, who sits in the pew to her left. Someone behind her honks noisily into his own hanky, and sniffles come from every corner of the chapel. With each new sob she hears, it gets harder to keep from giving in to the flood of her own tears, but she knows that once she starts crying it will be impossible to stop. She slumps forward, fighting the urge to bolt, and allows her father to rub circles on her back. His hand is large and warm through her jacket.

Reverend Justin Reid, a minister her mom had connected with shortly before she died, reads the poem that she chose for her own memorial service.

Do not stand at my grave and weep.
I am not there; I do not sleep.
I am a thousand winds that blow,
I am the diamond glint upon the snow,
I am the sunlight on ripened grain.
You feel me as gentle morning rain.

When you awaken in the morning's hush
I am the sweet uplifting rush
Of quiet birds in circled flight.
I am the soft stars that shine at night.
Do not stand at my grave and cry:
I am not there; I did not die.

Brenna frowns. *I did not die?* What is that supposed to mean? Her mother is dead. *Dead!* She liked the poem until he got to that line.

A poster-sized photo of her mom rests on a tripod beside the minister's podium. Brenna studies her face, that incredibly alive face. The picture was taken before her mother got sick. In it she is still beautiful. Her blue eyes gaze back at Brenna, eyes that lots of people think Brenna has inherited. Eyes that were always warm, always kind. Until the last few months, that is, when they were filled with pain or glazed over from the numbing drugs.

The minister takes two tapered candles from a shelf in the back of the podium and steps over to a chalice, where a lone candle flickers. He looks over at the sisters. "Brenna and Naysa, please join me."

Brenna grips Naysa's hand, and they take the few steps over to the chalice. The minister passes a candle to each girl. "Joanna has left two daughters behind," he says to the gathered people. "They will look to you, their community, to draw strength." He looks down at the girls. "You may light your candles now," he says quietly.

They each touch the end of their candle to the burning one. Brenna notices the tremble in Naysa's hand. She uses her own free hand to blot a tear she feels meandering down her cheek.

The minister reads from the pages in his hand. *"In our time of grief, we light a flame of sharing, the flame of ongoing life. In this time when we search for understanding and serenity in the face of loss, we light this as a sign of our quest for truth, meaning and community."*

Following the minister's quietly spoken instructions, the girls place their candles on either side of the one that was there and return to their pew. Brenna's father moves so that she can scoot past, so one daughter sits on each side of him. He opens his arms and draws them close. The sniffling around the chapel increases in volume. Brenna finally gives in to the tears and sobs openly.

"We will now listen to Johann Pachelbel's Canon in D, selected by Joanna herself," the minister says. "Following the music, Joanna's husband, Brett, will give the eulogy, and then anyone who would like to is welcome to come up to the sanctuary and light one of these for Joanna." He holds up a tray of small tapered candles. "Once it's lit, stand it in here," he says, lightly touching the side of a wide bowl filled with sand. "Then, if you wish, you may share a memory of Joanna."

With a shuddering sigh, Brenna slouches down and rubs her eyes. It feels like the service will never end, but she allows the music to wash over her, and her mind begins to drift. She has had months to prepare herself for this day—they all knew her mother was dying—but there is something about being gathered together like this, all the family, all of Joanna's friends, with all their combined pain, that makes it even more overwhelming. She knows the service is supposed to bring her comfort, bring some meaning to her mother's death, some closure, but if anything, the pain she's feeling now is even worse than in those last few agonizing hours before her mother died.

The music ends, and her father slips out of the pew to approach the podium. He pulls folded sheets of paper from his jacket pocket, smooths them out and puts on his reading glasses. He takes a long, deep breath but then removes his glasses and wipes his eyes with the back of his sleeve.

"Take your time, Brett," the minister says.

After a few more deep breaths, Brenna's dad begins to read from his notes. Brenna doesn't need to listen—she helped him write the eulogy. He seems to pull himself together as he reads, finding strength in the summary of his wife's life, but when he gets to the part where Brenna came into their lives, his voice quavers again. His eyes look up from his notes and meet her gaze.

"Brenna, you were truly a gift from heaven," he says, blinking back tears. "Every single day since you came into our lives, your mom thanked the young woman who trusted us to raise you as our own." He glances at the minister, who smiles gently.

Brenna nods at her father and blinks away her own tears. She's surprised that he mentioned her adoption. Not that it's a secret, but it isn't something they refer to very often, especially in public. She's been told that this minister was also involved in her adoption, though the details around that were never explained to her.

"And you, Naysa," their father continues. "You were a miracle, which is exactly what your name means. We were told that it was unlikely we'd be able to conceive children, and then along you came. That was one amazing day for us when you were born."

Brenna reaches for her sister's hand and gives it a squeeze.

Her dad returns to the scripted eulogy, but Brenna's mind wanders again, his words echoing in her brain... *the young woman who trusted us to raise you as our own.* In a sense, she thinks, she still has a mother out there, a woman she hasn't seen in almost sixteen years. She wonders how that woman would feel if she knew that the mother she had chosen especially for her baby had died before her daughter's sixteenth birthday. She doubts that was part of the plan.

When her dad finishes, he takes his place again between his daughters. Then, one by one, a dozen or more people line up at the front of the chapel, light candles and begin to share stories. Many are poignant. Just as many are funny, and tears are punctuated with laughter. The line of people seems to grow longer rather than shorter, and the light from the flickering candles gets brighter as more and more are added to the bowl. There's a sense of desperation, as if they can somehow keep her alive as long as they are sharing the moments of her life.

"Joanna hired me when I first moved to Canada," a male voice says. The Australian accent is familiar.

Brenna looks up from the tissue she is slowly shredding and makes eye contact with the young man at the podium. She knows him. He works on Grouse Mountain, where her mother had worked and where she herself now volunteers.

"She never forgot my name," he continues. He's still looking at Brenna. "Whenever I ran into her, she always took the time to ask how I was. She was so kind. I'll never forget her."

He nods at Brenna and returns to his pew. Brenna returns to shredding the tissue, but her mood feels marginally lighter. Her mom really was kind, and even a cool guy like Ryan saw that. He said he'd never forget her. It helps.

Eventually the line dwindles, and when there are no more people to share stories, the minister returns to the chalice that holds the three tall candles. He steadies a candle snuffer over the center flame and looks out at the gathered people. "We extinguish this flame to mark Joanna's physical death," he says, snuffing out only the center candle.

Brenna crumples in the pew.

"Yet the memories of her special character and gifts remain in our lives, as we can see by the glow of candles that continue to burn. Her beautiful spirit is indomitable," he continues, his voice deep and gravelly. "As long as we keep her in our hearts and in our thoughts, she lives on.

"Amen."

Brenna accepts another hug and excuses herself from the stranger. The reception is agonizing. Everyone feels they have to seek her out, offer their condolences and then after an awkward silence, melt away into the crowd or over to the food table. She looks around for Naysa, wondering if she's faring any better. She sees her pressed up to their father's side, his arm wrapped protectively around her. Brenna takes the opportunity to slip out of the room and back into the chapel. With a sigh of relief she slumps into a pew and closes her burning eyes.

A moment later she hears the door to the chapel creak open and feels the pew groan slightly as someone sits at the far end. She opens her eyes and sees the minister there.

"I hope I'm not disturbing you," he says.

"No." She shakes her head. "It just got to be a bit much in there."

"I can imagine."

They sit in comfortable silence for a while. Then the minister clears his throat. "Obviously, you don't remember, but I was at your birth."

"You were?" Brenna regards the man, taking in his kind eyes, his long narrow face. "I knew you had something to do with my adoption…"

"Your birth mom, Kia, was a friend. Back then I ran a church youth group, and Kia was in the group. I wasn't a minister yet."

Brenna nods, encouraging him to continue.

"I haven't seen your parents since the day they took you home, but I was deeply honored that they tracked me down and asked me to officiate at her memorial service. I guess they learned from Kia some time ago that I had gone into the ministry."

Brenna is not surprised. Her family doesn't attend a church, and it would be like Joanna to find someone she had a connection with to preside at her service. A stranger wouldn't do.

"I've often wondered about you, Brenna. I held you the moment you were born, and nothing in my life has ever come close to being as amazing as that. Witnessing life's first breath? Well" —he wipes his eyes—"I'm getting seriously choked up just thinking about it."

Brenna can only stare at him as he pulls himself together. After a moment he smiles at her. "I'm so glad I've had this chance to meet you again, even if it is under such sad circumstances." He takes a business card out of his pocket and hands it to her before stepping out of the pew and into the aisle. "I'll leave you in peace," he says, "but please feel free to call me if you need anything. I'm a good listener."

The door to the chapel creaks open and shut again. Brenna glances at the minister's business card and then looks into the eyes of her mom, whose picture still sits at the front of the room. "Thank you," she whispers.

When one person is missing, the whole world seems empty.

(PAT SCHWIEBERT, *TEAR SOUP:*
A RECIPE FOR HEALING AFTER LOSS)

Someone flicks the overhead lights to get everyone's attention. All heads turn to look toward the kitchen doorway, where Naysa is holding a birthday cake with sixteen burning candles.

"*Happy birthday to you,*" sings Brenna's father. "*Happy birthday to you.*" The whole family joins in. "*Happy birthday, dear Brenna, happy birthday to you.*"

Naysa sets the cake down on the coffee table. "Make a wish."

Brenna closes her eyes. *Make a wish.* There is only one thing she wishes for now: that her mom hadn't become sick and died.

"No boyfriends?" Grandpa Will asks when the candles have been extinguished.

Brenna shakes her head and attempts to smile, humoring her grandfather.

"Well, maybe no boyfriends, but definitely hundreds of admirers," he says.

Brenna notices that the crinkles that appear around his eyes when he smiles are identical to the ones around her father's eyes. She studies the faces of the other people gathered in their living room. This is her family: her father, her sister, both sets of grandparents, aunts, uncles and seven cousins. In the past they rarely managed to get everyone together to celebrate birthdays, but this summer has been different. In the month since her mother passed away, they've seen a lot of each other.

Half of the family—those on her father's side—are of Asian descent. The other half are Caucasian. Naysa is a blend of both races. Brenna knows that she too has some Asian roots, but she looks more Caucasian than Naysa does.

As she eats her cake she notices other family similarities. Her cousin Danika, and Danika's mom, Brenna's aunt Tamara, have the exact same laugh. Joe and his father, Uncle Brian, both stroke their noses when they're listening. Jillian and Michelle look more like sisters than cousins, right down to the way their hands flutter about when they talk. She wonders if she shares any similarities, any at all, with her family. Certainly not eye color. She is now the only one present with blue eyes. Joanna had been the other one.

When the cake has been taken away, presents and cards are placed on the table in front of her. As she unwraps them, Brenna notices that a lot of thought has been put into each one. Her aunt Laura, her mom's sister, gives her a necklace with an angel charm strung onto it. There is a diamond chip at its heart.

"Her heart sparkles, like your mom's did."

"Thanks. It's really special." Brenna puts it around her neck, and her aunt closes the clasp. Brenna sees her blink back tears as she admires it.

The remaining gifts include candles, books and framed photos. Her grandmother hands her a scrapbook filled with pictures of Joanna, badges she'd earned as a Girl Guide, certificates of achievement from school, copies of scholarship offers she received upon her high school graduation.

"That's for both you and Naysa," her grandmother says. "But I thought this would be a good occasion to give it to you."

Brenna nods at her grandmother, and Naysa slides onto the couch beside Brenna to look at it. Every member of the family is somehow represented on these pages, in photos and sidebar notes. On the second-to-last page is a picture of her mom and dad holding her, a newborn baby, beside another one of them holding newborn Naysa. On the final page is a photo of the entire family, everyone in the room, taken shortly after Joanna received the news of her cancer. She'd rallied everyone together without mentioning why it was so important to get it done promptly. They only figured that out after the fact.

The afternoon drags on, but as hard as everyone tries, it does not feel particularly festive. Joanna's presence is huge in its absence. There are gaps in the chatter as everyone seems to notice, at the same time, that something is missing.

Finally the cousins gather in the family room, and Joe pulls the game of Cranium off the shelf. He quickly divides them into teams, and the game begins. Brenna finds she can't concentrate. Her mind keeps wandering back to the scrapbook. She wishes everyone would leave so she could leaf through it again, absorbing her mother's life.

"Brenna!" Joe barks. She looks up and sees everyone staring at her. "Spell *tarantula* backward."

Slowly, and with long pauses, she begins to spell. "*A...l...u...t...n...a...r...a...t.*"

"You got it!"

As Brenna's teammates move their marker around the board, she sits back and lets her mind wander again. Looking up, she finds Naysa's eyes on her, those sad brown eyes. She's having trouble concentrating on the game too. Brenna gives her a little smile. Naysa nods back. Thank goodness we have each other, Brenna thinks. No one else can really know what it's like.

Earlier in the afternoon Danika had trapped her in the hallway when she stepped out of the bathroom. *How are you doing?* she'd asked.

All Brenna could do was shrug.

Danika had leaned into her. *I've heard that it's the first time for every occasion that's the hardest after a death,* she said.

The first birthday, first Christmas, first Mother's Day and so on. Next year will be easier. She spoke with authority, like she was imparting great wisdom.

Yeah right, Brenna thought. Easy for her to say. Her mother is alive and well.

Brenna had shrugged again and pushed past, leaving Danika standing in the hall.

When the day is over and everyone has finally gone, Brenna retreats to her bedroom with the scrapbook. Sitting on her bed, she flips through the pages slowly, savoring the unfolding story of her mother's life. She pauses at the page with the picture of her parents holding her, a brand-new baby. They are smiling into the camera, and clearly they are happy...but there's something else in their expressions, something Brenna can't quite read.

A soft tap on her door breaks her trance. The door opens and her dad's face appears. "May I come in?" he asks.

Brenna nods, noting once again the dark circles under his eyes. A stab of worry passes through her—what would happen if her dad up and died on them too? She couldn't handle it.

He sits on the end of her bed, and it's then that she notices the wrapped packages in his hands. "I hope your birthday was okay, honey, as good as it could be, anyway."

She nods. "Thanks for the driving lessons. I know they cost a lot."

"You're welcome. They say it's not good for a parent to teach their kid to drive, not good for their relationship."

"You'd be a good teacher," Brenna tells him, "but you can get tested sooner if you take lessons."

He nods. "So I heard."

A silence falls between them, and Brenna wonders what's going through his mind. And what's in the packages? Why didn't he give them to her earlier? When he doesn't say anything, she turns back to the scrapbook. "Dad?"

"Uh-huh?" He looks up, clearly coming out of some deep thought.

"Who took this photo of us?" She hands the scrapbook to him and watches as he studies the picture. He stares at it for so long that Brenna wonders if he's forgotten the question. She asks another one. "Where was the picture taken?"

"In the hospital." There's another long silence before he adds, "In the chapel of the hospital."

"The chapel?"

"Uh-huh. Your birth mom's minister had created an adoption ceremony."

Brenna doesn't comment but watches her father's face as a range of emotion sweeps across it.

"It was a beautiful ceremony. He reflected on what a momentous day it was in our lives and also acknowledged all the feelings in the room."

"What kind of feelings?"

"Well, your birth mom was grieving because of what she had to do—give you up—but your mom and I were overjoyed to be receiving you, yet…" He doesn't finish the sentence.

"Yet?"

"Yet…" He pauses. "Yet our hearts broke for her too. And for her parents, who were also there. It was terribly hard for her to hand you over to us."

Her parents. Brenna's biological grandparents.

Brenna had been given the facts about her birth mom, Kia, and why she felt she had to give her baby up for adoption, but she'd never understood how hard that would have been. She peers into the faces of her parents, their sixteen-years-younger faces. That explains their bittersweet expressions; they were feeling sad for her birth mom.

"So was it my biological father who took the picture?"

Her dad shakes his head, still staring at the photo. "No, your biological father was a teenager who…who wasn't there. Apparently he struggled with your birth mom's decision to go through with the pregnancy."

Brenna doesn't say anything as she absorbs this information. She wonders why she's never asked about him before now. "So who took the picture then?"

"Justin, I guess—or Reverend Reid as he's now known. He was Kia's friend then, before he became a minister, the one who spoke at your mom's service. There were just the eight of us in the chapel," he says, remembering, "including you and Kia's minister. So it must have been Justin."

"Was Justin her boyfriend?"

"No, I don't think so. He was quite a bit older than Kia, and he ran the church youth group."

"He spoke to me after Mom's service and told me he was at my birth."

As Brenna's dad continues to stare at the photo, she remembers something. Climbing off her bed, she goes to her dresser and pulls open the bottom drawer. She slides her hand under the folded T-shirts and pulls out a large, thick envelope. Back on the bed she opens it and shakes out a bunch of greeting cards.

"Why did she quit sending these to me?" Brenna asks her dad, picking one up and reading the inscription on the inside.

Dear Brenna,

Wishing you tons of fun, presents, cake and surprises on your 4th birthday!

I love you so much and think of you every day.

Love, Kia

She rummages through the rest: Valentine's Day, Easter, Christmas and birthday cards. She'd enjoyed receiving them—they made her reflect briefly on the woman she'd never known—but she hadn't thought about it much when they stopped arriving. Until now.

"I don't know why she stopped sending them, honey. Kia would be…hmmm, about thirty-three now. I think the last one came when you were around twelve. Who knows what may have happened. Maybe she's had more children, and it was too hard for her to keep on pining for the one she couldn't keep."

Or maybe she forgot about me, Brenna thinks.

"Anyway," her dad continues, "it's interesting that we're talking about her…"

Brenna meets his gaze. He looks concerned. She cocks her head, waiting.

"I have two more gifts here for you, but…well…"

"What, Dad?"

"They might be a little painful to receive."

"Then don't give them to me." She flops back against her pillows. The day had been challenging enough already, with her mom being so noticeably absent from her birthday party.

"I promised your mom."

That catches Brenna's attention. "Well then, let's get it over with." Her mind is whirling, trying to imagine what her mother may have left behind to be given to her on her sixteenth birthday.

Her dad hands her one of the two packages. She opens the card first. The outside flap says *For My Daughter*. When she turns to the inside, she's startled to see the words *Love, Mom* written in her mother's elegant handwriting below a poem. A folded sheet is tucked inside.

"She signed it before she died," her dad explains. "Obviously."

Brenna unfolds the enclosed letter with trembling hands.

Dear Brenna,

I'm sorry if it feels creepy to receive this letter after I'm gone, but I had always hoped to pass this gift on to you on the occasion of your 16th birthday.

This journal was given to your father and me during your adoption ceremony. Kia (your birth mom) told us that she started writing it when she first discovered she was pregnant. She didn't realize she was writing it for you, but the night before you were born she reread it and thought that you should have it. She felt that by reading it you would understand what she'd been through and why she chose to give you to us.

I always felt you'd be ready for it when you turned 16, the same age your mother was when she conceived you.

We haven't talked about Kia for a long time, but I want you to know that she was a lovely young woman, sensitive and wise. I often see her again when I look at you because you've inherited her beauty, both inner and outer.

The nature vs. nurture debate—which component has the greater influence on a child—has always intrigued me, but of course there is no doubt that it is nature that gave you your physical qualities. However, I'd like to believe that your father and I provided you with an environment in which you could thrive and reach your potential. That is what we promised Kia we would do.

My early death changes everything, of course, but I have had almost 16 years with you and hope you'll always feel that I was the best mother I could be in that time. I have loved you with all my heart. I hope you know that. How I would love to see you finish growing up, and maybe even get to know my grandchildren, but it seems that is not to be.

Happy 16th birthday, my darling daughter, and I hope this journal helps you better understand who your birth mother is. I can now feel satisfied that I have carried out her wishes in delivering it.

Love,

Mom

Brenna looks up from the letter, a lone tear running down her cheek. Slowly, carefully, she unwraps the small book. The cover is rough, made from recycled paper. Seeds and delicate flower petals are pressed into it. She fans through the pages, noticing the neat handwriting. Each piece of paper is unique, as delicate as butterfly wings and flecked with bits of pastel-colored tissue that has bled, creating a mottled effect. She notices an inscription on the front flap.

To my wise friend Kia. Your words deserve special paper. Keep on writing, girl!

Luv ya, Shawna.

Brenna closes the journal but continues holding it between her hands.

"Are you okay, honey?" her dad asks after a few moments.

She nods but continues to sit in silence, staring at the cover of the journal, a numbness spreading through her. Suddenly she opens the top drawer of her night table and slams the book inside. It's too much.

After a moment her father offers her the second gift. She knows before she pulls off the paper what it will be— it's the exact same shape as the other journal.

The cover is beautiful, with a large abstract heart painted on it, much like a child's drawing. A small tile with the word *love* on it is glued into the center of the heart, and other tiles cascade down the side to form the phrase *live with your whole heart*. She opens it to the first page and notices the inscription on the inside cover.

To Brenna,

May you find solace in writing down your thoughts, just as Kia did.

Love you deeply,

Mom

Brenna sinks back on the bed and holds the journal to her chest. The tears stream unchecked down her cheeks. With a final pat on her shoulder, her father gets up and quietly leaves the room.

You said move on; where do I go?

(KATY PERRY, "THINKING OF YOU")

"So, what did you get for your birthday?" Georgialee asks as she rubs sunscreen onto her legs.

The swimming pool in Georgialee's backyard lies aqua blue and undisturbed in front of them. The girls are sprawled out on side-by-side loungers. Bentley, Georgialee's chocolate-brown Labradoodle, rests his heavy head on Brenna's thigh, staring adoringly into her face. She scratches him behind his ears.

"Lots of things. A necklace, some clothes, driving lessons."

Brenna feels Georgialee's glance and remembers that Georgialee's parents had provided lessons for her, not as a gift but as if it was their parental responsibility. Their gifts were always extravagant.

"Anything else?"

"My grandmother put a scrapbook together for me and Naysa."

"A scrapbook?" Georgialee frowns, puzzled.

"It was filled with pictures of my mom and lots of stuff from her life."

"That sounds nice," Georgialee says with a total lack of enthusiasm. It doesn't surprise Brenna. Georgialee always steers the conversation away from talk of Brenna's mom and her death. She seems to think her role as a friend is to distract Brenna from her grief. Brenna decides not to tell her about the journal from her birth mom.

"I sure wish you'd let me throw you a party," Georgialee says. "Pool parties are a blast."

Bentley places a paw on Brenna's leg, reminding her to keep scratching. "Thanks for not throwing one," Brenna says.

"Everyone deserves a sweet-sixteen party."

"I would have hated it." She puts both hands under Bentley's chin and scratches, smiling down at him.

"Brenna," Georgialee says. She waits until Brenna looks at her. "It's been almost two months. You've really got to start moving on."

Brenna holds Georgialee's gaze for a moment, stunned at what she's just heard. Instead of responding, she gently pushes Bentley out of the way, climbs off her lounger and walks over to the edge of the pool. Bentley pads along beside her.

Brenna dives into the pool and floats underwater, the weight of her misery holding her down. She can hear

Bentley's muffled barks growing more and more hysterical before he too plunges into the water and noses her inert body to the surface.

Aug. 17

My mother has been "laid to rest." What does that mean? Is she simply resting? No, she is dead. Dead dead dead. She is not in the sunlight or in the stars. She is not the rain or the wind. She is dead. Gone forever. I will never see her again. And Georgialee thinks I should "move on." Fuck Georgialee.

Brenna rereads her entry and slams the journal shut. She knows she shouldn't have used that language on the first page of a brand-new journal, yet it's exactly what she's feeling, and her mom had hoped she'd *find solace* by writing out her thoughts. Oddly enough, she does feel better.

Sliding open the drawer to return the journal to its place, she notices the letter from her mom, neatly folded in half. It lies on top of Kia's journal. Kia probably didn't mar her journal with swearwords. Well, fuck her too, Brenna thinks, and immediately feels better yet.

She takes out the letter from her mom and rereads it, stopping at the line *How I would love to see you finish growing up, and maybe even get to know my grandchildren...* She refolds the letter and then picks up Kia's journal. A fresh wave of grief washes through her. She stares at the cover but cannot bring herself to open it. After a moment she returns both the journal and the letter to the drawer but takes her own journal back out. She adds a note to the bottom of the day's entry.

Two mothers. One dead who wants to see me grow up, and the other alive but who chooses not to be in my life.

"Great to see you back, Brenna. I've missed you." He smiles.

"Thanks." Brenna quickly meets Ryan's eyes before looking away. The last time she saw him was at her mother's memorial service, when he'd lit a candle and talked about how kind her mother was. His Australian accent charms her, even now. She struggles to act like talking to a cool guy is something she does every day.

Ryan is one of the "trammies" who operate the two Grouse Mountain trams that travel up and down the mountain, carrying passengers to the "Peak of Vancouver." In the winter the one-hundred-passenger tram, called the Skyride, delivers skiers, snowboarders and winter sports enthusiasts to the snow-covered slopes, but in the summer it is mostly tourists and hikers.

"I hear Grinder and Coola have missed you too," he says; referring to the two orphaned grizzly bears that Brenna helps care for as a wildlife-refuge volunteer.

"I bet," she says, her skin burning at the attention.

The Skyride quickly fills up, and Brenna steps to the back, allowing a large family group to move between her and Ryan. The doors close and she feels the jolt as the tram leaves the valley station and begins its eight-minute ascent to the peak. A moment later Ryan's voice is heard through the intercom, welcoming the tourists to the mountain and pointing out the landmarks in the view unfolding below them. She knows the spiel by heart but still enjoys listening to his voice. As the tram glides over the tower that marks the halfway point of the trip, it sways and there's a chorus of "ooohs" from the tourists. Brenna looks toward Ryan and finds him watching her. He rolls his eyes. She smiles and looks away.

At the summit Brenna follows the tourists off the tram.

"Hi to the bears from me," Ryan says as she passes him in the doorway.

She thinks about him as she crosses the alpine meadow on her way to the bear habitat and realizes that apart from his being a flirt and Australian, she doesn't know much else about him. She figures he's over eighteen—too old for her—but she likes his playful teasing. And for the duration of the tram ride, her numbing grief has been relieved.

At the Refuge for Endangered Wildlife, Brenna busies herself preparing bear food. Into pails go twenty-five sweet potatoes and thirty apples. With a knife she tops thirty-six carrots, wondering again why the bears won't eat the nubby ends. She doubts that grizzlies in the wild would be such picky eaters.

Mark, the wildlife manager, comes into the cabin while she's measuring out two buckets of protein kibble.

He has a watermelon under each arm. "Hey, Brenna, great to see you back," he says, echoing Ryan's words.

"Thanks. How are the bears?" she asks quickly, trying to divert the conversation away from the reason for her absence.

"They're good. Mostly hangin' out in the ponds, keeping cool, entertaining the tourists with their antics. The usual."

"Special occasion?" she asks, taking a watermelon from him.

"No," he says, laying the other one on the counter. "But they need to start packing on weight for hibernation. We've been giving them salmon too."

As Mark outlines the chores that need to be done, Brenna reflects on how much more comfortable she is with her responsibilities now than she was a year ago. Her mom, who had been manager of human resources for the mountain, had helped her get this position so Brenna could start accumulating the volunteer hours she needed for graduation. She'd wondered whether she'd be welcomed back once her mom was gone, but recently she'd received a card from the owner of the mountain resort, saying that her friends on the mountain had made a contribution to the World Wildlife Fund in her mother's memory and that they hoped Brenna would be back to her volunteer work soon.

The bear habitat encompasses five acres of land that closely resembles the environment they'd live in if they were in the wild. Carrying the pails, Brenna walks around the fenced enclosure, tossing in food so the bears can forage for it. She thinks about how much her mom loved this mountain resort. Just being here makes her feel a little closer to her.

～o～

"Grinder was found abandoned as a very small cub," Mark tells the group of tourists that has gathered around him for the morning ranger talk. "He would never have survived on his own in the wild."

Standing to the side, Brenna listens to the familiar story.

"Coola was found the same summer. His mother had been hit by a truck on a highway and killed, and he was also a very young and helpless cub."

The bears and I have something in common now, Brenna thinks. Dead mothers.

"Will they ever be released?" a tourist asks.

"Unfortunately, no," Mark answers. "They're far too accustomed to humans so might pose a threat if they were released. But we maintain their habitat to match— as closely as possible—what they would have in the wild."

Brenna feels a presence directly behind her.

"I told you they'd missed you," a voice whispers in her ear.

She jumps, startled, and swings around. Ryan grins down at her.

"What are you doing here?" she asks quietly, not wanting to disrupt Mark's presentation.

"It's my lunch break," he whispers. "I thought I'd come and check on my favorite bears."

Their gazes return to the habitat. The bears have discovered the watermelons, and the tourists are laughing in delight. Each bear has cracked one open and is sitting back on his haunches, eating the sweet red flesh inside. Brenna watches as a couple of ravens hop about near the bears, hoping for some watermelon fall-out. Coola gets up and lumbers away, half a watermelon clamped firmly in his mouth.

"They're beautiful, aren't they?" she says, more to herself than Ryan. She never grows tired of watching them.

"They really are."

A few minutes later Grinder gets up and follows Coola into the forest. The tourists begin to move away.

"I really did like your mom," Ryan says softly.

Brenna's shoulders stiffen.

"She was kind of like a surrogate mother to me. My own mom is so far away."

Brenna nods, feigning intense interest in the ravens who are feasting on the leftover watermelon.

"Anyway, I wanted you to know that."

"Thanks." She clears her throat. "And thanks for speaking at her service."

A fresh breeze sweeps across Brenna's face. She takes a deep breath.

"I lost a brother a couple of years ago," Ryan says. "I kind of know what it must feel like."

Now Brenna does glance at him. "What happened to him?"

"Car accident. He was the passenger." He stares into the distance. "The driver walked away. They'd been partying. A familiar story, I know."

"Oh my god. How old was he?"

"Sixteen."

"I'm so sorry," she says quietly and looks away. Why did he have to share that story? She has no tolerance for any more sadness right now.

"Thanks. My mom never got over it. I felt like such a jerk when I moved here." Ryan hesitates, as if trying to choose the right words. "She must feel like she's lost two sons."

Brenna nods and glances at him, suspecting that he has left something unsaid. She wonders how her own mom would feel if something ever happened to her or Naysa, then remembers that this will never happen to her mom. She died first.

"I have to get back to work," Ryan says, snapping her back to the present. He squeezes her arm and looks directly into her eyes. "Hang in there, Brenna."

She blinks and looks away. Why does sympathy always make her start crying again? She can only nod.

After a moment her gaze falls on his back, and she watches as he crosses the mountaintop on his way to the chalet.

Aug. 16

Is giving a baby up for adoption as tragic as losing a child to death? Probably not. With adoption, you know (or hope) the child will be fine, but the pain might be the same.

Brenna slides her journal back into the drawer and glances at the other one, still unread. With a shake of her head she shuts the drawer. She turns off her reading light and pulls the quilt up to her shoulders, hoping sleep comes quickly and that she can stay asleep all night. She knows her dad has resorted to sleeping pills.

"This is so disgusting." Georgialee pinches her nose with one hand while bagging Bentley's droppings with the other.

Brenna shakes her head, unsympathetic. "You should try shoveling grizzly-bear poop. Dog poop is nothing."

"I don't know how you do it," Georgialee says, knotting the bag. "Or why." She drops the heavy bag into a nearby garbage bin.

The two girls continue rollerblading along the Stanley Park seawall, Bentley galloping beside them. As they pass under the Lions Gate Bridge, Brenna notices two girls jogging toward them. Their blond ponytails swing in unison, like a pair of windshield wipers.

"Hey, Georgialee!" one of them says, slowing her pace as they pass each other.

"Julia!" Georgialee glides to a stop. "Hey, hi!"

The joggers keep running on the spot, keeping their heart rates up, Brenna figures. She doesn't know them but decides they must be sisters, they look so much alike. Georgialee quickly introduces them before Brenna takes Bentley's leash from her and lets him pull her away from the little group.

"Getting ready for the Terry Fox run?" she hears Georgialee ask.

"Yeah, and the Turkey Trot at Thanksgiving. How 'bout you?" They've slowed to walking on the spot.

Brenna catches Georgialee's eye before Georgialee answers. "I think I'll do both. Just taking it a bit easy with Brenna today. She's more of a walker, so we're blading, kind of a compromise. But there's still six weeks to train."

Brenna moves farther away, out of hearing range of the conversation. She sees them all turn to look at her at one point, before continuing their discussion. She figures Georgialee has told them about her mom. She wonders if, when she gets back to school, she'll be known as the-girl-whose-mom-died-of breast-cancer. She'd hate that but knows she'd probably categorize other people the same way if she didn't know them. Being the-girl-who-was-adopted might be another label that people could use to describe her.

Bentley tugs on the leash, and she follows him down toward the water. She sits on the barricade and sets him loose to explore the rocky beach. Looking across the busy harbor, she sees Grouse Mountain towering above the north shore of the city. From this vantage point the tram looks like a tiny red speck ascending the steep slope. She wonders if Ryan is on that tram, going through his spiel.

After a few minutes Georgialee's friends jog off, and Brenna and Bentley rejoin her on the seawall. "Where do you know them from?"

"That's Julia, from my running group. I'm sure I've mentioned her to you."

"And her sister?"

"No, that's her mom."

Brenna glances at Georgialee, wondering if she's joking.

"I know," Georgialee says. "She looks so young. Actually, she is young. She had Julia when she was, like, fifteen or something."

They continue to roll along the seawall. A seaplane buzzes through the harbor, ascending quickly to fly over the bridge that is now behind them.

"Can you imagine being a mom already?" Georgialee asks, breaking the comfortable silence. "She would have had Julia by the time she was our age."

Brenna doesn't answer. Her own birth mom wasn't much older when she had Brenna.

"But Julia thinks it's great," Georgialee continues. "She says it's only ever been the two of them, and they do everything together. They're more like sisters than mother and daughter. I'd like a mom like that."

I'd just like a mom, Brenna thinks.

Aug. 18

Would Kia and I be like sisters if she had kept me? Would we hang out together? Share clothes? How would I feel if my mom was mistaken for my sister? Do we look alike? Maybe not. Maybe Kia is Caucasian and my birth dad was Asian? For some reason I picture her looking like an older version of me.

Would I even want a sister as opposed to a mother?

They looked so happy together.

Brenna pushes mashed potatoes and peas around her plate. Would they ever get used to the empty chair, the one at her mom's place at the table? Maybe they should invite a guest to dinner each night to keep the chair filled. No, she decides, if they did that, they'd have to carry on a cheery conversation, and none of them has enough energy for that.

"Only a couple of weeks until school starts," her dad says.

The sisters both nod but don't reply.

"Is there anything you're going to need? School supplies, clothes…?" he asks.

The girls glance at each other and shrug. The new school year doesn't have that fresh-start feel that it did in other years. It's just something else to get through while they wait for the grief to ease, if it ever does.

"Well, let me know if you think of anything," he says. They finish their meal in silence.

⌒

Brenna stares blankly at her computer screen. The house is still, but she knows that both her dad and Naysa have retreated to their respective rooms, Naysa with an iPad and her dad with his laptop. With her mom gone it's like the heart of their family has stopped beating. She longs for the soft sound of her mom's voice as she chats on the phone or her boisterous laughter when her dad shares a funny story. She even misses the steady hum of it as she helps Naysa with her French homework. No one bothers to play music anymore either. The music would probably bring up a fresh surge of Mom memories.

A notification from Facebook appears in her email program.

New message from Angie Hazelwood

Brenna studies the name. Hazelwood. It's familiar, but she can't immediately place it. She stares at the message but hesitates to open it. And then she remembers.

Putting her laptop aside, she pulls out the big envelope of greeting cards from her bottom dresser drawer. She flips through them until she finds one that was put back in its envelope. In the corner is a return label: *Kia Hazelwood*.

Back on her laptop she stares at the name, trying to get her head around it. Someone related to her birth mom has sent her a message via Facebook. What could it possibly be about? She moves the cursor to the message but suddenly changes her mind and shuts down the page. She lies back on her bed, aware of how fast her heart is pounding. She tries to slow her breathing, but it's hopeless.

What is the matter with me? she wonders. Why can't I read the journal or open that message? So many questions might be answered.

She lies motionless, waiting for her breathing to return to normal. And then it comes to her. Yes, she might find some answers, but she might not like what she finds. Perhaps her birth mom is dead too. That might tip her over the edge.

Once her heart rate feels somewhat normal again, Brenna pads down to the family room, where she turns on the TV and channel-surfs until she comes across a rerun of *Survivor*. She places the remote on the table and sits back, ready to lose herself in the artificial world where no one actually dies and there is always something the people can do to save themselves. She feels first Naysa and then her father settle onto the couch beside her. They watch in silence.

Inhaling deeply, Brenna holds her breath for the count of five and then exhales slowly. She hears the woman on the next mat release her breath and wonders how much success that woman is having at clearing her mind.

"Give your thoughts wings," the yoga teacher instructs. "And let them simply float away."

Brenna's thoughts refuse to float away. The name Angie Hazelwood keeps flapping to the front of her mind, like a bird that can't quite make its landing. Who is Angie Hazelwood and what does she want? Should Brenna read the message? What harm would it do? She wouldn't have to respond...but what if it really is more bad news? Brenna reminds herself to breathe.

Yoga is something she'd practised with her mom, mostly because her mom loved it, but they'd stopped coming when she became too weak. Brenna hadn't expected to come back after her mom died—it wouldn't be the same—but she'd found herself here this morning, knowing she needed something to calm her fretfulness. She tries not to focus on anything but the postures as the class proceeds. It takes a while, but as she lies back into that final pose, *savasana* or corpse pose, she realizes that the anxiety has lifted and a sense of peace has settled over her.

Back in seated posture, the class is instructed to breathe deeply one last time. As Brenna exhales, she notices again how calm her mind is.

"May you find the inner strength to face all the challenges the day presents," the teacher says, bringing the class to a close. "Namaste."

"Namaste," the class replies in unison.

As Brenna bows toward the teacher, she knows what she has to do.

At home she goes straight to her room, flips open her computer and stares at the message notification for a long time, feeling the strength she'd had at the end of class already seeping away. She takes another deep breath, moves the cursor to the message and clicks. The message appears with a tiny picture of Angie Hazelwood staring out at her from the corner.

Dear Brenna,

I hope you don't mind me contacting you like this. I'm your biological aunt, your birth mom's sister. A couple of days ago I ran into Justin Reid, who was my sister's good friend, especially when she was pregnant with you. He told me that your adoptive mother had passed away.

I was so sorry to hear that. I was just nine when you were born, so I didn't understand much about what was happening, but I have often wondered about you and hope you are well, though I guess you're not so good right now with the loss of your mom.

Anyway, please excuse me for writing to you like this. I don't want to interfere with your life, but I haven't been able to stop thinking about you and your mom. I wanted you to know how sorry I am.

Angie Hazelwood

Brenna sits back and exhales, realizing she's been holding her breath the whole time she was reading the letter. So, she has an aunt. Someone younger than her mom. Brenna has never even wondered whether Kia has brothers or sisters.

This aunt, Angie, sounds like a nice person, taking the time to write to a stranger—even a related stranger —to give her condolences.

Brenna reads the letter again. Strange that she didn't say anything at all about Kia. Maybe she thought Brenna didn't want to know anything.

When she goes to Angie's Facebook page, Brenna discovers it has high privacy settings. She considers requesting her as a friend but decides against it. There must be some reason she wants her privacy. She wonders if Angie has checked out her page. What impression would Angie have of her after seeing her pictures and posts?

Brenna jumps, startled, when her cell phone rings. It's Georgialee. She decides not to answer it. Georgialee's chatter will keep her from doing what she knows she has to do next, before she loses her nerve.

Knowing that her dad and Naysa will be out for at least a couple more hours, she takes Kia's journal from her drawer and stares at the cover. Then, after taking one more deep breath, she turns to the first page.

Her absence is like the sky, spread over everything.

(C.S. LEWIS, *A GRIEF OBSERVED*)

<u>Jan. 1</u>
Virgin paper, fresh, crisp, clean
It's only an illusion.
It's recycled, not pure at all.
Illusion...do I look different?
Can anyone see what is happening to me?

<u>Jan. 5</u>
Blue.
The blue of tropical water, the surf pounding the shore.
The blue of the sky on a brilliant spring day.
The blue of a speckled robin's egg.
The ice-blue of Derek's eyes.
The blue ring in the water.
It's confirmed.

I am.
Blue.

Jan. 10
May the fleas of a thousand camels infest his Tommy Hilfiger
jockey shorts.
No, a swarm of bees—same place.

Brenna rereads the first two entries, and a wave of understanding washes through her. Kia had just discovered she was pregnant. The blue she referred to must have been a pregnancy test. Brenna knows that with home tests something changes color to indicate a pregnancy.

She rereads the next two entries and a few more before snapping the book shut and flopping back on her pillow. She closes her eyes.

It feels wrong, reading Kia's intimate thoughts, especially the passages where she describes the steamy attraction between her and Brenna's birth father...

She goes to the kitchen and takes a soda out of the fridge. Deep breaths, she reminds herself. Deep breaths.

While she fills a glass with ice she thinks about the journal entries. They're poignant and arranged almost like poetry. No wonder the girl named Shawna who gave Kia the journal and inscribed it said that her words deserved special paper. They really did. She wonders if Kia is still writing.

Grabbing a granola bar from the cupboard, she goes back to her room, climbs on her bed and continues reading.

Jan. 13
Two hearts beating...
Inside of me
Are they in unison
Or does each have its own rhythm?

Jan. 16
Is the date of my death already determined?
Like the date for the tiny soul living inside me?
How long will I get to live?
Who decides when it's over for me?

Jan. 17
Who is in control of me or of this tiny new life?
Me, or him?
Control—does IT have any?
No, IT depends on me.

If you are not born, do you have a soul?
Can you die?
Is birth or conception the first moment of life?
Tomorrow IT dies.
Will IT forgive me?

The ringing of her cell phone snaps Brenna back to the present again. She ignores it but pauses before turning the page in the journal. Had Kia really planned to abort her? What happened? She swallows hard and keeps reading.

After a few more minutes Brenna closes the book and slides it into her night table. Kia has described, in detail, the night that she was conceived. How many people really want to know about that? Not her. And it was not what she expected to find in Kia's journal either, the journal she wanted Brenna, her own daughter, to read.

Brenna slides the shovel under the bear scat and dumps it into the black plastic bag she's been hauling around the enclosure with her.

"That looks like fun."

Looking up, Brenna sees Ryan standing on the other side of the fence. She gives him her best don't-be-ridiculous look. He laughs.

"Where are the bears?" he asks.

"Probably having an afternoon nap somewhere in the shade." She wipes her forehead with the back of her sleeve.

Ryan takes a bite of the sandwich he's holding. "I'm assuming you're safe in there."

"Yeah. The bears like me. No worries."

"Are you serious?"

"No!" She laughs, and it feels good. "They're locked off on the other side of the enclosure. I triple-checked before I came in."

"Glad to hear it," Ryan says, finishing his sandwich. "Lunch hour?"

"Lunch half hour."

"Too bad the bears aren't around."

"That's okay. It was you I came to see today."

Brenna glances at him. "You want me to act like a grizzly bear?" she teases.

"Ha! It is kind of weird seeing a human on that side of the fence."

She smiles, feeling shy again.

"I was wondering, do you ever do the Grouse Grind?" he asks.

"No, I've heard the trail is kind of steep."

"You'd have no problem with it."

"Climbing an entire mountain? I think I'd have a problem No, I know I would. You're a grinder?"

"Yeah, but not a serious one. I was hoping you'd keep me company." He cocks his head.

"When are you going?" She feels alarm rising in her throat.

"Today, after work."

"Oh, I'm not really…" She looks down at herself.

"You're dressed perfectly. I'll provide the water."

"I'm usually pretty tired after working here."

"Okay, how 'bout on a day you're not working then?"

"Okay." What could she say?

"Like tomorrow?"

She laughs. "You're persistent."

"It will be fall soon, you'll be back at school, the days will be short…"

"Okay, okay. What time?"

"Four o'clock. We'll meet at the trailhead, okay?"

"All right."

Ryan waves as he turns and begins his walk back to the chalet.

Brenna watches him and wonders what she's gotten herself into. He turns and catches her staring at him. He waves again.

Blushing deeply, she heaves another pile of bear scat into the bag.

～

"What does he look like?" Georgialee asks, way too enthusiastically.

Maybe it should be her meeting Ryan for a hike, Brenna thinks. She's certainly in better shape. "Kind of average."

"And he's from Australia? I love Aussie accents."

Brenna considers that. He does have a nice voice… and his looks are better than average, but she didn't want to get Georgialee going.

"What are you planning to wear?"

"Whatever people usually wear when they hike… shorts, a T-shirt—"

"You can't wear any old shorts or T-shirt."

Brenna regards her friend. They're sprawled out on the leather couches in Georgialee's living room. "Listen, this isn't a date or anything. We're just doing the Grind together."

Georgialee cocks her head. "You are kidding me, right? He walks clear across the mountain on his lunch hour to find you and invite you to do the Grind? I call that a date."

"Lunch half hour," Brenna corrects, smiling as she remembers their conversation. "He wanted me to hike after my shift today. I found an excuse, but then he asked about tomorrow, and I wasn't quick enough with another excuse. So it's not a date. It's a hike."

"Whatever. Just don't wear any old T-shirt and shorts."

"I'll wear clean ones. For you."

"Brenna! You know what I mean. That pink tank you have, the one that dips pretty low—"

"I'm not wearing that on a hike! Besides, he's way too old. I don't want him to think I'm coming on to him or anything."

"How old is he?"

"Over eighteen. Maybe twenty? He's finished school."

"That's nothing. My dad's ten years older than my mom."

"It's too old for me. My parents…" Brenna pauses, realizing her blunder. "My dad would freak."

"You're impossible."

"No, you're impossible."

They glare at each other across the room.

Brenna had come over with vague hopes of talking to Georgialee about Angie Hazelwood's Facebook message and Kia's journal, but something made her share the news about Ryan and their hike first. Now she doesn't have the strength to bring up the other stuff. Not today, anyway.

~

Aug. 24

It's hard to read about Kia's feelings...they're so intimate...so intense. Maybe if it was someone besides my own birth mom it would be easier? Kind of like reading a steamy novel? I don't know.

Will I ever have feelings like that for a guy? Georgialee has. But how could you feel like that and then have it vanish so quickly? Poof. Gone. Maybe it's because she was so young.

I can't imagine being pregnant. What would I do?

~

"I'm climbing the Grouse Grind with a friend tomorrow afternoon."

Brenna's father looks up from the newspaper he's reading. "Who's the friend?"

"A guy I met at Grouse. He works there."

"He must be a special guy." He cocks his head, eyebrows raised.

"Why would you say that?" Brenna glares at him.

"The Grind's not an easy climb for an inexperienced hiker. I'm sure you know that."

"So?"

"So...I don't think you'd say yes to the Grind unless it was someone you really wanted to spend time with."

"Well, you're wrong about that. He suggested it, and I couldn't think of any good reason to say no."

He shrugs and turns the page of the newspaper. "At what point should I call Search and Rescue?"

She sticks out her tongue before stomping out of the room.

Despite what she said to Georgialee and her dad, Brenna finds herself trying on various combinations of T-shirts and shorts, trying to mask the little roll that is developing around her tummy. She decides on a pale-blue tank top and black Lululemon shorts. Checking herself in the mirror, she notes how the shirt brings out the blue in her eyes.

Blue eyes! She remembers what Kia said in her journal: *The ice-blue of Derek's eyes.* So that is where her blue eyes came from! That means he was probably Caucasian. She's noticed that her aunt, Angie, looks at least partially Asian in her Facebook profile, so Kia is likely part Asian too. What do Angie and Kia's parents look like—her biological grandparents?

Her mind returns to the ice-blue description of her biological father's eyes. That didn't make him sound very warm and friendly.

Ryan has blue eyes too, but not ice blue. His are very dark, royal blue, and she remembers the pain in them when he spoke of his brother.

She tosses a long-sleeved sweatshirt into her backpack. In the kitchen she adds a couple of granola bars, apples and water.

Brenna chews at a hangnail on her thumb as she rides the bus up Capilano Road to the base of the mountain. What will they talk about for the entire hike? There's only so much you can say about grizzly bears. Maybe she can ask him more about Australia and where he went to school. She'll steer the conversation away from family.

Forty-five minutes later, with leg muscles on fire and her tank top streaked with sweat, Brenna almost laughs at how misplaced her worries were. Ryan has stepped to the side of the trail many times to let her catch her breath, and she is dismayed at how many people, young and old, jog past her, straight up the mountain.

When she thinks they must be nearing the top, they come across a sign that says ¼ *mark*.

"Only one quarter? Are you kidding me?" she says, bent at the waist to catch her breath. "How many more stairs?" she asks, referring to the wooden steps that go straight up.

"Lots." He laughs. "All first-timers freak when they get to this sign. But if a hundred thousand people a year can do it, you can do it too."

"I'm not sure, Ryan. Maybe we should head back down. I really wasn't prepared for this."

"We'll take our time. There's no rush."

Brenna struggles up another long set of steps. Worrying about what to talk about had been stupid—she's breathing way too hard to even think about talking. But somewhere near the three-quarter mark she begins to relax, knowing that the end is actually within reach, and the trail is somewhat less steep here. Two hours after they left the base, they step into a clearing outside the chalet. The red tram pulls into the dock above them. Ryan gives her a high five.

"You did it!" he says.

She flops down on a grassy patch. "Barely!" Her breath comes in great heaves. She can't believe she actually worried about what she was going to look like on this hike. Survival should have been her only concern. Her dad was right after all.

"Let me buy you a cold drink," Ryan says. "You deserve it."

"Let's do it again sometime," Ryan says as he steers his old Mazda into Brenna's driveway.

"I don't know," she says, climbing out of the car. "I hurt all over."

"It gets easier, I promise."

"I bet you could have climbed it, ridden the tram back down and climbed it again in the time it took me."

"Forget about the time." He shakes his head. "You did it. That's what counts."

After thanking him for the ride, Brenna tries to walk to her front door without showing how stiff she's already become, worried that he might be watching. Should she take a yoga class in the morning to try to stretch out her muscles?

In the house she warms up some leftover casserole. Her dad and Naysa are having dinner at her uncle's. She sits at the table and finds she's relieved to be alone. Being with either of them seems to intensify the ever-present ache. Is it because their grief inflames hers, or because she can't do anything to ease theirs?

Her first plate of dinner disappears in mere seconds, so she spoons out a second helping. While she waits for it to heat in the microwave, she does a quick inventory of the food in the freezer. It's still well stocked with casseroles that their friends and family delivered to them when her mom was sick and then again following her death. If all these people had provided recipes with their meals, she could have compiled a cookbook, *Comfort Casseroles*.

After she's eaten, Brenna puts on pajamas and stretches out on her bed. The hot shower and big meal have left her fully relaxed. She's feeling so good she decides to read more from Kia's journal so pulls it out and turns to the page where she left off.

Feb. 1
I came to a bend in the road. I took the turn.
My life is not ruined. It's only changed.

Feb. 5
I hate myself.
I don't deserve this family.
Maybe I'll wake up and find this was all just a bad dream.
I wish.

Feb. 6
I have redefined myself.
No longer the perfect child.
I feel release.

March 1
This detour is full of pitfalls.
What's so great about that?
I'm not even a real mom yet, but I've already had to give up
so much.
What's the big deal about being a parent anyway?

Brenna closes the journal with a snap. The euphoria of a few minutes earlier is gone. The front door creaks open as her dad and Naysa come into the house. Her dad pokes his head into her room.

"How was the hike?" he asks, smiling down at her, but his smile evaporates when he sees her face. He glances at the journal on her lap. "Maybe it was too soon to give that to you," he says softly.

Brenna shrugs. She has no words.

"Do you want to talk about it?"

"Talk about what?" Naysa asks, peering around her father, but after one glance at Brenna's face she changes the question. "Are you okay?"

With a huge effort Brenna pulls herself back to the present. "I'm okay," she says, looking first at her father and then at Naysa. "The hike was really, really hard. You were right, Dad. I'm going to go to sleep. I'm exhausted."

"Are you sure?" her dad asks. "We're going to watch a movie. It's Friday night, after all…"

Friday night. When her mom was alive they always stayed in and watched a movie together. Pizza, popcorn, movie. They hadn't done that since she died.

Brenna climbs off her bed slowly, stiffly. "You guys go ahead. I really am tired." She hugs her dad and tugs Naysa's ponytail. "I'm gonna brush my teeth and go to bed." She squeezes past them in the hall. "I'll see you in the morning."

Brenna can hear the drone of the TV as she climbs into bed. She shoves Kia's journal into the night-table drawer and pulls out her own.

Aug. 25

Why did she want me to read her journal? Didn't she consider how it would make me feel when I read that being pregnant with me sucked? That she would have to give up so much? I DIDN'T ASK TO GET BORN!! IT'S NOT MY FAULT THAT SHE WAS PREGNANT WITH ME!!!! So why do her words make me feel so guilty? Like I somehow wrecked her life? And I don't want to know that my father was a jerk!!! (A hot jerk, obviously.)

I am half him!! Does that make me half a horrible person? Right now I hate her. Maybe I do take after Derek. What I didn't seem to inherit was his sex appeal. All that talk about

ENERGY

DESIRE

HEAT.

I seem to be in the camp that prefers to use words.

Well, not lately. They seem to have dried up. Maybe this journal will help me find them again.

Maybe not.

I wonder what Derek is like now...16 years later. Is he still hot? Maybe he has a beer belly and a comb-over. Maybe he grew horns in that shallow head of his.

What is Ryan doing tonight? Is he sore all over too? Probably not. I was such a slug today. How embarrassing. Did he regret inviting me? The hike sucked—I barely made it.

But...

At the top I realized I hadn't thought of Mom the whole time. The physical pain made me forget for two full hours. Except for when I sleep, that's the longest break I've had since she died.

Brenna closes her journal and reaches for her laptop. She signs on to her Facebook page and rereads Angie Hazelwood's message. Taking a deep breath, she types in the name *Derek Klassen*.

I know it aches, how your heart it breaks.
You can only take so much. Walk on.

(U2, "WALK ON")

Six Derek Klassens appear on the screen. Brenna studies their profiles. One is forty. Too old. One is twenty-five. Too young. Three of them have brown eyes. The sixth lives on the other side of the country and, apparently, has lived there all his life. For some reason her biological father—blue-eyed, thirty-three-year-old Derek Klassen—doesn't appear to have a Facebook page.

Very reluctantly she types in *Kia Hazelwood*, but there are no results.

Returning to Angie's message, she rereads it once again, then hits *Reply*.

Dear Angie,

Thanks for your message. It's been a very sad time. I miss my mom so much.

I have to admit, hearing from you really took me by surprise. I have been told about my mother, Kia, but never anything about her family. You might be interested to know that after they adopted me, my mom and dad did end up having a child of their own, so I have a sister.

Thanks again,

Brenna

Brenna rereads her note. Part of her desperately wants to ask about Kia, about her biological grandparents and even about Derek, but a bigger part of her is terrified at the thought of going there.

With a deep sigh she presses *Send*.

Brenna's heart sinks as she steps into the tram the next morning. The operator is a girl, someone Brenna doesn't recognize. She'd told her dad she was taking extra shifts at the wildlife refuge to cover for vacationing volunteers, but it isn't completely true. She's discovered that what she really wants is to see more of Ryan. He takes her mind off her mom, and, as he pointed out, school will be starting soon, and her shift will switch to a weekend day. She doesn't know if he even works weekends.

He could be operating the other tram, she realizes, but if he doesn't know she is on the mountain, there's no hope of him coming to visit her on his lunch break. As the two trams meet at the midway point, she tries to see who the other operator is, but there are too many people inside, and the two trams pass each other quickly.

"Will the bears have babies?" a visitor asks Brenna. The mountain is busy with tourists, and Mark is checking the fencing, so she is left alone to talk to the visitors who have gathered around her. She stands on the bridge that divides the upper and lower ponds.

"No, they're both male," she answers.

"Oh, one of them is smaller. I thought he must be a she."

"The reason Grinder's smaller," Brenna explains, "is because he comes from the interior of BC. Interior bears don't have as much protein in their diets as the coastal bears. Coola is a coastal bear, so he comes from a line of bears that have access to a lot of salmon. That seems to explain why they grow larger." She's heard these grizzly-bear facts so often she simply spews out the memorized information.

"Is it true that bears have bad eyesight?" This question comes from behind her, and the voice is familiar. Brenna swings around and finds Ryan standing there, grinning at her.

She returns the smile but can't find the words to answer the question. After a long moment she breaks eye contact with him and sees that the tourists are waiting for an answer. "Actually," she says, "grizzly bears, or brown bears as they are scientifically known, have good vision, probably about the same as our own. But it's their sense of smell that's really amazing. These boys can smell one hundred times better than us and ten times better than a bloodhound."

There's a chorus of "oohs" from the crowd before a splash from the upper pond catches their attention and they move as a group to the other side of the bridge, where Grinder and Coola are now play-wrestling in the water.

"I thought you might not be working today," Brenna says to Ryan, who has not moved away with the rest of the visitors. Immediately she regrets her words, not wanting it to be obvious that she hoped to see him.

"Hey, didn't you know? I practically live up here."

Brenna smiles and then realizes she has no idea where he really does live.

"I saw you arrive at the base this morning," he says. "My tram was leaving the valley station and I looked down and saw you walking from the bus loop toward the coffee shop."

Brenna nods, remembering how she'd just missed a tram, which had given her time to grab a hot chocolate.

"I have a present for you," he says.

"You do?"

"Uh-huh." He looks around. "Is there somewhere we can go that's a little more private?"

Seeing that the tourists are temporarily distracted by watching the bears in the pond, Brenna leads Ryan into the little cabin called Ski Wee that's used by the wildlife team in the summer and the ski school in the winter. After a quick glance around the room, Ryan slides the pack off his back, unzips the top and pulls out a small bag. He hands it to her.

"What is it?" she asks.

"Check it out."

She glances at him suspiciously, wondering if this is some kind of practical joke, but he only looks pleased with himself.

Opening the plastic bag, she pulls out a deep-green T-shirt.

"Look at the front," he says, smiling at her puzzled expression.

She unfolds the shirt. Printed on it, in bold type are the words *I Survived the Grouse Grind*.

"Aha!" She laughs, holding the shirt up to herself. "I will wear it proudly."

"Good," he says. "You should. And by this time next year, you will have shaved an hour off your time."

"What?" Brenna frowns.

Ryan looks a little sheepish at his outburst. "You'll have shaved an hour off your time," he repeats. "I'm hoping you'll keep hiking with me, and if you do, for sure you'll find it gets easier."

Brenna folds up the T-shirt and puts it back in the bag. "But I don't want to do it again. I didn't enjoy it at all. My muscles are still hurting. I can hardly walk."

"Will you think about it?" he asks.

Brenna lowers her head. It is true. She did hate it, but she does like Ryan, and the constant inner ache eased for the time they were hiking. That has to count for something.

"Why do you want me to hike?" she asks. "I'll slow you down."

"Because I need a hiking partner. See? It's all about me. It's not safe to hike alone."

Once again Brenna realizes how much she enjoys hearing him talk—his Australian accent stirs something up in her. "Yeah right. You're never alone on the Grind. That trail is like a hiking highway."

Surprisingly, Ryan doesn't have a comeback for that.

"And besides, the Grind closes over the winter," Brenna points out.

"That's when we start doing the Snowshoe Grind," he says, smiling brightly.

"The what?"

"There's a Snowshoe Grind that goes up Dam Mountain, west of here."

"Are you serious?"

"I am, and besides, there are dozens of other local trails we can hike in the winter."

Brenna sighs and plunks herself onto a bench. "I haven't had the energy to do much of anything lately," she admits.

Ryan sinks onto another bench, facing her. "I know," he says. "I remember exactly how it feels."

She picks at her fingernails before looking up and making eye contact. Then she looks back down to her hands. "Why me?" she asks softly.

"Why not you? I like you."

She glances at him again, wondering if he's teasing. His elbows are on his knees and he leans toward her. He looks completely serious.

"And because I really liked your mom."

That startles her. "What does that have to do with anything?"

"Well…" He pauses, as if looking for the right words. "I believe that not only will exercise help you get stronger physically, but it will also help you build up your strength emotionally too. Helping you get stronger can be my way of giving back to someone who was kind to me."

Brenna doesn't respond.

"Your mom came into my life when I was at my lowest point," Ryan says. "Maybe it's time for me to pay it forward."

Brenna rolls her eyes. Ryan laughs, and the awkward moment vaporizes. His phone buzzes. "I've got to get back to work," he says, glancing at it, "but promise me you'll think about it."

She nods, and he whoops in triumph.

"You can give me your answer when you're heading back down. Wait for my tram."

"I only said I'd think about it," she repeats, but he's already out the door and jogging away.

Ryan swipes Brenna's pass before she climbs onto his tram for the trip back down the mountain at the end of her shift. "What did you decide?" he asks, already swiping the pass of the person behind her in line.

"I'll let you know," she says.

"Don't wait too long."

Aug. 26

Was he serious? Does he really think he's returning a favor to my mom by getting me to take up hiking? I don't buy it. Besides, do I want to be his service project?

I am going to say no.

But...I like being on "Mom's mountain." I feel close to her there. And I like being with him. He didn't ask me to take up skiing. I would have said no to that.

Does he think I look so out of shape that I need to be his project?!?!

Brenna finds herself checking her Facebook messages every few hours. Will she hear back from her biological aunt? Part of her wants to see the name Angie Hazelwood appear, and part of her fears it will.

"You already have way more volunteer hours than you need," Georgialee says. She's propped up on her bed, applying polish to her toenails. "You don't need to waste a day of every weekend up there."

"I'm not wasting my time. I like being with the bears." Brenna sits on the carpeted floor with Bentley snuggled up beside her. His large head rests on her leg, and she massages his floppy ears. She doesn't bother mentioning that being on the mountain also makes her feel closer to her mom. Georgialee wouldn't understand that. How could she? Her own mother is alive and well and cooking dinner in the kitchen one floor below them. "And I've decided to keep doing the Grouse Grind too," she says, surprising even herself. She hadn't come to a decision until that very moment. Now that the words are out of her mouth, she's going to have to follow through. A wave of exhaustion sweeps over her.

"Is this with or without that Australian trammie?" Georgialee asks, the nail-polish brush poised over a toe, momentarily forgotten.

"With."

Georgialee sits up straighter, but Brenna doesn't give her a chance to say anything. "Don't even go there, Georgia," she cautions. "He needs someone to hike with, and, well, I need to get in better shape."

"Reeeeally." Georgialee drags the word out as she studies Brenna's face. "That first date must have gone better than you reported."

"It's not what you think," Brenna says, surprised at the defensive tone of her own voice. She doesn't know why she can't be completely honest with Georgialee about this. What is she hiding? There was a time when they shared everything. Not anymore. When had things changed between them?

Georgialee returns to her nails. "Whatever. I don't care why you're hiking, I'm just glad you're going to stop moping around your house."

Brenna's head snaps up.

"Sorry," Georgialee says quickly. "That came out all wrong. It's just good to see you...to see you moving on."

Brenna pushes Bentley's head off her leg and gets to her feet. "I've got to go."

"I'm sorry, Brenna." Georgialee scrambles off the bed and tries to block the doorway. "I really didn't mean it that way. Sometimes things come out all wrong."

"Whatever." Brenna pushes her way past Georgialee and runs down the stairs, nearly crashing into Georgialee's mom, who is at the front door, bringing in the mail.

"Brenna!" she says, startled. "Is everything okay?"

Brenna shakes her head and brushes past her. She doesn't glance back.

Aug. 27

Moping. My mother is dead and she thinks I'm moping. Her mother asked if everything is okay. What does she think?

NO! NOTHING IS OKAY ANYMORE!!!!

Brenna closes the journal and flops back on her pillows. For a long time she lets the tears spill, but then, with a deep, shuddering breath, she reopens it and picks up her pen. She stares at the page and then begins to write.

Would I have been any different if it were her mom that had breast cancer?

Would I know what to say? To do?

What do I want her to say? To do? Is there a right thing to say when someone dies? Maybe there are only wrong things.

Ryan gets it. He had a brother who died. He doesn't have to say or do anything. He just knows.

Brenna watches Naysa pour milk over her cereal. She's shocked to see the dark smudges under her sister's eyes. When had they appeared? With a guilty pang she realizes she hasn't spent any time with her sister lately. She thinks back to her mom's last words to her. *Take care of Naysa for me.* At the time, Brenna had resented the words. After all, who was going to take care of her? Now she felt she was letting her mother down.

"How are you feeling about starting high school today?" Brenna asks.

Naysa shrugs. "I don't think it will be much different from my old school."

"Actually, it is," Brenna says. "The teachers expect you to be more independent."

Naysa nods but continues eating in silence.

"There are a lot more kids too, so you can make new friends if you want."

Naysa still doesn't respond.

Brenna wonders if Naysa's friends are any better than Georgialee is at finding the right things to say. She swallows a mouthful of her cereal but finds she has no appetite so pushes her bowl away.

"At least going back to school will be…a distraction," Brenna says. There's no need to say what the distraction is from.

Naysa shrugs again and then wipes a lone tear off her cheek.

Brenna knows she hasn't helped at all. In fact, it seems she's made things worse. "Text me if you get lost or anything. I'll find you."

Naysa finally looks up from her bowl. Brenna can see the misery in her eyes. Do her own eyes look like that?

"Thanks," Naysa says. "I'll be okay."

But Brenna knows she won't be okay. The only way that either of them would ever be okay again is if they could turn back the clock, back to the time before their mother got sick.

No matter how bad your heart is broken,
the world doesn't stop for your grief.

(FARAAZ KAZIR)

Dear Brenna,

Thanks for your message. I wasn't sure if I was completely out of line contacting you, but somehow I felt I needed to.

How cool that you have a sister! I think you must have just turned 16, right? That must mean you are in your final few years of high school. It's weird, I still think of you as a baby. How silly. I'm certainly not the little girl I was when you were born, so I don't know why I can't imagine you growing up too.

I hope you're coping okay during these sad days following your mom's death. Know that I am sending kind thoughts and strength your way.

Angie

Brenna stares at the words. They say so little, and yet Brenna feels a surge of relief that Angie has at least responded. It is a link, however fragile, to her biological mother. The mother who is still alive.

The first day of school had been agony. There were so many people she hadn't seen or spoken with since her mom died, and the awkward moments became overwhelming. Some of her classmates tried to ignore what had happened, said hi cheerfully and then quickly looked away. Others apologized for not contacting her sooner. They didn't know what to say. They'd been so busy. Brenna found herself having to assure them that it was okay, that she understood. A few others collapsed in tears when they saw her and simply hugged her. They didn't try to say anything. Although these hugs made her cry too, she preferred them to the more awkward verbal responses. She'd had lunch with Georgialee, and neither of them said anything about Brenna's hasty exit from Georgialee's house a few days earlier. At least Georgialee knew enough to drop that subject.

Brenna wonders how Naysa survived her first day. She expects the reaction of Naysa's classmates will have been much the same but probably even more awkward, as they are younger and would have even less idea about how to respond to a classmate whose mother has died. She knows she should go talk with Naysa, offer some comfort, but, just like many of her own peers, she doesn't know how. She heard Naysa come home, heard her bedroom door click shut, but that was it.

Brenna thinks about writing to Angie again, asking about Kia, but what would she say? Instead, she pulls Kia's journal out of the drawer. She holds it for a moment, letting her thoughts drift to her "other" mother. Where is she now? Why didn't Angie say anything about her?

She turns the pages and begins to read from where she'd left off.

March 5

A picture is worth a thousand words.

I've seen her. She's real. This detour is worth every extra mile, pitfalls and all!!

I don't care about baseball or summer camp. I'm busy growing a baby. She's all there. I am creating her. It is so amazing.

And Justin is there with me.

Brenna flips back a page and rereads the previous entry before skimming the new one again, startled by the change in tone. Kia has gone from resenting her unborn child to being elated with her pregnancy. If only she'd read one more entry the last time she was reading the journal. It would have spared her a lot of anguish. She turns the page, wondering if Kia's mood will flip-flop again.

March 12

Shawna is wrong.

He is the perfect partner.

Our feelings are mutual and right.

It can work.
It will work.

Turning to the inscription on the inside cover, Brenna remembers that it was Shawna who gave Kia the journal. Shawna was clearly a good friend. So what was she so wrong about? And is *he* Justin the minister?

She keeps reading.

March 24
There are so sides. Me against everyone else. Why did I say anything? Now that I've said it I can never go back. It changes everything.
Dear Peanut,
I haven't felt you move yet, but I know you're there and I luv you. It's so easy for everyone else to tell me I have to give you up— you are not a part of them. But you are as much a part of me as my own heart is. There is no one to talk to anymore. I thought Justin understood. I thought we had the same feelings for each other. I thought wrong. I'm so stupid.

So Kia hadn't hated her! She'd loved her!

The knock on Brenna's door is soft, but she flinches, startled from her thoughts.

She quickly slides the journal back into the drawer. "Come in," she says. The door opens and Naysa is standing there, holding a sheet of paper. "Hey, Nayse," she says, trying not to show how much she doesn't want to be interrupted right now. "How did your first day of high school go?"

Naysa shrugs noncommittally and holds up the sheet of paper. "Wanna see my courses?"

Brenna notices Naysa's puffy, red-rimmed eyes. She slides over and pats the bed beside her. "Come here. Let's see what teachers you have."

Naysa props herself up beside Brenna, and together they go over her courses and discuss the teachers. Brenna tries to be enthusiastic, sharing stories about the teachers and giving advice, but her mind is only partly there. Kia's feelings for Justin—is that what Shawna is wrong about? And does Kia continue to love her unborn baby, or does she go back to resenting it?

When their father gets home, they move their conversation to the kitchen so they can help get dinner started. Brenna escapes the chatter by folding a load of laundry while they wait for the rice to cook, but she still has to field first-day-back questions from her dad while they eat their stir-fry.

Now Naysa decides that she really does need some school supplies, so after dinner they drive to the mall. Brenna quickly grabs some paper and binders, but Naysa seems to take forever, weighing the merits of different pens, sticky notes and index dividers. In the meantime their dad gets distracted in the electronics department. Brenna waits in the car, wishing she'd brought the journal along.

Finally they're home again, and Brenna is free to read some more. She brushes her teeth, puts on her pajamas and climbs under her comforter. She pulls the journal out of the drawer and holds it for a moment, running her hand over the coarse cover and thinking about Kia and how she reached for this journal each time her mood either spiked or plummeted. She'd bared her soul here, not realizing that the unborn child she was writing about would someday read it.

April 4
Dear Peanut (I have to think of another name for you),
Feeling you move is too amazing! I can't believe I have a little person inside of me who I've never met. It almost seems like you're an alien! But keep moving, it's so awesome.
I wish I could read Justin's mind. He seems as fascinated by all this as I am. Is it me that turns him off? My age? Or is it just because I'm in the Youth Group?

April 11
What will be worse?
Liking them and having no reason NOT to give her up?
Or not liking them and having to choose again?

Brenna holds the journal to her chest. It's too painful to read. Clearly, the decision that Kia was writing about was what to do with her, Brenna, when she was born. Kia was so right—her decision really would decide the fate of Brenna's life...*did* decide the fate.

Brenna pulls her own journal out of the drawer.

Sept. 3

Reading her most intimate thoughts...about me...it feels so strange. I feel like I know this girl, but she is no longer a girl...she is a woman. How does she feel now about the decision she made... to give me up for adoption? What would my life be like if she'd raised me herself? She loved me before I was born. Would that have changed if having me felt like it wrecked her life?

I can't imagine not having Mom and Dad as parents. But if they hadn't adopted me, I would never have known them so I wouldn't miss them. I wouldn't even know Naysa. Weird

Kia got pregnant with me by accident. She didn't want me but grew to love the baby growing inside her. My father, Derek—it appears he never did want me or grow to love me. Yet he is my "real" father. Or is he? What is real? Mom and Dad chose me. They told me they desperately wanted me. That should be enough, shouldn't it? Wouldn't that make them "real" parents? But now that Mom is gone...how would Kia feel about me now? Would she be able to dig up that love she once felt for me? Or has she moved on, purposely forgetting that time in her life, and the baby she conceived...

Angie sounds like a nice lady...did she tell Kia about my mom dying? How would that make Kia feel? Why hasn't Angie said anything about her in her messages? I could ask Justin what he knows.

Sighing, Brenna closes her journal and puts them both away. She has too many questions, just as Kia once had.

〜

"I swear this mountain has gotten steeper since last time." Brenna moves to the side of the trail to let a couple of hikers pass. She leans forward, hands on her knees, trying to catch her breath.

Ryan steps beside her and rubs circles in the middle of her back, just as her dad often did. "You'll be jogging up here in no time," he says.

Despite being aware of how sticky with sweat her T-shirt must be, Brenna enjoys the feel of his touch, the pressure exactly right, so doesn't straighten up too quickly. A few more hikers climb past them.

"I don't know, Ryan," she says, starting up the trail again. "Maybe some of us aren't cut out for mountain climbing." On her previous volunteer shift she had told Ryan that she'd decided to be his hiking partner. He'd whooped and high-fived her. She'd tried to set aside her reservations about being his "service project" and think only about getting stronger and doing that on her mom's mountain, but the doubts lingered. "And I should have known not to do it after working my shift," she complains. "Doing both in one day is too much."

Ryan ignores her whining and changes the subject. "How did the first week back at school go?" he asks.

She shrugs. "It was all right." It was, after the initial day, and it had been somewhat of a distraction, as she'd promised Naysa. "What year did you graduate?"

Ryan doesn't answer immediately. Brenna looks over her shoulder at him, noticing the slight frown on his forehead.

"I didn't, actually," he says.

"Oh, but I thought…"

"I know. I probably implied that I came to Canada after I finished school…"

Brenna keeps climbing the steep path, curious about this sudden change in his story. She hears him sigh and glances back again. He is staring at the ground, still frowning.

"My uncle lives just down the road. He's been in Canada for years."

"So you live with him?"

"Yeah, he took me in when things…when things got too bad at home. My mom, well…"

Brenna moves to the side of the path again. "I'm sorry. I didn't mean to pry."

Ryan steps around her and begins to lead the way. "You didn't. I just don't usually like to get into the reason that I ended up in Canada. It was because my brother died, but it wasn't actually my choice. I'm sorry I wasn't completely honest."

"That's okay." Brenna doesn't know what else to say. "My mom, the one you knew, she wasn't my real mom," she blurts out, as if she should now share a secret too.

"Huh?" Now it's Ryan's turn to glance at her, puzzled.

"I was adopted."

"Your parents adopted you?"

"Uh-huh."

"Then I think that makes Joanna your real mom."

"Well, yeah, but you know what I mean."

Ryan doesn't respond. They hike in silence for a few minutes.

"So you didn't really choose to come to Canada?" she says.

"No, I didn't want to leave Mom when she needed me."

"So why didn't you stay in Australia then?" Struggling for breath, Brenna finds it hard to talk.

Ryan steps off the path. Brenna joins him and reaches into her pack for water.

"It's complicated," he says after a moment. "But my mom isn't well, and my uncle felt I'd be better off with him for a while." He takes a long sip from his own water bottle.

"Where's your father?"

"I've never met him."

"Oh." Brenna is at a loss for words.

"Anyway," he continues, "I'm sure it was for the best, and now that I'm making a life here, I'm reluctant to go home."

"So stay."

"Not so easy. For a lot of reasons." He sighs. "But let's talk about other things."

He smiles brightly, but Brenna can see it's forced. She decides to confide some more in him, though she doesn't know why. "My biological aunt recently messaged me via Facebook," she tells him as they start up the trail again. It seems to be a day for sharing secrets.

"Really? Have you met her?"

"No, I didn't even know she existed until a few weeks ago."

"Huh."

Brenna is about to tell him more but is interrupted by more hikers passing them. She feels a drip on her head, and then a second one. "Uh-oh." She looks up, but the canopy of trees prevents her from seeing the sky.

"Did you bring a rain jacket?" Ryan asks.

"No. Did you?"

"No, it was completely clear when we started out. We'd better hustle."

"Hustle?"

Ryan smiles at her. "Okay, hustle's the wrong word. But we'd better concentrate. We're at the three-quarters mark. Not far to go now."

Three-quarters may sound close, Brenna thinks, but it still feels incredibly far. She does her best to keep up with Ryan, but it's hard. She's almost grateful for the sudden downpour, as it keeps her cool. When they finally reach the top, Ryan leads her directly to the tram. "We may be okay now, but we'll get chilled if we don't get home and changed into something dry soon."

Brenna nods and steps into the tram behind him. He greets the trammie and she listens to their easy banter. She thinks back to their early conversation, and how he admitted that it wasn't actually his choice to come to Canada. He hides his troubles well. She wonders if people would say the same about her.

She lets him drive her home again, even though she now realizes how far he has to travel out of his way.

A shiver runs through her as they pull up to her driveway.

"You're getting chilled," he says. He pats the dashboard. "Sorry, no heat in Big Red. Get into a hot shower and you'll be good to go."

"Thanks for the ride."

"Same time next week? Or could you squeeze one in some evening?"

She rolls her eyes. "I think it took me a week to recover from the last one."

"It will get easier faster if we do it more often."

"Wednesday night?"

"That's the spirit!" he says, raising his hand to smack hers. She responds grudgingly. "See you at four o'clock on Wednesday then."

She lets herself out of the car. "Okay."

He beeps the horn and waves as he pulls away, and she wonders how he remains so cheerful given that he too has a mom who can't be there for him.

The rain continues throughout the weekend. Finding herself alone on Sunday afternoon, Brenna takes Kia's journal to the family room. She settles in the big easy chair and tucks her legs up beside her, noticing how sore all her muscles are but not really minding. In a way it feels okay, like she's used them in a good way. She thinks again about going to a yoga class and stretching them out. Maybe later.

As she opens Kia's journal to where she left off, she notices the tug of anticipation in her belly. She hopes Kia doesn't go back to resenting her, the unborn baby.

April 14

I feel like I have a split personality and both of me are having a big fight inside my head. I can't stand it. It goes like this.

Me #1—They're perfect. Brett's cool. Joanna's wonderful.

Brenna blinks, startled by seeing her parents' names. It's surreal hearing about them before they'd even adopted her.

Me #2—But this is our baby. Giving it away—even to THE PERFECT PARENTS—will be like giving away an arm, a leg, even our heart!

Me #1—But we'll be able to go visit. She'll know we are her birth mom.

Brenna stops reading again, wondering about this. Had Kia ever actually visited her?

Me #2—Maybe she'll know she is our flesh and blood, but her real mom will be Joanna. Joanna will be the one rocking her to sleep, kissing her scrapes and bruises, reading her bedtime stories...

Me #1—Quit being so romantic! Joanna will also be changing stinky diapers, getting up in the middle of the night and listening to her whine. We'll just get to enjoy her.

Me #2—My baby won't whine.

Me #1—Get a life.

Brenna smiles at Kia's writing—she'd had a sense of humor even though she was clearly struggling.

Me #2—I can't give her away. Even to THE PERFECT PARENTS.

Me #1—Yes, you can. And you will.

Me #2—Not if I can help it.

Me #1—I've got our parents and Justin and Sadie on my side. Now I've got Brett and Joanna too, as well as every other living person we know!

Me #2—Yeah, but...

Me #1—But what?

Me #2—I've always had more pull than you.

Me #1—LOL We'll see now, won't we?

Me #2—(deep sigh) Yes, I guess we will.

Brenna sinks back and closes her eyes. What a struggle. She'd never imagined the decision had been so difficult. She glances at the entry again, and her heart aches a little, knowing Me #1 won. Even though she knows it's foolish, Brenna feels sad for the loser, Me #2.

May 3
I have to give her up.
There.
I've said it.

Brenna puts the journal down and stares out the window, feeling deeply for this girl, this girl who is now a woman. She has to remind herself that she was the baby who was soon to be given up.

Needing a distraction, she picks up her phone. She doesn't have his number, but she thinks about talking to Ryan. She'd love to hear his voice—he'd make her laugh, snap her out of the mood that reading the journal has brought on. She puts the phone down. Even if she had his number, she wouldn't call. That would be pushing it. He's okay with going on hikes with her—she's his service project, after all—but chatting with her between hikes? That's not part of the deal.

She checks Facebook for another message from Angie. She thinks about responding, coming right out and asking about Kia, but a little part of her doesn't really want to know. For some reason Kia had stopped sending cards, had stopped visiting—if she ever had. Brenna is afraid to know why. Maybe she simply stopped caring about her.

She picks up Kia's journal and with a deep sigh continues to read, trying hard to process the struggle Kia endured. She learns that Kia's pregnancy also impacted her parents and her sister. She reaches the final few entries.

<u>July 28</u>

I'm scared. It's going to hurt so much! The birth, the adoption, everything!

I don't want to be me.

<u>Aug. 14</u>

She called me courageous and generous.

What a joke. I'm scared and greedy.

I don't want to share my baby.

I want her all to myself.

There's a second entry for August 14. Brenna flips the page and sees that it is the last one, and it appears to be a letter to her, the unborn baby.

<u>Aug. 14</u>

Tomorrow is your "birth" day. We will finally meet face to face, even though I already feel like I know you. I have never felt a love like this before.

You will be going home with Joanna and Brett and I believe their love for you is every bit as strong as mine. They want you as badly as I do. Their love must feel different than mine, for you are a part of me, and loving you is really like loving myself, but their love is just as real.

I know they will make excellent parents. After all, I chose them especially for you. You'll know from reading this journal that giving you away is not what I wanted to do, but what I had to do, for your sake. It is the best thing for you, even though it doesn't feel *like the best thing for me right now. My hope is that you'll learn wisdom, compassion and love from Joanna and Brett, for they have so much of it to offer.*

I will love you always, little daughter.

Your mom,

Kia

Closing the journal, Brenna wipes away the tears that are running down her cheeks. Kia was right—her mom and dad did have a lot of wisdom, compassion and love to offer, but so did Kia, even though she was only seventeen years old.

Curling into a little ball in the big armchair, Brenna wonders where Kia is now. Did she still love her like she said she always would? If she did, why did she stop communicating with her? Me #2, the part of Kia that had wanted to keep her, said she'd keep on visiting. What had happened to that?

There is one person who would know. Angie. But for some reason, Angie has not yet mentioned Kia's name. And Kia has not contacted Brenna herself.

seven

...nothing remained but loneliness and grief

(LOUISA MAY ALCOTT, *LITTLE WOMEN*)

Brenna stares at her planner, numbly processing the schoolwork that is piling up: a math quiz to study for, three chapters to read for biology, an essay to write for English. She also has the new-drivers' manual to study. She slumps back in her chair, unable to tackle any of it.

After a few moments she slides her laptop in front of her. Signing into Facebook, she begins to compose yet another message to Angie.

Hi again,

I've just finished reading the journal that Kia wrote when she was expecting me. In it she said she was going to visit me after I was adopted. Can you tell me why she never did?

She stares at what she's written and then deletes it. Part of her really doesn't want to know the answer.

Swiveling her chair around, she stares at her bed. It looks so inviting. Maybe a short nap. Her aunt had told her it was okay to nap, that sometimes people sleep more when they're sad.

Her phone rings. Georgialee again. She can't avoid her forever.

"Hey, Georgialee." She can hear the lack of enthusiasm in her own voice.

"Brenna! What's going on? How come you haven't been answering my calls?"

A bunch of lame excuses come to Brenna's mind, but she doesn't say anything.

"Okay, you're mad at me. I can be insensitive. I get it. Let's get together next Saturday and take Bentley for a long walk, and we'll talk."

Brenna almost smiles. It's astonishing to hear Georgialee admit to being insensitive. "I have my volunteer shift on Saturday."

"Are you still doing that? I thought we agreed that you already had more than enough volunteer hours."

"*We* didn't agree on anything. *You* thought I should quit."

Georgialee is quiet for a moment. "Is it that guy...what's his name? Ryan? Is that why you keep going up there?"

Brenna shakes her head. How can she explain that being on the mountain helps her keep her mom's spirit alive—in a good way, as opposed to a sad way, as it was the rest of the time? Ryan being there? That was just a bonus. "No."

"Okay, how about Sunday afternoon then?"

"Can we make it Sunday morning?"

"No, my group has a run. What are you doing in the afternoon?"

Brenna considers lying. If she mentions the hike, Georgialee will know it is with Ryan, and then there'll be more questions, but she can't come up with anything else. "I'm hiking."

"Hiking?"

"The Grouse Grind."

"Again? With that same guy?"

"Uh-huh. I told you I was going to keep doing it. He's trying to make a Grinder out of me."

"Brenna, you're keeping secrets from me!"

"It's not a secret. It's just something that has…evolved."

"Right."

Brenna knows Georgialee doesn't buy it, but she doesn't have the energy to argue with her. "Okay, then," she says, "how 'bout one day right after school? We won't have as much time, but at least we'd be together."

Brenna can hear Georgialee turning the pages in her planner. "Hmm, I've got soccer practice Monday, field hockey Tuesday. What about Wednesday?"

"I'm hiking that day too."

"Are you kidding me?"

Brenna doesn't respond. She can't think of anything to say.

"There's got to be more to this than you're telling me, Brenna."

"There's not, really."

"Okay, how about Thursday, or are you hiking then too?"

"Thursday works," Brenna says, ignoring the sarcasm.

"Good." Georgialee's voice softens. There's a long pause and then she says, "Bentley misses you, Brenna."

Brenna smiles. She knows Georgialee isn't just talking about the dog. "I miss him too. Give him a hug from me."

"I will, and I'll see you at school tomorrow."

"Yep." Brenna ends the call, knowing she may get glimpses of Georgialee at school, but the reality is they aren't in any of the same classes this year, and Georgialee belongs to so many clubs that she's usually attending meetings during the lunch hour.

Brenna falls onto her bed and pulls a blanket across her shoulders. She presses the soft fabric to her face. She used to be busy at school too. She'd been a founding member of the Social Justice Club. She'd also been one of the grade reps on the student council, but when her mom got sick she'd pulled away from these groups and hadn't found the energy or passion to resume. No one was pushing her to get involved again either. Were they just giving her space, or did they not like being around her anymore—the-girl-whose-mom-died-of-breast-cancer? She must be such a downer.

Sept. 8

So much work...so little energy.

Will I ever go back to being "me"?

Maybe I am not "me" anymore.

I am a new person. A sad, heavy, numb person.

I don't like this new me.

Brenna reads her journal entry and realizes that it sounds like something Kia would have written. Can you inherit your biological mother's writing style?

She stares at the poster hanging on her wall. The round brown eyes of a baby orangutan stare back at her. She'd hung the poster as a reminder of the dream trip she and her mom had planned, a trip to Borneo to visit the Matang Wildlife Centre, where they wanted to volunteer with the orangutan project. Another dream that would never come true.

"Are you going to the fall dance?" Naysa asks, peering into the fridge.

Brenna finishes her bowl of cereal. "I don't know. I'm not sure I'm really into it this year. But you should go."

"My friends are all going," Naysa says. "That's all they talk about. What they're going to wear. Who they want to dance with."

And probably how to get drunk without getting caught, Brenna thinks, remembering her own eighth-grade year.

"I'm hiking after school today, so I won't be here when you get home."

"Who with?" Naysa asks.

"Ryan. The trammie."

Naysa gives her a meaningful glance.

"No, no. We just hike. That's it," Brenna says, answering her sister's unspoken question.

Naysa pours herself a tall glass of chocolate milk.

"You want to come along?" Brenna asks.

Naysa frowns. "Are you kidding me? I did the Grind once. That was enough."

Brenna thinks about telling her how the agony of the hike helps her forget the other kind of pain but decides not to. It's something you have to discover on your own. And besides, her love for the mountain and the wildlife on it is something she shared with her mom—it isn't Naysa's thing.

"I'll probably hang out with Amber after school," Naysa says.

"Who's Amber?"

"A girl I met in math. She seems nice. She went to Lynnmour," she adds.

"What about Sasha and Lauren?" Brenna asks. "How come I never see them around here anymore?"

Naysa shrugs and takes a last swallow of her chocolate milk. She places her glass in the sink with a bang.

Brenna glances at her and wonders again if Naysa's old friends are finding it hard to relate to her now that her mom has died. "Dinner will probably be a little late," she says. "Maybe you could get it started? I'll take something out of the freezer."

Naysa doesn't answer, but Brenna can see the frown that crosses her face as she leaves the kitchen.

Brenna doesn't blame her for being cranky. Starting dinner was something their mother always did, while they shared cleanup duties with their dad. Now they do both.

"So the last time we were hiking, you mentioned something about an aunt contacting you on Facebook."

It is a clear fall day. They had spent the first part of the hike catching up on each other's week.

"Yeah, her name's Angie. She messaged me out of the blue. It was so random."

"Really? Something must have prompted it."

Brenna takes a deep breath and lets it out slowly. "She'd run into the minister who officiated at my mom's service. He'd been a friend of my birth mom. He told her my mom had died." Her voice is barely audible, and she feels her energy sag as she says the words. It hasn't gotten any easier. "She wanted to say she was sorry."

"Are you going to stay in touch?" Ryan's voice is gentle.

Brenna doesn't answer for a moment. She's suddenly aware of the bird sounds coming from the canopy of trees above them. The air is cooler today, and the scent of the forest is earthy. "I don't know," she says finally.

"We've exchanged a few messages, but…" She can't finish the sentence.

Ryan glances back at her but keeps climbing. "I guess it's complicated," he says. "I know all about complicated."

Something about Ryan's words makes Brenna feel safe enough to talk about what she hasn't yet been able to share with anyone else. "I really want to ask her about Kia, my biological mom, but something stops me every time I start to message her. Maybe I'm afraid of what I'll find out."

"How much do you already know?" Ryan asks. He is slowing the pace a little, to Brenna's relief.

"I know she was seventeen when she had me. She didn't want to put me up for adoption but felt she had to. She chose my adoptive parents for me."

"She did a good job of that," Ryan says. "Well, your mom anyway. I don't know your dad."

"Yeah, she did. But I wonder how she'd feel if she knew my mom had died while I was still young. Maybe she does know now."

Ryan stops to pull a granola bar out of his pack. He passes it to her, and she breaks a chunk off and pops it in her mouth before passing it back.

"I can imagine you'd be curious about your other family, but you run the risk of…of what is it they say? Opening a can of worms?"

"Worms? You're calling my relatives worms?" She smiles at him.

"You know what I mean."

"My biological mom kept a journal while she was expecting me. After I was born she gave it to my mom and dad to give to me when they felt I was ready to read it."

He tilts his head. "And?"

"And I just finished reading it."

"Oh." He breaks off another piece of the granola bar and passes it back to her.

She takes it and feels him studying her face. "It was really bizarre, reading about how it felt to be expecting me."

"Yeah, I can imagine."

"She sounded like a pretty cool person though."

"That doesn't surprise me. Look at what she produced." He smiles down at her.

"Very funny."

"I wasn't trying to be funny."

Brenna rolls her eyes but feels the heat in her cheeks, and not just from the exertion of the hike. They start back up the steep trail with Brenna following Ryan again. "In the journal," she says, "Kia said she was going to visit me. I don't know that she ever did. And she used to send me greeting cards on special occasions, but then she stopped. I'd like to know why."

"I'm sure she has her reasons."

"I'd like to know what those reasons are."

"Don't forget about that can of worms."

They've arrived at the ¼ mark sign on the trail. Ryan reaches into his pocket and pulls out his phone. "Go stand by the sign," he says. "I want to take your picture."

"No way," she says. "I'm all sweaty."

"You look good when you're sweaty," he says. "Get over there."

"You get in the picture too," a passing hiker says to Ryan.

"Thanks." Ryan hands the stranger his phone. He grabs Brenna by the arm and pulls her over to the marker.

"Say cheese," the stranger says, holding the phone up to take the picture.

In that second Ryan flings his arm around Brenna and pulls her in close. She smiles in surprise. The hiker clicks the button and looks into the small screen. "Good one," he says and hands the phone back to Ryan.

Ryan checks it and smiles. He hands the phone to Brenna. She glances at the picture and tries not to show how relieved she is that she actually looks okay in it.

"Thanks," Ryan says to the hiker before he strides away.

"Will you text it to me?" Brenna asks.

"Not a chance. You didn't want your picture taken, so why should I send you a copy?" He tucks the phone back into his pocket.

"What?" Brenna smacks his arm in mock fury.

He laughs and pulls the phone back out. "Okay, what's your cell number?"

Once the picture is sent, they continue up the trail. The conversation about Kia is dropped, but Brenna notices that she feels lighter simply from having shared her thoughts with someone.

〜

"Dad, did Kia ever come to visit me when I was a baby?"

Brenna tries to maintain a casual tone as she stacks her plate in the dishwasher, but she's ultra aware of her father's body language as he scrapes out the bottom of a casserole dish.

"Yeah," he says. "She did. Most weekends for the first year she would come by to see you."

"Just for a year?" She hasn't noticed anything unusual in his tone or behavior.

"She went away to school after that. Then, for a few years, she'd come by to see you when she was home for holidays or on summer break."

"Oh."

Her dad drapes the tea towel over his shoulder as he pulls out the stopper in the bottom of the sink. The water goes down the drain with a swoosh. He turns to lean against the counter, folds his arms across his chest and looks at Brenna. "I remember the day she arrived to see you when you were about three. She was really excited, as always, but that year you were shy with her. You hid behind your mom's legs and refused to go on the outing Kia had planned."

Brenna sinks onto a kitchen chair.

"You okay?" her dad asks.

"Yeah, my legs are aching from the hike," she says, but that's not the only reason she had to sit down.

"I think that was very hard for Kia," he continues. "She came by less frequently after that, and you continued to be shy with her. Mind you, you were shy with most people in those days." He regards his daughter thoughtfully. "Have you finished reading her journal?"

She nods.

"Do you want to talk about it?"

"No."

He scans her face again before squeezing her arm. "I have some office work to catch up on," he says, leaving the kitchen.

She hears him walk down the hall and into his office. He shuts the door behind him.

Sept. 11

No wonder she quit visiting.

I rejected her.

I had it backward.

I thought she'd rejected me.

Hi, Angie,

I've noticed that you haven't mentioned Kia, and I'm wondering why. Can you tell me where she is and how she's doing? Thanks.

Brenna hits *Send* before she can delete the message again.

eight

Goodbyes are only for those who love with their eyes.
Because for those who love with heart and soul
there is no such thing as separation!
(RUMI)

Bentley tugs hard on the leash, pulling Brenna away from Georgialee. They're walking north along a trail that follows the winding Seymour River. Although they're only a few minutes from Brenna's neighborhood, it feels like they're miles from anywhere, as the forest is thick and unspoiled around them.

"You can let him go off leash here," Georgialee says.

Brenna unclips the leash and smiles at Bentley's joy as he leaps away.

"So how was your hike yesterday?" Georgialee asks.

"It was hard. It always is."

"I don't want to know about the hiking part," Georgialee says. "It's the hiking-with-Ryan part I want to know more about."

"There's not much to tell. Honest. I'm his service project. When he was going through a rough time, my mom came along and helped him out. He's paying it forward by trying to help me out."

"Hiking the Grouse Grind is his idea of helping you out?"

Brenna feels a wave of defensiveness wash through her. "He says that if I get stronger physically, I'll also get stronger in other ways."

"And? Is it working?"

"All I know is that when I'm on the Grind and every muscle from the waist down is screaming in pain and I can hardly get my breath and I'm soaked in sweat, well, I forget about the other pain for a while."

Georgialee starts to say something but stops herself. Brenna knows it took her a moment to figure out what *the other pain* refers to.

"Did someone die in his family?" she asks quietly.

Brenna nods. "His brother. A car accident."

They walk along the trail in silence for a while.

"Can I give you some advice, Bren?"

"Yeah. What?"

"If you like this Ryan guy, you should find something else to do with him."

Brenna frowns. "Why?"

"Because the image of you all stinky and sweaty with your face twisted in pain...well, it's not too attractive."

Brenna swats her friend's arm. "I'm not trying to be attractive."

Georgialee shakes her head.

They've reached the place where the river widens into a pool with a deep center before spilling over an edge of rocks to continue its winding journey to the ocean. The pool is a popular spot for swimming in the summer months, but it's deserted today. Brenna walks across the rocky beach. She finds a flat-topped boulder and sits on it.

"Scootch over." Georgialee sits beside her, their shoulders pressed together. They watch as Bentley paddles at the shoreline.

"There's something I want to talk to you about," Brenna says, finally finding the nerve to bring up the topic that's troubling her.

"What's that?"

"I got a Facebook message from my biological aunt."

Georgialee turns to look at her. Brenna proceeds to fill her in on the messages they've exchanged as well as telling her about Kia's journal. "And last night I finally got up the courage to ask Angie about Kia. I want to know what's going on in her life."

Georgialee doesn't say anything. After a few moments she climbs off the large rock and starts searching the beach for flat rocks. When she's collected a few, she flings one into the center of the swimming hole, trying to make it skip. Bentley thinks it's an invitation to a game of fetch and swims toward the place where the rock entered the river, but after a quick search he realizes there is nothing to retrieve and paddles back. Georgialee continues to throw rocks and Bentley continues his futile attempts to retrieve them. Brenna wonders what is going through her friend's mind.

Eventually Georgialee returns to the boulder and sits back down. Bentley follows her up the rocky beach, and when he reaches Brenna he begins shaking the water off. "Bentley!" she screams, turning away from the spray.

Bentley simply looks up at her, his tongue hanging out the side of his mouth. It's clear to her that he's smiling. She shakes her head and smiles back. His presence is almost as good as the Grouse Grind for making her forget.

"So do you really want to reunite with your birth mom?" Georgialee finally asks.

"Who said anything about that?"

"Well, that's where this is going, isn't it? You've continued to write back and forth with this Angie. Why would you bother unless you wanted to reestablish ties with Kia?"

It was just like Georgialee to get right to the heart of things.

"I don't know."

"Then I think you should figure that out before you keep exchanging messages with Kia's sister."

"My aunt."

"Yeah, she's your aunt biologically, but she's never been an acting aunt. You have good aunts. Women who care about you. Real aunts."

"What makes them more real than Angie?"

Georgialee shoots Brenna a look. "You don't need me to answer that question."

Brenna doesn't respond, but she remembers that Ryan asked her much the same thing, only in different words. He called it *opening a can of worms.*

Sept. 12

It's easy for her to say.

She has a biological mom, alive and well.

She doesn't know what it's like to have a whole family out there, people she's never met. An aunt, grandparents. A <u>mother</u>. A father. Maybe they've had more children, which could mean I have other brothers and sisters. They could live in my neighborhood—right next door—and I wouldn't even know.

I love Dad and my family, but I can't stop thinking about my biological ones. Do I have the same mannerisms as them? Do I like the same food? Who did I inherit my double-jointed fingers from? My long legs? Is my love of spicy food inherited, or is it unique to me? I want to know these things!

Brenna huddles under the overhang of the Ski Wee cabin. Grinder, followed by Coola, glances at her as they amble past on the other side of the fence.

"I know," she says to them. "It's gross. Go into your bear den and stay dry. No tourists are going to be crazy enough to come out today."

As if they understand, they continue across the enclosure through the drizzling rain and finally disappear into the fog. Brenna shivers as a gust of wind drives the rain straight at her.

A human figure emerges from the fog on her side of the fence, carrying a cup in each hand. As soon as she recognizes him she adjusts the ballcap she pulled on when it started raining.

"Hey," she says as Ryan joins her under the overhang. He hands her a cup. She can smell the hot chocolate even though the cups have lids. "You read my mind. I was just thinking I needed something to warm me up."

"Yep, I heard your thoughts clear across the mountain." He leans back against the building and takes a sip. "Where are the boys today?"

"They just walked by. With no tourists to entertain, they've probably decided to have an early nap. And maybe they wanted to get out of the rain, though I never really thought it bothered them much. Their coats are so thick."

"Yeah, it's a really nasty day. Only Grouse employees on the tram today. Lots of prep to get the mountain ready for the ski season."

Brenna takes a long swallow. The hot chocolate is rich and creamy. She thinks about the approaching ski season. It will mean that the bears' habitat will become smaller as the fencing is taken down and stored until spring. The bears will eventually go into their man-made bear den for winter hibernation, oblivious to the skiers, snowboarders and snowshoers.

"So what's new with you?" Ryan asks after a few moments of comfortable silence.

Brenna continues to warm her hands on her cup. "I got up the nerve to write to my biological aunt and ask her what had become of my mom," she blurts out.

"Kia."

"Right."

"And?"

"That was Wednesday night, and she still hasn't responded."

Ryan doesn't say anything. He's watching a whiskey jack that has landed on the fence beside them. It fluffs up its feathers, trying to shed the raindrops.

Brenna reaches into her pocket and pulls out a couple of peanuts. She stretches her arm toward the bird. He tilts his head, regarding her, and then flies off the fence, perches on her hand for as long as it takes to swallow the peanuts and flies off.

"Cool!" Ryan says.

"The tourists love it," Brenna tells him.

"Did you train him to do that?" he asks.

"No, whiskey jacks are really bold. My mom used to feed them when we went camping. I was too scared to in those days."

The memory is bittersweet. Every time a new one surfaces, she feels a pang of sadness. Will she ever stop missing her? It seems like the more time that goes by, the worse it gets. So much for the theory that it will get easier with time.

"You're not afraid of them anymore?"

"No." She smiles. "I can't even remember why I was so scared of them."

"So…" Ryan pauses and then says, "How are you going to feel if you never hear back from Angie?"

"Rejected. Again."

"Again?"

"It feels like Kia rejected me by not staying in touch. Though actually," she adds, "Dad told me that it was really me who rejected her in the end. I was too shy to go on outings with her."

Ryan nods.

"But she was the grown up. I was just a kid. She could have kept trying." She takes a deep breath and sighs. "I guess I could call Justin, the minister, and see what he can tell me."

There's a movement in the bear habitat, and Coola reappears through the mist.

"I guess it isn't naptime after all," Brenna says.

They watch as the huge grizzly lumbers past. "He's gotten fat!" Ryan comments.

"Yeah, they've been getting a lot more food these last few weeks. They need to put on a couple hundred pounds each before hibernation."

"Whoa. That's so cool."

"I know."

"What do you do when they're in hibernation?"

"I'll take the winter off and come back in the spring when they wake up."

"Good thing you're my hiking partner then."

She glances at him.

"So that I still get to see you." He glances at his watch. "I've got to go. Same time tomorrow?"

"Yep, and thanks for the hot chocolate. I really needed that today."

He crumples up his cup and drops it into a garbage bin as he walks away. Brenna expects him to head back across the mountain, but he turns and walks toward her instead. He pauses in front of her and then pulls her into a hug.

"Angie may have good reasons for not wanting to talk about her sister. Try not to read too much into it," he says.

Brenna is so startled by the hug that she doesn't return it. After a moment he releases her but quickly kisses her cheek and then runs back into the bank of fog. He turns once to wave before he disappears.

Brenna sinks into the scented bubbles. She's still chilled to the core from her day on the mountain, but the warm bathwater immediately brings relief. She sighs and closes her eyes. Her thoughts return to Ryan, and she smiles.

She'd missed his tram on the trip down the mountain, but she'd seen him in the one going up, which was empty except for him, as the two trams passed each other. She'd waved and he'd waved back, and he kept waving until she couldn't see his tram anymore.

Sept. 14
It was just a hug and a kiss on the cheek.
It probably means nothing.
I know it means nothing.
I haven't felt this good in months.

Brenna checks her Facebook messages, hoping to find one from Angie that she might have missed, but there is nothing. She scrolls through the posts from her friends. Most of them contain links to other sites, and she can't be bothered to open them. She's about to shut it off when a new message appears.

Hi, Brenna,
Here's my email address. Write to me here and then I'll have yours, and we can communicate that way. angiehazelnut@hotmail.com
Thanks,
Angie

As quickly as she can, Brenna copies the address, opens her email account and pastes it in the *To* field.

In the subject line she types *My email* and then hits *Send*. She sits back and stares at her inbox. Five minutes pass. Ten minutes. She realizes how fast her breathing has become. What if Angie doesn't get back to her tonight? Not able to sit still any longer, she gets up and stretches, then bends into a forward fold. She raises her arms, stands and flows into a sun salutation. After five of them she glances at her computer, but there are no new messages. She drops to the floor, lies on her back and moves into a twist, first on the right side, then on the left. She holds them as long as she can. When she looks up at her computer again, she sees that there is a new message in her inbox. Scrambling back into her chair, she clicks on the message.

From: angiehazelnut@hotmail.com
To: brennayoko@gmail.com

Hi, Brenna,

This is better. Thanks.

So, you asked about Kia. She works for an organization called Aid-A-Child International. Her job is to supervise volunteers working in orphanages in Africa. She has a passion for children. Most of these kids have AIDS. She's been in Uganda for over a year.

I should tell you, I don't think Kia would be very happy to hear that we are connecting this way. I really only wanted to write to tell you how sorry I was about your mom and couldn't see the harm in that. I didn't anticipate that we'd stay in touch, but I'm glad we have.

Tell me a little about yourself, Brenna. What school do you go to? What do you like to do when you're not at school? I'm finishing up my university degree this year. I took time off after high school to work and travel. I hope to teach high school in the near future.

Angie

Brenna reads the letter twice. Kia? Working with orphans? She quickly googles Uganda and brings up a map of Africa to locate the country. It is on the east side of the continent and straddles the equator. Kia couldn't get much farther away. Then Brenna looks up Aid-A-Child and reads about the work it does. It would be difficult, in hard conditions. Working with orphans, especially the ones with AIDS, would be especially hard.

Brenna shuts off the computer without responding to Angie. She lies on her bed and stares at the ceiling. Eventually she picks up her journal again.

I should be proud of Kia.
I'm not.
She's so far away, doing important work.
She's probably forgotten me.
I know those children need her.
But I need her too.

Brenna lies in bed on Sunday morning, still trying to absorb the new information about Kia. She picks up her pen and continues to write.

Sept. 15

Why would she be unhappy that Angie has contacted me? That hurts.

She's not going to step back into my life. I am so stupid.

Everything sucks. What's the matter with me? And I am not going to be Ryan's project. I'm so pathetic.

She picks up her phone and texts Ryan.

Hey, Ryan. I'm not up to hiking today. Actually, I don't think the hikes are working out. Thanks anyway. I'll probably see you on my next shift.

nine

The cure for anything is salt water—sweat, tears, or the sea.

(ISAK DINESEN, *OUT OF AFRICA*)

Brenna slams the fridge door. "There's nothing good to eat in this house."

Naysa and their father glance at each other. "Put whatever you're craving on the grocery list and I'll pick it up next time I'm shopping," he says. "You know the deal," he adds quietly.

"Are you hiking today?" Naysa asks. She's doing homework at the kitchen table.

"No, I gave that up."

"Oh." Naysa glances at her father again. He shrugs.

Brenna stomps back to her room and checks her phone. There's a message, a sad-face emoji, from Ryan. She throws the phone onto her bed.

The weather has cleared overnight, so she grabs her biology textbook, Kia's journal and a soft blanket and goes outside to the sundeck. Pulling a lounge chair into a sunny corner, she snuggles down under the blanket, opens the textbook and turns to where she left off, but even though her eyes skim the lines of print, nothing reaches her brain. She leans back in the deck chair and closes her eyes. The sun is warm on her face.

An hour passes. She's aware of the doorbell ringing but has drifted into a dreamlike state. It's probably a neighbor dropping off yet another casserole. Or brownies. She's grown tired of casseroles—they still receive a few each week. But she also knows that when they stop coming, she will wonder if it means people are beginning to forget her mom. She'd happily continue eating casseroles if it kept her mother's memory alive. Gifts of comfort food are symbols of love—

"Hello, Brenna."

A deep voice startles Brenna out of her light nap. Sitting up, she swivels around and finds Ryan standing on the deck behind her.

"Your dad let me in."

"Oh." Brenna slumps back down in the chair, embarrassed. "Hi."

"Can I join you?" he asks.

She nods and uses a foot to push a chair toward him.

"I came to see if you're okay," he says, "and to find out why you suddenly quit hiking."

"I never actually liked hiking—you know that."

"Maybe not, but you were willing to give it a try, and you liked being on the mountain."

She doesn't answer, and for the first time since he's arrived she looks up and meets his eyes. He's studying her face.

"Was it something I said?" he asks. "Or something I did?"

She knows he's referring to the hug and kiss on her cheek. "No," she says, quickly looking away. "It's just too hard. I don't have it in me right now." She closes her eyes again.

"Is that Kia's journal?" he asks, referring to the small book on her lap.

"Yeah."

He doesn't respond. After a moment Brenna opens her eyes to see if he's even still there. He is.

"We could do a different hike today," he says. "An easier one. I was probably being a tyrant about doing the Grind so often when you haven't worked up to it."

Brenna shrugs.

"There's a really nice one just down the road. Quarry Rock."

"I've done Quarry Rock. The whole world has hiked Quarry Rock."

"Then you know it's not hard. Come on. We could be done in an hour and a half and you could get back to your book." He takes the biology textbook off her lap and scans the cover. "Obviously a riveting read."

She smiles a little despite herself.

"So, what do you say?"

She hesitates but then looks into his face. The warmth of his smile melts her resolve. "Okay. I'm not getting much studying done anyway." She climbs out of her chair. "Let me get changed."

Ryan holds up his hand for a high five. "Attagirl!"

She smacks it, but her hand is limp.

After sliding into some yoga pants and a T-shirt, Brenna finds that Ryan has joined Naysa at the kitchen table. "Your little sister is a math genius," he tells Brenna. He hands her a sheet with 10/10 scrawled across the top. "This is her first math quiz of the year, and she nailed it."

"Yeah, Naysa got all the brains in this family," she says, then realizes how stupid that is. It isn't like they share the same genes.

At the Quarry Rock lookout they find at least a dozen other hikers sprawled across the flat outcrop, enjoying the view. Ryan takes Brenna's hand and pulls her closer to the cliff edge. "Want to sit here for a bit? Soak up some rays?"

She nods but she hardly notices the rays. A pulse of electricity had jolted her entire body at the touch of his hand.

The sunlight sparkles on the water far below them. Indian Arm, as the fjord is called, is speckled with

DANCING IN THE RAIN

recreational boaters enjoying one of the last Sundays of the boating season.

Ryan lets go of Brenna's hand as they sit down, but he takes it again and squeezes gently. "I never get tired of this view," he says.

Brenna wonders if her hand is sweaty or if she should squeeze back. Why did he even take her hand?

"It's so different than the view from Grouse," he continues. "Up there, you see the city with the high-rises and bridges, all the engineering genius of humankind. Here you see only ocean, sky and forest."

"The engineering genius of Mother Nature."

Brenna senses, rather than sees, Ryan's smile. "Or God's genius," he says.

"Different names, same thing."

He squeezes her hand again. "That so sounds like something your mom would have said."

She laughs. "She did. I stole the line from her. I've been waiting years for the chance to use it."

Ryan lets go of her hand and wraps his arm around her shoulder, pulling her against him. "You're too funny, Brenna."

She leans into him and tries to relax, noticing how her dark mood has lifted. All her senses have heightened, and she can practically feel the endorphins bouncing around in her bloodstream. Breathing in a lungful of fresh air, she watches as a sailboat comes about in the water below the lookout. It seems to be heeling precariously low in the water.

Ryan leans his face against her hair. She senses him inhaling deeply, breathing her in. "Did something not so good happen this morning?" he asks.

Brenna feels those same endorphins scramble back to where they came from. She sits up straighter. "Not really."

Ryan remains quiet.

"I got an email from Angie last night," she admits finally.

"Oh." Ryan doesn't say anything for a moment. His arm begins to feel heavy on her shoulder. "You didn't like what she said?"

Brenna shrugs. She feels her eyes begin to well up with tears, but she blinks hard, forcing herself to remain in control. "Apparently, Kia, my birth mom, works for Aid-A-Child. She oversees volunteers who work in orphanages."

She feels Ryan sit up, and he pulls his arm off her shoulder so he can turn to look more closely at her. "Is that a bad thing?"

"No. But she's working in Africa. With kids who have AIDS."

"Whoa! That's so cool!"

Brenna shrugs. "And Angie didn't think Kia would be happy that she had contacted me."

"Did she say why?"

"No."

"It could be for a lot of reasons."

"I guess."

Ryan picks up her hand again and cradles it in both of his. She stares at the white crescents at the base of his nails.

They continue to watch the boating activity in silence. A breeze sends little ripples across the water, while a shiver ripples up Brenna's spine.

"You're cooling off," Ryan says. "We should head back down."

Brenna nods, but she's reluctant to let go of Ryan's hand. Sometime in the last few minutes their fingers have intertwined. She likes the feel of his strong fingers squeezing hers, and she no longer cares if hers are sweaty. Ryan doesn't seem to mind.

As she follows him down the twisting trail she wonders about his life, feeling a twinge of guilt that they're always talking about hers. "Did you say you never actually finished high school?" she asks.

"No, not *actually.*" He smiles at her over his shoulder. "Another reason I appreciated your mom for hiring me. It's hard to get a job without a high school diploma."

"You didn't want to go to school in Vancouver?"

He shrugs. "I never intended to stay in Canada this long. I always thought I'd go back and finish school at home."

"But you haven't."

"Not yet. But I will."

Brenna thinks about that. Another person who will eventually leave her. Her mood plummets further. She doesn't respond.

"When my mom is released from the treatment center she's in, I'll go help her out. And I'll have saved up enough to take care of her for a while. That's the plan anyway."

Treatment center? Brenna decides not to ask. "And you'll finish school then?"

"Hopefully. Or do it through distance education."

They have reached a wooden bridge that spans a stream meandering down Mount Seymour. As they lean against the rail they look up at the trickling water. Ryan puts his arm around her shoulder again.

"I think I'll contact the minister," she says. "He was Kia's friend, and he encouraged me to contact him if I wanted to talk. I'll see what he can tell me about Kia. Maybe we can meet at a coffee shop or something."

"Let me know if you want me there," he says. "Moral support."

"Thanks, that would be nice." She leans into him. "I guess I'm opening that can of worms, aren't I?"

"Yes, I'd say you are." Ryan turns and leads the way back down the trail. "But I always rather liked worms."

Brenna rifles through her desk drawer until she finds what she is looking for—the business card she was given at the chapel where her mom's service was held. It has all of the minister's contact information on it. She decides to send him an email and chooses the more informal-looking address of the two that are listed.

From: brennayoko@gmail.com
To: justintime@yahoo.com

Hello Reverend Reid,

After my mom's service, you said it would be okay to contact you if I wanted to talk about anything. I hope that offer is still open. I was wondering if maybe we could meet and include Angie Hazelwood. I have some questions about my birth mom, Kia.

Thank you.

Brenna Yokoyama

Sept. 15

Ryan has "mother issues" too. What else do we have in common?

Kia wrote about that instant/magnetic/physical pull between her and Derek. (My father. Weird.) It's different for me and Ryan. Ours is like a friendship that is becoming closer. It felt so good to hold hands, to feel his arm around me. If Dad hadn't been in the yard when we got home, would he have kissed me again? A real one this time?

I think so.

Did I want him to?

Yes.

Mom's only been gone 2 months. Is it wrong to feel this way???

⌒

"Whatcha doin'?" Georgialee slides into the chair next to Brenna in the school computer lab.

"Nothing." She quickly exits the website she's been browsing, but it's too late. Georgialee has seen it.

"Aid-A-Child?" Georgialee asks.

"Just researching a project for the Social Justice Club," she says. Her skin burns with the lie. She can't meet Georgialee's eyes.

"Are you joining again?"

Brenna shrugs.

"Why Aid-A-Child?"

"I've always been interested in them."

"You have?"

"Uh-huh."

"I didn't know that."

Brenna can hear the skepticism in her friend's voice. "They do good work." She knows she should tell her the truth, but she's not ready to do that. "Did you know that 2.4 million children under the age of fifteen in Uganda have lost one or both parents to HIV/AIDS, the most of any in the world? And many of those children also test positive for HIV."

Georgialee studies Brenna's face. "Social Justice Club is starting up again on Thursday," she says. "Will you be there?"

"I'm thinking of it."

"That's great, Brenna! Everyone will be glad to see you again."

Brenna knows she should tell the truth now, before the lie grows any bigger, but she can't find the words.

"And are you going to the school dance on Friday night too?"

"No. I'm not feeling it."

"Too bad. I was hoping to meet Ryan."

"What makes you think I'd bring him?"

"Wishful thinking, I guess. I think it's time I meet him. Make sure he's good enough for my best friend."

"I'm his service project, Georgialee." She knows she's stretching the truth again, so she changes the subject. "Keep an eye on Naysa for me."

"Oh. My. God." Georgialee shakes her head. "I can't believe Naysa's actually old enough to go to a school dance. I still think of her as a little pesky kid."

"I know. Me too."

ten

Tears are words the mouth can't say nor can the heart bare.

(JOSHUA WISENBAKER)

From: justintime@yahoo.com
To: brennayoko@gmail.com

Hello, Brenna,

First of all, please call me Justin. Reverend Reid makes me feel so old! And stern. ☺ I'm so glad you contacted me. I'd be delighted to meet with you and hope Angie will also join us. Evenings and Saturdays work best for me.

Justin

Brenna stares at Justin's email. Connecting with Angie via email is completely different than meeting her in person. She decides to send the invitation before it's too late.

From: brennayoko@gmail.com
To: angiehazelnut@hotmail.com

Hi, Angie,

Justin Reid and I are planning to get together to talk. We're wondering if you'd like to join us. Evenings and Saturdays work best for Justin.

Let me know.

Brenna

Brenna quickly hits *Send* before she loses her nerve.

From: angiehazelnut@hotmail.com
To: brennayoko@gmail.com

Hi, Brenna,

I'd love to meet you! Just tell me when and where. I'll be there!

Angie

Sept. 17
The can of worms has been split wide open.

⌒〜

"I got myself into a bit of a bind with my friend Georgialee," Brenna tells Ryan. They've passed the halfway point on the Grind and have stepped to the side of the trail to catch their breath.

"Oh yeah?" Ryan wipes his face with the red bandanna he's had tied around his head.

"Uh-huh." She wonders why it's so easy to share things with him. "She caught me looking at a website with info about Ugandan orphans."

"Oh no! Not that!" He feigns horror. "Now she's going to hack into your illegal baby-smuggling operation!"

Brenna swats his back as he replaces the bandanna and resumes his lead up the steep trail. "I don't know why, but I haven't told her what I found out about Kia."

"That's understandable. It's pretty personal," he says.

"Yeah, but I lied and said I was researching a project for the Social Justice Club."

"Uh-oh." Ryan glances back at her. "Lies have a way of coming back to bite us in the butt."

"Exactly. So now I either have to go to the first meeting tomorrow and suggest a project or admit to Georgialee that I was lying."

"Which is worse?"

"I don't know. Probably admitting that I was lying, 'cause then she'd want to know why."

"Then I guess you'd better come up with a project."

Brenna sighs. "Like what?"

"It's a no-brainer," Ryan says. "Raise money to send to Aid-A-Child to help with those orphans. No one has to know your connection to it."

Brenna stops dead in her tracks as the possibilities settle over her. This would be the perfect way to reconnect with Kia. Why hadn't she thought of it herself?

"You okay?" Ryan asks, retracing his steps to stand with her.

Brenna nods but doesn't say anything. Her mind and heart are racing.

"Maybe it wasn't such a good idea," he says, misunderstanding her reaction.

"Or maybe it was!" She starts to move again, ideas pinging through her brain. "Any thoughts on how we can raise money?"

"I always liked cupcake sales," Ryan teases.

Brenna rolls her eyes. "Just what I need," she says. "Cupcakes. My freezer is still full of brownies and Nanaimo bars."

"Maybe you could sell those too."

"Yeah, maybe." She smiles.

"But I think what you need to do is figure out how to sell this idea to the club first," Ryan says. "And then figure out how to raise money."

"You're right. I'll do some more research tonight." The decision gives her a rush of energy, and she picks up her pace, pushing past Ryan.

"Hey!" He grabs her daypack, pulling her back so he can scoot ahead of her again. "I'm the leader here."

"Oh yeah?" She snatches at his arm as he's maneuvering past, but he hip-checks her and takes the lead again.

Brenna then grabs his pack, causing him to lose his balance on the steep slope. He crashes into her and they both begin to slide downward. They quickly come to a stop, but by then Ryan has grabbed her with both arms to regain his balance. Laughing, he pulls her into a hug. She laughs too and squirms, but he doesn't let go and then they both become still. Brenna notices that their breathing, which is deep from the exertion, is in unison. He smells warm, earthy. She finally looks up and finds him looking down at her. The forest is still. Their faces are close. She lifts a hand to push back the bandanna, which is sliding down his forehead. He places his hand over hers, holding it against his face.

"Brenna..."

"Yes?"

Voices of hikers coming around a bend in the trail below snap them out of the moment. Ryan doesn't finish what he was going to say and slowly releases her. He gestures for her to take the lead. "After you, mademoiselle," he says, sweeping his arm out to let her pass.

"Thank you, kind sir," she says as she takes the lead. Thoughts of her Social Justice project have been replaced with thoughts of Ryan. What had he been about to say?

～

Forty-five minutes later, Ryan raises his fist in a gesture of victory. "We conquered it once again!" he shouts.

They've left the trail and are standing right below the chalet. "That's five Grinds under your belt now," he says. "Is it getting any easier?"

"I'm not wearing a belt," she says between heaving breaths, "and no." She gulps down the remainder of her water, not caring that half of it spills down her chest. The intimacy of the moment on the trail is gone.

Ryan glances at his watch. "I think you're wrong. We've already shaved ten minutes off our time. That's two minutes less per Grind."

"You've been keeping track?"

"Yeah, why not?"

"I don't know. Too much pressure."

"Have I been pressuring you?"

Brenna pushes him in the chest. "I wouldn't be here right now if you hadn't pressured me to take up hiking!"

"You've got a point." He smiles and cocks his head.

"And if I'd known you were timing us, I wouldn't have taken so many breaks."

"That's why I didn't tell you," he says.

"But now I know, so I'll feel the pressure next time!"

He rolls his eyes. "Forget I said anything." He leads the way to the Skyride. "But ten minutes is ten minutes."

They both stare at the view unfolding below the tram. "We won't be able to hike in the afternoon for much longer," Ryan says.

"No," Brenna agrees. The sun is beginning to set behind Vancouver Island in the far distance. "It's getting dark earlier and earlier."

"We'll just have to go twice on the weekends," he says.

"Are you serious?"

"Yeah. The first snow will probably fall in November, and then we'll have to quit for the season."

"That's when we start the Snowshoe Grind."

"That's right! You remembered." He smiles down at her.

"I've never snowshoed before."

"Neither had I before I moved here. You're going to love it."

Brenna watches the valley station as it comes into view. She doesn't know about that, but she's glad to have a reason to keep on seeing Ryan.

"Whatcha doing?" Naysa asks, peering into the fridge.

Brenna closes the website she was browsing when Naysa came into the kitchen. She had spent the last couple of hours researching information to bring to the next day's Social Justice Club meeting, knowing she'll need a good pitch to sell her idea. The first meeting of the year is when everyone has a chance to suggest projects. "Homework."

As Naysa walks around the kitchen table, she glances at the screen of Brenna's computer. The photo of her and

Ryan on the Grind is on her desktop. "He seems like a nice guy."

"He is. So what's up with you?" Brenna asks, wanting to change the subject.

"What do you think I should wear to the dance?" Naysa asks, spooning chocolate pudding into her mouth.

"Nothing too warm. It gets really hot in that gym." Brenna scans Naysa's body, noticing with surprise that Naysa has put on some weight too. Damn those desserts their neighbors keep delivering. "Why don't we go to the mall after school tomorrow? Find you something new to wear?"

Naysa's eyes light up. "Really? That would be awesome!"

"I know Dad wanted to buy you some back-to-school clothes anyway."

Naysa smiles. "Thanks, Brenna!"

From: justintime@yahoo.com
To: brennayoko@gmail.com

Hi, Brenna,

Would next Friday work? (I have plans for this week.) Check with Angie. If it's a go we can choose a location.

Justin

Brenna shows the Social Justice Club a YouTube video clip from the Aid-A-Child organization. The camera work is professional, the music draws viewers in, and although the story of the orphaned children is tragic, it has a positive spin. It's both heart-wrenching and inspiring. She shuts off her computer. "So you see?" she says to the group gathered around her computer. "If we get involved, we can make a difference."

"You want us to go to Uganda?" Jas asks and then smiles at the laughter from the rest of the group.

Brenna ignores him and continues with her well-rehearsed conclusion. "These children just need proper medicine, nutritious food and some loving care. Aid-A-Child is an organization that is there right now doing the work. But they need money, and that's where we come in." She looks around the room. "Any questions?"

There's a long pause while the group processes the information. "Why did you choose Uganda?" Georgialee asks, and Brenna recognizes the skepticism in her voice. "There are organizations all around the world that are crying out for donations."

"Like I told you, HIV has hit Uganda hard. There are so many children who have lost both parents to AIDS. Why not Uganda?" Brenna doesn't make eye contact with her friend.

"There must have been something that made you aware of this organization."

Brenna simply shrugs.

"Last year we decided we wanted to take on social-justice issues close to home," Courtney reminds her.

"And our mandate is to educate rather than fundraise," Blair adds.

"So, this is a new year," Brenna says. "And we can educate people about the orphaned children of Uganda while also fundraising for them."

The room grows quiet.

Brenna begins to panic. While doing the research, her plan had become cemented in her heart. She knows she only has a few more minutes to sell her idea and through it make a connection with Kia. "What I really like about Aid-A-Child," she says, "is that they discourage their orphans from begging on the streets by teaching them skills, like dancing or singing. Then the kids perform to raise money to help themselves."

"Then why do they need our help?" Blair asks.

"What they earn doesn't nearly cover what they need. But at least they're not just sitting around waiting for handouts."

The bell rings, ending the lunch hour. "Let's think about it over the week," Courtney says. "And if anyone else has any project ideas, they can present them next Thursday."

Naysa steps out of the boutique's change room. She's wearing a short snug skirt with a long loose-fitting blouse that flows as she moves. She also has a scowl on her face, the same one she's been wearing since they started shopping.

Brenna nods. "That's better. What do you think?"

Naysa steps in front of the full-length mirror and turns to look at her backside. "I don't know…"

"This suits you way better than all those snug tops," Brenna tells her sister. "This blouse is glam. And you have great legs. The skirt lets you show them off."

Naysa's eyes fill with tears. They've been on this mission for two hours already, and they are both frustrated. "I'm not trying to look glam!" she says. "I want to look like everyone else!"

Brenna sighs. She knows the feeling. At a school dance everyone wants to look as hot as they can, but they also don't want to stand out by looking different. The trouble is, what everyone else will be wearing doesn't suit Naysa's changed shape. "Let's put this outfit on hold, just in case we don't find anything else. But we'll keep looking."

"Maybe I won't go to the stupid dance," Naysa mumbles, slamming the change-room door shut behind her.

Brenna leans back in the armchair in the waiting area. She feels like she's Naysa's parent instead of her sister. What would her mom have done in this situation? She sinks deeper into the chair. Her mother wouldn't have had to deal with this. Both of her daughters have gained weight as a result of her dying. When she was alive and healthy, she cooked delicious meals, and they were lighter than the cheesy casseroles they've been eating for months now, and dessert used to be a rare treat. Maybe it's a good thing the supply of donated food in the freezer is beginning to dwindle.

The quest for the perfect outfit continues without success. An hour later they're back in the same shop, purchasing the skirt and blouse. With a grim face, Naysa takes the bag from the salesgirl and leads the way out of the mall.

"I'm going on a diet," Naysa grumbles. They're sitting on a bench at the bus stop.

Brenna doesn't respond. She knows there's no right thing to say, but in her mind she thanks Ryan for getting her moving again. Knowing she doesn't have the will-power to diet, she can at least burn off those casserole calories. She sees the bus in the distance, and an idea hits her. "C'mon, Naysa." She grabs her sister's arm. "We're going to walk home."

"We're what?" Naysa asks, pulling her arm away.

"We're going to walk home. It will be good for us."

"It's at least five miles!" Naysa says, appalled.

The bus pulls up to the curb and the doors swing open. The girls remain on the sidewalk, glaring at each other.

"In or out?" the driver asks.

"C'mon," Brenna urges. "Let's go."

Naysa hesitates.

"Well?" the driver asks.

"In." Naysa steps onto the bus. She flashes her bus pass at the driver.

Brenna follows her up the steps, feeling powerless. Naysa selects a seat right behind the driver, and there's a woman in the window seat, so there's no room for Brenna.

She gets the message and moves to the rear, where she takes a seat and rides home alone.

Stepping onto the Skyride, Brenna sees that the trammie is not Ryan. She considers stepping off and waiting for the next tram but quickly decides against it. She could text to let him know she's on the mountain, but she chooses not to do that either. He knows her volunteer shift has reverted to Saturday mornings. She tries to see into the passing tram at the halfway mark, but it's too crowded. The weather has become unseasonably warm, and there are a lot of visitors heading up.

Her phone rings as she's walking across the alpine meadow toward the bear habitat. She pulls it out of her pocket, hoping to see Ryan's name on the call display, but it's Georgialee. "Hey, Georgia."

"Brenna! Did you have your phone on mute last night?"

"Yeah, but not until I went to bed."

"Oh yeah, I guess it was kinda late when I called."

Brenna thinks back to the evening. Naysa had been at the dance, and her dad had shut himself in his office after she declined his invitation to watch a movie together. She'd wanted to spend the evening researching fundraising ideas and reading more about the Aid-A-Child organization. She desperately needed to find a reason why Ugandan orphans were the ideal choice for the Social Justice Club project, and not just because Kia worked there.

"How was the dance?"

"Okay. Same old. It got really hot."

"Temperature hot or hot hot?"

"Both. Steamin' hot."

Brenna smiles to herself. Maybe she should have invited Ryan to the dance after all. "So you phoned to report on who hooked up with whom?"

"No, though we'll get to that later. I phoned about your sister."

"Did something happen?" Brenna's entire body tenses up. Ever since her mother died, she's become ridiculously overconcerned about her sister's and her dad's well-being.

"Remember you told me to keep an eye on her?"

"Yeah."

"Well, about halfway through the night I saw her on the dance floor with a bunch of girls I didn't recognize. They weren't the kids I used to always see at your house." Georgialee pauses. "I wanted to say hi to her, so I went and started dancing with them."

"And?" Brenna has almost reached the bear habitat, so she slows her pace.

"Well...I think she was drunk."

Brenna comes to a complete halt. That was the last thing she expected to hear. "Naysa? Are you sure?"

"Ninety-nine percent. When she saw me she practically fell into my arms. Apparently, she was that happy to see me.

I thought I smelled booze, but when she started introducing me to her friends I realized they were all pissed. I'm not sure how they got past the teachers at the door, but there are ways."

Brenna collapses on a bench. "Are you sure, Georgia?"

"Yeah. Sober girls don't dance like that. There was a lot of dirty dancing going on in that gym, but these girls were almost out of control."

Brenna is beyond stunned. "They didn't get busted?"

"Not that I saw."

Naysa had made plans to sleep over at a friend's after the dance. The oldest trick in the world.

"Listen," Georgialee says. "You didn't hear about this from me, okay? I don't want to be the bad guy."

"Okay."

"And go gentle on her. She's probably feeling like hell today."

"Yeah yeah. Thanks for letting me know."

Brenna goes into Ski Wee and counts out the bears' carrots, potatoes and apples. She tosses them in the buckets, but she struggles to stay focused. Naysa has always been a sweet kid and an excellent student. Getting drunk at her first high school dance doesn't seem like something her sister would do. She'll have to talk to her, but she won't tell her dad. He doesn't need anything else to worry about right now. The feeling of being a surrogate mother settles over her; she's not ready for the responsibility.

The morning disappears quickly. Once again Brenna finds that the mountain air makes the cares of "real" life evaporate. Even the worry about Naysa eventually dissipates as she talks to the visitors about the bears. She finds herself glancing in the direction of the chalet a few times, hoping to see Ryan coming toward the refuge, but that's only because he's become a frequent visitor. When her four-hour shift is over, she walks slowly back to the chalet, reluctant to leave her mountain sanctuary.

Ryan is the first person she sees when she steps into the chalet. He's sitting on a couch in front of the giant fireplace, his back to the door. He's with three female Grouse employees, all wearing matching Grouse fleeces. They have gathered close, focused on a story he's sharing. His arms wave about as he speaks.

Brenna steps back outside, not wanting to be noticed, but she watches through the window. It must be a good story, she thinks. The girls are smiling and leaning in toward him, waiting for the punch line. When it comes they all throw their heads back with laughter.

Ryan seems to be enjoying the attention. She watches him launch into another story, or perhaps he's just continuing the one he was telling. The girls are being seduced by his charming Aussie accent, she thinks. After all, that's what charmed her into thinking there was something going on between them.

She takes the outside stairs to the Skyride station.

Sept. 21

I am not his girlfriend.

Why am I getting so bent out of shape?

I should quit hiking, At least with him. I've got all the turmoil I can handle for now. I don't need to invite any more my way.

I'm up. I'm down. I just want to coast.

It's the middle of the afternoon. Brenna knocks lightly on Naysa's door, and when she gets no answer she peeks inside. Naysa is in bed, sound asleep, and she's still wearing the new blouse she wore to the dance. She really must have tied one on last night, Brenna thinks. She decides to let her sleep it off.

Lying on her own bed, she stares at the ceiling. She tries to let all her thoughts flow by, the way they tell you to during the meditation part of yoga, but it's too hard.

The chime on her phone signals an incoming text message. She reaches for it and sits up when she sees Ryan's name.

G'day, Brenna! Sorry I missed you this a.m. Was at a staff training session all morning. I might be getting promoted!! ☺ Grind day tm? Same time/place?

She doesn't respond.

⌒⌣

"Can we have something other than casserole tonight?" Brenna sits down beside her father on the couch. He's watching a nature documentary on TV. "Mom's favorite channel," she comments, noticing.

"Yeah, I was thinking that too."

"About the casserole or the TV channel?"

"The TV channel." He glances at her. "But I'm tired of casserole too. What do you suggest?"

"Maybe I'll go through Mom's recipe file and find something."

"Good idea," he says, but his eyes don't leave the TV screen, where a lone butterfly lands on a milkweed bloom. The butterfly's wings flutter delicately.

"Because of the eradication of the milkweed plant from widespread herbicide use," the commentator says, "the monarch butterfly's numbers have declined by 44 percent this year alone."

"That would really have upset Mom," Brenna says.

"Yeah, it would have. I guess it's a blessing she's been spared any more news about how we're messing up the planet."

"That's a weird kind of blessing."

"I'll take any blessings I can get," he replies.

Brenna retrieves the recipe file from the kitchen and brings it back to the family room. She pulls out one card after another, all written in her mom's perfect handwriting.

"That's a good one," her dad says, looking over her shoulder. It's a recipe for red peppers stuffed with quinoa and a lot of chopped vegetables and beans.

"Yeah, but it's also lots of work. I'm not quite up for that tonight."

She continues to pull out cards. Spinach soup. Greek frittata. Black bean salad.

"Could I have this?" she asks her dad, referring to the recipe box.

"Have what?" Naysa's standing in the doorway, her hands on her hips. Her hair is wrapped in a towel, and she's wearing her housecoat.

"This is an odd time of day for you to be showering," their dad says, glancing at his watch.

Naysa shrugs. "I didn't want to shower at Janine's house."

"Oh, right. So how was the dance?" he asks. "You must not have slept much at Janine's." He takes a hard look at her. "Are you okay? I was surprised to find you napping in the middle of the afternoon."

"I'm fine. It was fine," she snaps. "What does Brenna want to keep?"

"Mom's recipes," he says.

"What if I want them?"

"Well, then, we'll have to discuss that, won't we?"

Naysa plunks herself on the other side of Brenna. She pulls out a card. *Pasta Puttanesca*. "I always liked this one."

Brenna glances at it. "Me too."

"How about this one?" their dad asks. He's holding up the recipe for curried cauliflower.

Brenna takes it from him and skims the directions. "It's not too much work either. Do you want it tonight? We can have it with rice and a salad."

"I'm not too hungry," Naysa says.

Brenna glances at her, sees she's a little pale and remembers why. "More for Dad and me then," she says.

"And I don't want you giving Mom's stuff away without asking me," Naysa says. The snarky tone is back in her voice, and there's a deep frown etched across her forehead. She continues to pull recipe cards out of the box.

Her dad clears his throat. "I'm glad you've brought up the subject of your mother's things," he says. "Aunt Laura has asked if she can come over and help us clean out Mom's closet."

"No. I'm not ready." Naysa's voice trembles.

"I'm not either," her dad says. "But I don't know that I ever will be. I think we should find a time when we're all free and go through her closet together. You can keep anything you want."

"No!" Naysa flings the recipe cards into Brenna's lap before stomping out of the room. Brenna begins the task of slotting each one back into the box.

"Maybe we'll stick with casserole tonight," her father says. "I don't really feel like picking up groceries anyway. We'll make the curry tomorrow."

Back in her room, Brenna rereads the message from Ryan. She's tempted to cancel again, but that didn't work for her last Sunday. She sends a text, agreeing to meet, but vows not to fall under his Aussie spell again. She's hiking to get stronger. Period.

⌒

Their father leaves Brenna and Naysa in the kitchen to clean up the dinner dishes while he retreats to his office. Brenna knows this is her chance to talk to her sister about the dance, but Naysa hasn't stopped scowling since she emerged from her nap. She's combed out her hair, but she's still in her housecoat.

"So seriously," Brenna asks, stacking the dishes in the dishwasher, "how was the dance?"

"It was fine. I told you already."

Brenna decides to ignore Naysa's attitude. "Did you dance with anyone?"

"Yeah. Lots of people."

"Like who?"

"Like my friends, okay?" Her phone vibrates and she picks it up. Brenna watches as Naysa returns a text. She places the phone back on the counter and puts the jug of milk in the fridge.

"So, who *are* your friends these days?"

Naysa stares at her sister. "Who do you think you are? My mother? It's none of your fuckin' business!"

Brenna watches, shocked, as Naysa turns and stomps out of the kitchen. A moment later she's back. She meets Brenna's eyes briefly, but in that moment Brenna can see the depth of her pain. Naysa grabs her phone off the counter. "And I'm going out tonight."

Brenna knows better than to ask where. She closes the dishwasher and leans against the counter, dumbfounded. What the hell is happening to her little sister?

She knocks softly on her father's office door before entering his room. Then she shuts the door behind her. Her father's eyebrows arch.

"I'm worried about Naysa."

Her father pulls off his reading glasses. "Why is that?"

Brenna sinks into a plush chair. "She hasn't been herself for a few days. Way more cranky than usual. And she has new friends that I think…well, I'm not sure if they're a good influence on her."

"Oh."

"She says she's *going out* tonight. She's been so snarky to me that I don't dare ask where, but I don't have a good feeling."

Her father thinks for a moment. "I know she's been a bit irritable, but I put that down to her age and, well, you know, everything else. Are you sure you're not overreacting?"

"I'm sure."

"Okay then." He sighs. "What do you think I should do?"

"For starters, don't let her go out tonight."

"Why not?"

"Cuz like I said, I don't think her new friends are good for her."

"Brenna. Be reasonable. Unless you know that she's done something she shouldn't have…"

Brenna doesn't respond.

Her father puts his glasses back on and turns to his computer screen. "Okay, I'll keep a closer eye on her. I trust your instincts. And I'll ask to meet her new friends and try to connect with their parents. Other than that"—he looks over at her—"unless you can give me something more concrete to go on…"

Brenna gets up to leave, but in that moment the office door flings opens. Naysa is standing there, glancing from one to the other. She's changed into her old too-tight clothes.

"Why was the door closed?" she asks.

"No reason." Brenna brushes past her as she leaves but hears her sister informing their father that she'll be sleeping over at Janine's house again that night. She stops in the hall to hear what her father will say.

"No, I'll pick you up at eleven," he says. "Only one sleepover per weekend. That's the rule."

"Since when?" Naysa argues.

"Since now," he says. "Obviously you didn't get enough sleep last night, because you had to sleep all afternoon today. It's not healthy to have two late nights in a row."

"We're going to bed earlier tonight."

"You heard me, Nayse. Eleven o'clock. And I can drop you off and maybe meet her parents at the same time."

"I'm walking over with Maddi."

"Okay, then leave me the address so I can pick you up, and maybe I can meet her parents then."

"Don't be stupid. It'll be way too late for that, and I'll be the only person who has to go home."

"That's the end of the discussion, Naysa." Brenna can hear an edge creeping into his voice. "There's no need to talk like that."

Brenna tries to duck into her room before Naysa sees her lurking in the hall, but she doesn't make it.

"What did you say to him?" Naysa demands. Her eyes squint accusingly.

"Nothing."

"Yeah, right." She slams the door to her room, leaving Brenna standing there, staring after her. The slamming door brings her dad into the hall, carrying an empty mug. He gives her an I-did-my-best shrug before going into the kitchen to pour himself more coffee.

Sept. 21

I'm starting to get why Kia put me up for adoption. I'm sooo not ready to be a mother either.

eleven

Life isn't about waiting for the storm to pass.
It's about learning to dance in the rain.
(VIVIAN GREENE)

"So have you made plans to meet up with Justin?" Ryan asks.

"I have," she says, huffing along behind him on the Grind. She's tried hard to remain cool, unaffected by his charm, but she's finding it difficult. He's just so refreshingly open and interested in her.

"And?" he asks. "Do I get to tag along?"

"I don't know. Are you free next Friday night? We're going to meet at the Daily Grind. Suitable name, right?"

"Perfect!"

"Angie's coming too."

"I'll have to check the work schedule," Ryan says. "But if I'm on that shift, I'll swap with someone. Your moral support will be there."

"Thanks." She follows along for a few minutes. *Moral support?* Is that how he sees himself? She figures she could tell him that he's completed his service project, that he's free to hike with one of his coworkers from the chalet yesterday, but she keeps her thoughts to herself.

"So tell me about your potential promotion," Brenna says.

"There's an opening in mountain maintenance."

"What's that?"

"Mostly shoveling snow, erecting signs, driving some of the machines. There are lots of things that need maintaining all winter."

"Sounds harder than being a trammie."

He smiles. "I've liked being a trammie," he says, "but honestly, some days I think I'd rather jump off the tram than recite that spiel one more time. I bet I've rattled it off, like, thousands of times already. Sometimes I try to add a new twist or make a joke to change it up, but then I forget where I'm at, so I figure it's best to stick with the script. The maintenance guys get to do different things all the time, depending on what's needed."

"I'll keep my fingers crossed for you."

"Thanks. The timing's good. My work visa will probably expire about the same time the winter season winds down. If your mom were here," he adds, "the job would be mine for sure. She always had my back."

"Mine too," Brenna says.

⌒

"Have you heard of the Seek the Peak relay?" Ryan asks. Once again she's accepted a ride home, though more reluctantly this time.

"Yeah, but I don't know much about it."

"It's a race that goes from Ambleside Beach to the peak of Grouse to raise funds for breast cancer research."

"Really?" She's surprised she doesn't know more about it, given that her mom had worked on the mountain *and* died of breast cancer.

"Yeah. It can be run solo or in teams, and the relay has four legs. The first runner goes from Ambleside Beach to Cleveland Dam. The second goes from the dam to the bottom of the Grind, the third runner does the Grind, and the last person runs to the peak of the mountain. It's put on every spring."

"I can't imagine running up the Grind."

"It's all about the fundraising and camaraderie, not the winning."

"Hmm."

Ryan glances at her and then continues. "I was thinking we could put a team together to run in your mom's memory this year," he says softly.

Brenna doesn't respond. They drive in silence until he pulls into her driveway. He turns off the ignition and turns to look at her.

"I think you should consider it, Brenna," he says. "We have months to prepare, and you'd be doing it to help find a cure so that no one else has to lose their mother to breast cancer. Or their sister. Or daughter."

Brenna sighs. Her legs ache. "How was our time on the Grind today?" she asks, ignoring the topic.

He takes a moment before responding. "We shaved off another five minutes."

"Maybe because we didn't take as many breaks."

"And maybe that's because we're getting stronger."

"I'd be the weakest link in a relay," she says, finally acknowledging his suggestion.

"No, you wouldn't. All kinds of people participate. Young, old, in shape, out of shape. And we'd prepare all winter and spring for it. You'd be fine."

Brenna sinks lower in her seat.

"We don't have to decide anything today," he says. "But it's something to think about."

She nods.

"Same time on Wednesday?"

"Okay."

"It will be our last afternoon Grind of the season, but we'll find something to replace it."

Brenna reaches for the door handle.

"Hey, Brenna?"

"Yeah?"

"I'm really enjoying our hikes."

"Yeah, me too."

He puts his hand on her arm, gently pulling her toward him. Georgialee's words about being all stinky and sweaty run through her head. She reaches for the door handle again.

"Even if I hadn't liked your mom so much, I'd still want to hike with you."

She glances at him. He looks completely sincere.

"I don't really like hiking," she admits. "But I like hanging out with you."

He smiles. "I was hoping you'd say that." He tugs her to him and pulls her into a hug. She tries to relax, to return the hug, but it's forced. She's too aware of how she must smell.

Ryan kisses her forehead and continues holding her. "The timing is wrong," he says. "I know it's only been a few months since your mom died."

Brenna feels even stiffer. Where's he going with this?

"I totally get that," he continues. "But whenever you're ready…"

She looks up and meets his gaze. Ready for what exactly?

"I'm already ready," he says, smiling. He gently kisses her lips before releasing her.

She sits for a moment, not knowing what to say. Then, without a word, she leans back into him and this time hugs him tightly. Tears stream down her cheeks, and her breathing becomes ragged.

Ryan doesn't say anything, just holds her tightly. When the moment has passed, Brenna dabs her nose with her sleeve and grabs the door handle again. "Sorry," she says. "I don't know where that came from."

"Nothing to be sorry about."

"I saw you in the chalet yesterday."

"You did?"

"Yeah, and you were with all those girls."

"And?"

"And...I felt kind of jealous."

"Really?" He grins. "That makes me happy."

She swats his arm.

"They're just my workmates, Brenna." He laughs. "It's you I want to hang out with after work."

"Wednesday?" she confirms.

He nods. "Can I call you before that?"

She smiles shyly. "Yeah."

"How old is that boy?" her dad asks as she steps into the house. She realizes he must have been watching them through the front window.

"I'm not sure," she admits. "Maybe eighteen or nineteen?"

"A little too old for you, don't you think?" He's drying his hands on a tea towel.

She doesn't answer as she leans over and unlaces her hiking boots.

"Maybe Naysa's not the daughter I need to be worrying about."

She gives him a withering look and places her boots by the door.

"What do you two have in common?" he asks.

"Ryan had a good relationship with Mom," she tells him. "That's what we have in common."

She begins to walk down the hall to her room. "And I'm sixteen now, Dad. I can handle it. You can quit spying on me."

"Curried cauliflower is on the menu for dinner tonight," he says to her retreating back.

Sept. 22

He kissed me he kissed me he kissed me he kissed me he kissed me he kissed me.

Ryan parks the car against the curb outside the coffee shop and shuts off the motor, but neither of them moves. They've arrived early for their meeting with Justin and Angie.

"You sure you're going to be okay?" Ryan asks.

She nods, but her stomach is anything but okay. After all, she's about to meet a biological relative for the first time.

She glances across the street to where a bunch of young teenage girls are gathered on the sidewalk. None of them are wearing coats, even though the evenings have become cool. Their skirts are short, they're teetering on high heels, and they are all wearing tight, low-cut shirts.

The door to a convenience store swings open, and Naysa steps out and joins the rest of the girls. Even from across the street Brenna can see how much makeup she's wearing. Naysa holds out a bag to one of the other girls, showing her the contents, and then squeals when the other girl pulls an item out of the bag. Brenna can't make out what it is.

"Hey," Ryan says, noticing where Brenna's gaze has gone. "Isn't that your little sister?"

Brenna doesn't answer, because right at that moment the girls start to cross the street and are about to walk right in front of Ryan's car. Brenna slides down in the seat, hoping not to be noticed by Naysa. When she thinks they've moved on, she glances up. Naysa has lingered behind and is just now walking in front of the car. Their eyes meet, and Brenna sees the look of alarm that crosses her sister's face. There is a moment when they simply stare at each other, and then Naysa scurries to catch up with the rest of the group. The girl who had pulled something out of Naysa's bag is carrying a pack of cigarettes. She too glances at Brenna before moving on.

"What was that all about?" Ryan asks.

"I don't know." Still feeling shocked at seeing Naysa there, she watches the girls as they move down the street.

Ryan checks his phone. "It's almost time. Shall we go meet your aunt?"

Brenna takes a deep breath and lets it out slowly. "Yeah."

Ryan comes around to the sidewalk and takes Brenna's hand. She can feel herself trembling, but Ryan doesn't comment. They walk toward the Daily Grind.

"Try to remember what we talked about," he reminds her.

She nods. On their Wednesday-afternoon hike and over a few phone conversations, they'd discussed all the questions she could ask.

"But not to worry—if you forget, I'll remember and ask for you."

She squeezes his hand, grateful to have him along.

He pulls open the door to the coffee shop, and she steps inside. Immediately her eyes lock on a woman sitting in a booth facing the door.

"Brenna?" the woman says, standing up and moving toward her.

Brenna can only nod. Her feet are frozen to the floor.

The woman pulls Brenna into a tight hug. "Oh my god!" she says. "I can't believe it's you!"

Even though Brenna is still being squeezed and can't see Angie's face, she's aware that Angie is crying. She can't hold back her own tears either, and the two of them stand in the doorway for a long moment, silently crying in each other's arms.

She hears Ryan beside her. "Hi, I'm Ryan," he's saying. She looks over and sees him extending a hand to Justin.

Angie releases her hold on Brenna. "Sorry," she says, wiping tears off her cheeks. She holds out her hand to greet Ryan. "I'm Angie," she says.

Justin looks down at Brenna and smiles. "Good to see you again."

Brenna is wiping her own eyes as Angie leads them back to their table. She and Ryan sit across from Justin and Angie.

"So," Angie says, still trying to pull herself back together. "It was almost like seeing Kia walk through those doors." She studies Brenna's face. "Except for your eyes. Kia's eyes are brown."

An awkward silence falls over the table. Ryan reaches out and takes Brenna's hand.

"What can I get for everyone?" Justin asks, standing up.

They tell him what they want, relieved to have something to say. After he excuses himself to get their drinks, Angie leans across the table toward Brenna. "She never stopped missing you," she says gently.

Tears spring to Brenna's eyes again. She'd been expecting at least some small talk first. "Then why did she stop coming to see me?"

"Things change," Angie says, sitting back. "For the first year I think she went to see you every weekend, but then she went away to university." Her eyebrows scrunch together as she tries to recall the details. "Like I told you," she continues, "I was young—I didn't really know what was going on. But I think my sister changed after you were born. When she came back from seeing you on weekends, she always seemed sad."

Justin returns to the table with a tray of hot drinks. He hands them around. "What did I miss?" he asks, sitting back down and taking in the serious expressions.

"I was telling Brenna that Kia seemed different after Brenna was born. Is that how you remember it?"

Justin thinks for a moment. "She was always responsible and level-headed," he says. "But she may have become more withdrawn after you were born."

"Yeah, withdrawn," Angie says. "That's the right word. Like I said, she couldn't wait to see you each weekend, but then she was really quiet afterward."

"Why did she go away to school?" Brenna asks.

Justin and Angie exchange glances. Angie shrugs. "I don't know for sure, but I suspect she needed a fresh start."

"That's how I remember it," Justin says. "Having a baby so young...well...I don't think she ever really felt like she fit in with her old group again. She'd grown up so much over that year."

"But going away didn't work out so well," Angie says.

Brenna notices how both Angie and Justin seem to sink into themselves.

"She struggled with depression," Angie continues. "She had planned to go into med school—she had the marks—but the summer before she was to start, the depression totally derailed her."

"Depression." Brenna shakes her head. She had realized from reading the journal that Kia had mood swings, but she knew depression was something entirely different.

"Yeah, she had to take a year off. She stayed home while she was in therapy."

"I remember talking to her around that time," Justin said. "She really struggled to find meds that helped her but that didn't have horrible side effects."

Brenna leans back in the booth. Ryan grips her hand.

"There were a few rough years," Angie says. "I was still in high school, and I remember that I never wanted to bring my friends home because I didn't know what Kia was going to be like. I hate to admit it, but sometimes she embarrassed me with the rants she'd go on. She was super into causes—which is cool—but for a while there she'd lecture my friends if they were wearing brand-name clothes or if we bought things that weren't locally made. Our parents didn't dare buy anything unless it was organic. We became vegetarians."

Justin smiles sheepishly. "I may be responsible for egging her on during that time. I thought that her passion for those things would help her heal."

"Maybe it worked," Angie says, "but sometimes it was hard to be her sister. She could be so self-righteous." Angie glances out the window. "Now that I'm older I respect her passion, but at the time I wanted a normal sister."

"I know a little about depression," Ryan says. It is his first contribution to the conversation. "And I think it's better to be passionate than to shut down completely."

Now it's Brenna's turn to squeeze his hand. She knows he must be thinking of his own mother.

"She did that too, at first," Justin says. "That's why I thought it was a good sign when she was getting passionate about things again."

Brenna studies the man who'd been Kia's close friend, the man Kia had longed for. She can understand the attraction. His face is kind, and his voice is deep yet gentle. "Ryan thinks physical exercise will help me heal," she says. "From losing my mom."

Angie and Justin both nod at Ryan.

Angie continues. "Eventually Kia found the right meds, and she mostly returned to being the same old Kia."

"But she never found her way back to medical school," Justin adds.

"Not yet anyway," Angie says. "But she has a huge passion for helping people. She especially loves old people and children. I think it was you who sparked her interest in children, Brenna, and an old woman named Grace, who died right after you were born, who made her want to work with seniors in care homes."

"My middle name is Grace," Brenna reminds them.

"That's right! I'd forgotten that. Kia did work in a care home until she applied for the job with Aid-A-Child. She's been with them for five years now."

"And she's okay?"

"Yeah, though I always worry that she'll have a relapse if the stress gets too great."

"You'd think that working with orphans would be stressful work," Ryan comments.

"No," Angie says. "Not for her. She knows she's making a difference there. I think doing that job was what returned her to the old Kia."

Brenna takes a deep breath and lets out a long sigh.

Angie smiles at her. "Sorry, Brenna," she says. "That's a lot of information all at once. I hope I didn't upset you."

Brenna shakes her head and takes a sip from her mug of hot chocolate. "It's just weird," she says, struggling to collect her thoughts. "I read the journal Kia kept when she was pregnant with me. But I assumed her life had been happy-ever-after since I stopped hearing from her."

"Is anyone's life happy-ever-after?" Justin asks.

Brenna shrugs. Hers and Ryan's weren't. She wonders what stories Justin and Angie could share.

They sit quietly for a moment, Brenna trying to find the courage to ask the question that has been bothering her for nearly two weeks. Ryan must know what she's thinking, because he squeezes her hand again. It's just what she needs. "Why do you think Kia would be unhappy if she knew you and I were in touch?" She looks directly at Angie.

Angie's finger strokes the rim of her mug. She chooses her words carefully. "My relationship with Kia has been a bit shaky ever since she got sick," she says. "I said some stupid things, mostly because I was young and didn't know better. I told her she'd embarrassed me by having a baby and then I turned around and told her I thought she'd abandoned you." She shakes her head and slouches in the booth. "I can't believe I said those things. I was just mad. I really hurt her, and even though we've talked about it and she says she's forgiven me, I feel our relationship is still strained. She doesn't come home very often, so I haven't dealt with it. I know, though, that if she hears about us connecting, she'll think I'm interfering with her life."

"But...she's chosen not to have me in her life, right?"

"Yeah, but..."

"And I'm your niece."

"Technically, yes."

"Technically?"

"That's the thing about adoption. Kia made the choice to give you to someone else to raise. But it affected me too. And my parents."

"Do they know you're here?" Justin asks.

"No."

"How come?" He cocks his head.

She sighs, then looks at Brenna rather than Justin. "They're really good people, Brenna. You have to know that. But this is so complicated. They encouraged Kia to put you up for adoption because they loved her and felt her life would be way easier if she wasn't a teen mom. But it must have been hard for them too. Now they're at an age where they'd love to have a grandchild, but the only one they have was adopted into another family. They'd think that meeting with you now, after all this time and with what Kia's gone through, well, it'd be like opening a can of worms."

Ryan and Brenna glance at each other, startled by her choice of words.

"Brenna, did you tell your dad you were meeting us?" Justin asks.

Brenna shakes her head but doesn't meet his gaze.

"Same reason?" Justin asks.

"Kind of. He wouldn't forbid me to be here—I just didn't want to hurt his feelings. Until now, I was never very curious about Kia. That changed when my mom died."

Ryan, who's been sitting completely still, now leans his shoulder into hers. "Are you going to mention the social-justice project?"

Justin and Angie look at Brenna.

"Ever since you contacted me," Brenna says, "I've had a fantasy of reconnecting with Kia. When you told me she was working in Uganda, I lost hope of that ever happening, but then I suggested to my Social Justice Club that we raise money and send it to support her organization."

"You did?" Justin's eyes light up.

"Well, I haven't sold them on the idea yet, but I'm trying."

"Like mother, like daughter. Social activists." His smile is warm.

Angie is frowning. "God knows they can use the money, but there's a good chance Kia knows what school you go to because she knows where you live. Getting a donation from any school would be a surprise, but a donation from your school…well, it would be too big of a coincidence. Kia would figure out I told you where she is."

"Could you donate it anonymously?" Justin asks.

Brenna doesn't meet his eyes. If she donates it anonymously, it defeats the purpose. It was her way to connect with Kia.

"Perhaps you could support another organization," he suggests. He looks from Angie to Brenna, sensing the standoff.

"Maybe," Brenna says, knowing she never will but not wanting Justin to realize how selfish her motives have been. She's clearly not her birth mom's daughter after all. Justin was wrong about that.

The subject is changed, but so is the mood around the table. Justin and Ryan do their best to maintain a lightness to the conversation, but Brenna and Angie have each retreated into their own private worlds.

When they leave the coffee shop there are awkward hugs and handshakes, but Brenna doesn't know if she'll hear from Angie again, or even if she wants to.

Sept. 27

She never stopped missing me!!!!!!

So then why wouldn't she want to connect with me?

twelve

Love opens your heart, trumps fear, and paves the way
for healing in all aspects of your life.

(LISSA RANKIN, *MIND OVER MEDICINE*)

Ryan doesn't work on Saturday, but he picks Brenna up after her shift and drives her home.

"How old are you anyway?" she asks as he pulls into her driveway. Her father's car is parked outside, and it reminds her of their conversation a few days ago.

"Eighteen. Nineteen next month. How old are you?"

"Sixteen."

"I keep thinking you're older."

"Is that a problem for you?" she asks, not looking at him.

"Is what a problem?"

"That I'm only sixteen." Now she does look directly at him.

"Why would it be?" He smiles. "Is it a problem for you that I'm eighteen?"

"No." She smiles back. "But it might be for my father. Especially the almost-nineteen part."

"That's because he doesn't know me. Maybe you should invite him to hike with us."

"Are you kidding?"

Ryan laughs. "Okay, then invite me in. When he discovers how charming and clever and charismatic I am…"

Brenna laughs and opens the car door. "Come on in then," she says. "Let's see how clever you really are. Charming, well, yeah, I already know about that."

They find her dad and Naysa leaning over a jigsaw puzzle at a small table in the corner of the family room. Before Brenna has a chance to say anything, Ryan extends his hand to her father. "Hello, Mr. Yokoyama. We met once, briefly, at the door. I'm Ryan. I know Brenna from Grouse."

Brenna's dad clasps his outstretched hand. "Hi, Ryan. Please call me Brett. Do you know Naysa?"

"Yep, I've met the young math genius."

A flicker of a smile tugs at Naysa's mouth, but she doesn't respond. She's still in her pajamas.

"I'm going to get out of my bear-minding clothes," Brenna says. "I'll be right back."

When she returns to the family room, Naysa is gone and Ryan is leaning over the table, telling her dad about his work at Grouse.

"You've finished school then?" he asks.

"For now. I'll finish when I return to Australia."

"When will that be?" Brenna's dad slides a puzzle piece into place, and the completed eye of a bright-green frog stares back at them.

"Not yet determined." Ryan places a piece to complete the frog's mouth. It curls up into a pleased expression.

Her father's phone rings. He answers it and wanders out of the room and down the hall to his office.

"I think that went well," Ryan says. He grins at Brenna before returning his focus to the puzzle.

Brenna picks up a piece and examines it. She then studies the puzzle. They work in silence for a few minutes.

"Have you made any decisions about the Aid-A-Child fundraiser?" he asks.

Brenna glances at the door to the room, making sure no one is listening. "My heart's not really in it anymore," she says. "It was hard to admit to myself that it was never about the kids, only about me."

While Ryan searches through the remaining puzzle pieces in the box, Brenna's thoughts return to the meeting the previous night. Before they left, Justin had shared his involvement with Kia during her pregnancy.

"Justin seems like a really nice guy," she says. "Imagine being the birth coach when it's not even your own baby. I couldn't believe he'd even considered adopting me himself."

"Yeah, that was amazing."

"I wonder why he and Kia never hooked up. She wrote in her journal that she was attracted to him and thought they'd be good together."

Ryan looks up from the puzzle. "Because he's gay."

"He is? How do you know?"

"I sent him a friend request on Facebook when I got home last night. He accepted. You can tell from his pictures that his partner isn't a business partner."

"Oh. Well. That explains some of the missing pieces in the journal. Kia couldn't figure out why he wasn't interested in her as a girlfriend."

"Speaking of missing pieces," Ryan says, pointing to a hole in the puzzle, "I think this piece is missing. I've looked through the whole box and there are no more green ones."

"It'll show up," she says. "They always do."

"Spoken like a true puzzle nerd. I mean, master."

She gives his arm a friendly slap.

He grins. "By the way," he says, glancing at the door, "did you get a chance to talk to Naysa about last night?"

"No, not yet."

The doorbell chimes. Ryan glances at her.

"Probably a casserole delivery," she says. They can hear her father's footsteps going down the stairs to the front door. A moment later they hear a clatter of footsteps running up the stairs, and Georgialee and Bentley burst into the room. Georgialee drops Bentley's leash so he can gallop over to greet Brenna. She squats down to hug him. His whole body wiggles with joy.

"Hey," Ryan says. "You must be Georgialee."

"I am. And you're Ryan?"

"Yep." They both glance at Brenna, who is giving the dog a full-body scratch. "So that would be Bentley."

Brenna eventually stands up, and Georgialee retrieves the dog's leash. "What's happening?"

Brenna can tell she's sizing Ryan up.

"Your best mate—the puzzle pro—was giving me some puzzle-making advice," Ryan says.

"Out for a run?" Brenna checks out Georgialee's spandex tights and singlet, noting that she manages to look good even when she's all sweaty.

"Yeah, and I was running past your house and thought I'd see what you're doing tonight."

Brenna glances shyly at Ryan. They'd never spent a Saturday night together, and she didn't want to assume anything. "I dunno. Why?"

"A bunch of us are going out for sushi and a movie." She looks at the puzzle. "If you can drag yourself away from all this fun," she says, "you should join us. You too," she says to Ryan.

Before Brenna can open her mouth, Ryan responds. "I'm in."

Georgialee high-fives him. "Good," she says. "And try to drag Brenna along. I haven't seen much of her lately." She pulls on Bentley's leash. "I'll let myself out. See you guys later."

They clatter back down the stairs.

"She seems nice," Ryan says, returning to the puzzle.

Brenna's phone buzzes. She checks the screen and sees a text from Georgialee.

Not bad. 👍

She pulls a puzzle piece out of the box and slots it into the hole Ryan had thought was missing its piece. "Seems you're not so clever after all."

"Puzzle nerd."

～

On Sunday morning Brenna finds Naysa sprawled on the family room couch, channel-surfing. She glances out the window, checking for Ryan's car. She checks the time on her phone, sighs and steps over to the table where the puzzle lies unfinished. "So who was the friend you were with the other night?" she asks.

"None of your business."

Brenna is startled by the tone of her sister's voice.

"I was just asking. She must have a name."

"Why would I tell you anything? You'd go straight to Dad."

"I'm worried about you, that's all."

"Don't bother. I'm fine."

"You're not fine if you're drinking and smoking," Brenna says, her anger flaring.

Naysa glances at the door, obviously worried that their father will overhear them.

"Okay, you tell me who you were with at the Daily Grind, and I'll tell you their names."

Now it's Brenna's turn to glance at the door. "How do you know I was at the Daily Grind?"

"We were going to go in, but I saw you in the window. It was your birth mom, wasn't it?"

"No! She's way too young to be my birth mom."

Naysa flicks off the TV and steps over to the window. "Ryan's here," she says.

Brenna's heart stirs at the sound of his name, yet she has to know. "Why do you think—?" She doesn't get the question out.

"Because you look just like her."

The doorbell rings.

"I tried talking to Naysa this morning," Brenna tells Ryan. They're sitting on a bluff on Mount Seymour, looking over the city below them. Bentley lies at their feet, panting. Georgialee had willingly agreed to let him hike with them.

"How did it go?"

"Not good. She shut me right down. And then she asked who we were with in the coffee shop. Apparently she was spying on me."

"Did you tell her?"

"No, I don't want it to get back to Dad."

Ryan sighs. He scratches Bentley's ears. "Maybe if you shared that with her, she'd trust you with her stuff."

Brenna shrugs one shoulder.

Ryan changes the subject. "I had a good time last night. I like your mates."

"My *friends*." She corrects him with a smile. "You're in Canada now."

"Okay, your friends," he says. "The only people I know in Vancouver are the ones I've met at Grouse. It was nice to hang out with other people, though it reminds me how much I miss my mates back home. I mean...my *friends*."

Brenna leans into him, and he strokes her hair.

"But the best part of the night was the last part," he says quietly.

Brenna's whole body responds as she remembers the kiss they'd shared when he dropped her off. It had started soft and gentle, his lips simply caressing hers, and her body flooded with sensation. Ryan must have felt it too, because his fingers wound through her hair and his kissing became more urgent, almost rough. His hands had begun to explore her body before he suddenly broke away and sat back.

I think you'd better go in, he'd said. *We don't want to get carried away.*

She'd nodded but hadn't moved. There was a disconnect between what her brain told her to do and what her body had wanted.

Or maybe we do, he'd said and laughed a little as he reached for her hand. *A car is not the place though.*

Her breathing had eventually returned to normal, but she still hadn't wanted to get out of the car. *I'll see you tomorrow*, she'd said finally and leaned over to kiss the tip of his nose.

I think we'd better bring an escort, Ryan teased.

How about Bentley? she suggested.

Perfect, he'd said. *And we'll change it up and hike Dog Mountain. Dogs are welcome there.*

Now Ryan plunges his hand into Bentley's fur. "Kinda hard for a guy to hold back when the kissing is that good," he says, remembering.

"Kinda hard for a girl too."

He gives her a shy glance. "You're not on the pill or anything, are you?"

She can't meet his eyes. "I've never really had a boyfriend."

"A looker like you? I'm gobsmacked!"

She laughs at his choice of words and elbows him in the ribs.

"Then we'd better take it slow," he says.

She nods.

"But maybe I'll buy some condoms...just in case."

She sits quietly for a moment. "Okay. I wouldn't want to carry on the family tradition."

He looks at her, puzzled.

"Becoming a teen mom."

"Ah. Right. That family tradition." He drapes his arm around her shoulder and pulls her in close.

From: justintime@yahoo.com
To: brennayoko@gmail.com

Dear Brenna,

It was great to see you again the other night. I know you were disappointed that Angie didn't want you to contact Kia via Aid–A-Child. I hope you'll still consider raising funds and have someone else donate the money. The work she does is so hard and yet so important. Family secrets often have dire consequences, but that's the kind of secret I'd encourage. Such a beautiful gesture it would be.

Anyway, let's keep in touch. Kia would be so proud of the girl you've become. Maybe someday she'll be ready to connect with you again.

J.

Sept. 29
He's wrong. I'd be a big fat disappointment to Kia.

"Each week we could go downtown in groups of three or four and hand out food and warm clothes to the people on the Downtown Eastside. We could keep collection boxes outside the school office for donations."

Brenna listens as Jas pitches his social-justice project to the group.

"It fits into our mandate of doing something close to home," Jas continues, "and we won't have to fundraise. It's a service project that will make a difference to people in our own city. We will see firsthand what our efforts can do."

"Isn't that just a Band-Aid solution?" Georgialee asks. "We're not addressing the problem of why people are homeless."

"I say let the politicians deal with that," Jas responds. "It's too big for us to solve, but we can help keep people warm and fed."

Brenna's mind wanders as the discussion continues. They now have four social-justice projects to choose from. Two others were pitched last week. When there's a lull in the conversation, she speaks up. "I'm withdrawing the Aid-A-Child idea," she says. "That will make it easier to choose a project."

Everyone turns to look at her.

"Why are you withdrawing it?" Georgialee asks.

Brenna shrugs. "I just am. I don't really have the energy right now to spearhead it."

There's a quiet moment as they all regard her. Then Jas picks up a red marker and draws a line through *Aid-A-Child* on the list of projects written on the whiteboard.

Oct. 3
Sorry, Kia.
Sorry, Justin.

⌒〜

Brenna's phone pings with a text from Ryan.

I got the job!! I start tm! Going to a game with my unc 2nite. C U on the mt. tm. xo

Brenna smiles as she texts him back.

Congratulations! xoxoxo

Even though Brenna has withdrawn the Aid-A-Child project from the Social Justice Club's list, she still finds herself drawn to its website. She scrolls through it, following the links and reading the stories of many of the orphans. She's so immersed in it that she jumps, startled, when she hears the key in the front-door lock. She glances at the clock and sees that it's eleven fifteen. Naysa is fifteen minutes past her weekend curfew. Brenna hears the footsteps on the stairs and expects Naysa to poke her head into the room to say hello as usual. She doesn't. Nor does she go into the kitchen for a snack or stop by her father's room to say goodnight. There's just the click of her bedroom door as it shuts.

Brenna returns to the Aid-A-Child website, scrolling through the photos again, peering into each face, looking for an aid worker who looks like her, only older.

‿〜

When Brenna arrives at the bear habitat on Saturday morning, Ryan is already hard at work with a team of young guys, pulling down the fencing, preparing the mountain for the winter season when the habitat becomes part of the ski and snowboarding terrain.

Ryan waves and smiles when he sees her. He pulls off his ballcap and wipes his forehead with his sleeve. The temperature on the mountain has dropped considerably over the past week, but all the guys working with Ryan are red-cheeked with exertion. She waves and goes into Ski Wee.

"Hey, Brenna," Mark says. "You're looking happy today."

She is happy, Brenna realizes, and she's acutely aware of Ryan's presence as she goes through her morning routine. Often when she glances over at him, he happens to look back at her at the exact same moment. She feels a full-body rush every time their eyes meet.

The bears are getting extremely fat and are moving slowly. Mark tells her they've also been sleeping more and more each day. She remembers how much she missed them when they hibernated last year—it was like a physical ache—but there's a video camera in their den, so she can watch for their daily stretching sessions. The wildlife team has dubbed this activity "bear yoga."

When she's finished her shift she walks over to where the fence crew is working. Ryan steps away from them, taking a short break. He's panting from exertion.

"Want to hang out tonight?" he asks.

"Sure. Why don't you come over and have dinner with us? We can figure out what we want to do after that."

"Sounds good," he says. "What's on the menu?"

"Probably casserole," she says, laughing. "With brownies for dessert."

"Beauty, mate," he says. "After this day I'm going to be starved."

"This is delicious!" Ryan says, forking the pasta into his mouth. Brenna, her dad and Naysa watch with amusement how fast he shovels it in. "What's in it?"

Brenna shrugs. "I just pulled it out of the freezer. It didn't come with a list of ingredients."

Initially it felt odd to have someone sitting in her mother's chair at the round kitchen table. The chair had sat empty for months, like a gaping hole. When the extended family had come over, they'd moved the meals to the larger dining room table. Brenna's relieved that it's Ryan and not someone else sitting in this chair now.

"I start my driving lessons next week," she says, making an effort at light conversation. "And I need fifteen hours of practice time between lessons. I hope you'll be able to take me out," she says to her dad.

"I could go with you." Ryan takes his eyes off his plate just long enough to make the offer.

"Thanks, but it has to be someone over twenty-five," Brenna tells him.

"We'll set up some times," her father says. "And you can practice in your mom's car."

"You're not planning on selling it?" Brenna asks.

"I thought we'd keep it for you girls to use."

"Well, that's not fair," Naysa says. She's been quiet until now. "I'm not sixteen for another three years. It will be old by then. And Brenna doesn't have to share with anyone from now until then."

Brenna's glad Ryan is having dinner with them because she's pretty sure that either she or her dad would have lost their temper with Naysa otherwise. No one reacts for a moment, and then Brenna says, "Who knows where I'll be in three years. I could be working in Africa, and the car will be all yours."

"Africa?" her dad asks.

Ryan looks up from his plate long enough to glance at her before returning to his meal.

"Just sayin'," she responds. "And I'll be able to chauffeur you around until then, Nayse, so it will benefit you too."

Naysa pushes her plate away. "May I be excused?"

Brenna and her father exchange glances. "Yes, Naysa, you may," he says. "What are you up to tonight?"

"Hanging out with my friends."

"You've been doing a lot of that."

"What else is there to do?" She carries her plate to the dishwasher.

"Homework," her dad says and smiles.

Naysa throws him a look and leaves the kitchen.

"May I have another helping, please?" Ryan asks.

～

Brenna scrolls through the options on Netflix. They've decided to stay in and watch TV. The evening has turned wet, and Brenna lights the gas fire for the first time since last spring. Brenna's dad is in his office, and Brenna sits close to Ryan on the couch. He puts his arm around her shoulders, and she snuggles in closer.

"Shall we take Bentley on our hike again tomorrow?" she asks after they agree on a program and the opening credits roll.

"Yeah, he was a pretty good chaperone," Ryan says. "Didn't stop me from putting my moves on you."

Brenna smiles.

Ryan stretches out his legs. "Though you may have to pull me up the hill tomorrow. I'm stiff all over. Maybe I'm not cut out to be a maintenance guy after all."

The program begins, and Brenna relaxes. Five minutes later she feels Ryan's arm get heavy, and then he begins to snore softly. She lifts his arm off her shoulder and decides not to wake him. An hour and a half later she shuts off the TV and prods him in the chest.

"Ryan. Wake up."

He sits up with a start and looks around the room, momentarily confused.

"Did you like the show?" she teases.

"Oh man." He enjoys a full-body stretch and rubs his face.

"You were out cold."

He yawns and glances at the door. "Does this mean we've slept together?" he whispers.

"No, Ryan, it doesn't," she says sternly. "Because you were the only one sleeping."

He glances at the door again and then leans in to give her a kiss. She pulls away after only a few seconds.

"I guess I'd better head home," he says. "I'm sorry I've been such a dud tonight."

"You're not a dud, even when you're sleeping." She kisses him, lingering a little longer this time.

On his way out, Ryan stops at the door to her dad's office. "Thanks for having me over," he says. "Dinner was amazing."

"Maybe you should take the leftovers," Brenna's father suggests. "We're getting a little tired of that sort of thing."

"I won't do that, but if they're still in the fridge tomorrow I might eat them before our hike."

"It's a deal."

Brenna sees Ryan out before returning to her father's office. "I'm going to bed, Dad."

"I'm not far behind."

She gives him a kiss on the cheek before leaving the room.

"Brenna?" he says, calling her back from the hall.

"Yeah?" She stands in the doorway.

"He seems nice."

"He is."

"Take it slow."

She nods.

"Have you seen Naysa yet?"

"No."

He glances at his watch. "She's late."

"She was late last night too."

His eyebrows spring up. He picks up his cell phone. "I'll give her a call. See if she needs a ride."

As he punches the buttons, the front door opens and Naysa appears at the bottom of the stairs. "She's home," Brenna tells her father and goes straight to her room, closing the door behind her. Her father can deal with this new person who used to be Naysa.

Ryan really does arrive early to finish the leftovers on Sunday afternoon. They collect Bentley from Georgialee's and head back up Mount Seymour.

"I am sore everywhere," Ryan complains as they walk through the parking lot toward the trailhead.

"Maybe you should reapply for your trammie job," Brenna suggests.

"Maybe not."

Brenna unclips Bentley from his leash when they start the trail and he gallops ahead of them, celebrating his freedom. A moment later he's back, gazing up at Brenna, his tail wagging.

"Having fun?" she asks him.

He barks in response and bounds off again.

"I'm surprised you don't have your own dog," Ryan says, taking her hand as they reach a wide, flat section in the trail.

"Yeah, I'd like one," she says. "And Mom always did too, but until recently we lived in a no-pets condo, and then Mom got sick right after we bought our house. Without Mom on my side I don't know if I could persuade Dad to get one. Besides, I might be gone in a couple of years."

"Gone, as in working in Africa."

"Okay, I know that was a bit extreme, but maybe I'll go away to school or something. Who knows? And I probably couldn't leave my dog if I had one, so it's best not to get one. For now," she adds.

"I had to find a new home for my dog when I came to Canada," Ryan says. "Max. I miss him."

Brenna glances at his face and sees the sadness there. "I used to think about starting a dog-walking business," she admits.

"Hey, that's a great idea! But make it a dog-hike business."

"Right."

"No, seriously. Why not make a little cash while getting in shape for Seek the Peak?"

"Did I agree to do that?"

"Not yet, you haven't."

Brenna shakes her head. They both know his track record on talking her into things.

"I think it'd be great! I can't hike on Wednesday afternoons anymore because of my new job. You could do Quarry Rock with dogs after school every day, make some money, and we'll still have our Sunday hikes. Or snowshoeing, depending on the weather."

"Sounds like a lot of hiking."

Ryan stops to pull the water out of his pack. He takes a long drink, then looks up and down the trail. "Where's our chaperone?" he asks. Not waiting for an answer, he leans into Brenna and begins to kiss her. Brenna closes her eyes and loses herself in his kiss. The forest is still except for the odd bird chirp. She tastes the lingering flavors of his lunch and breathes in the saltiness of his skin. A moment later Bentley nudges her hand. "Right here," she says, breaking off the kiss. "Doing his job."

"Oh man," Ryan grumbles, and he follows Brenna along the trail.

$\sim$

"Have you thought any more about that dog-hiking idea?" Ryan asks. They'd made it to the lookout, where Bentley had rested while they stretched out under a tree, wrapped in each other's arms. They were now headed back to the parking lot.

Brenna laughs. She's feeling euphoric from the long, uninterrupted kisses. "When was I supposed to think about it? You only suggested it an hour ago."

"Yeah, but it's such a good idea. A win-win."

Brenna doesn't respond.

"I could come back to your house and help you make flyers to tack up around the community. You could post an ad on Craigslist and ask your friends to promote your business on Facebook."

"Maybe you should start a dog-hiking business."

"I already have a job."

They walk along in silence for a while.

"Tell me honestly, Brenna. We've been hiking for six weeks now. Are you feeling any different?"

She thinks about it. The hikes do seem less strenuous, and she'd noticed just yesterday that her jeans were feeling looser.

"I bet a lot of people could really use the services of a dog hiker."

Brenna still doesn't respond. She wonders what her mom would have thought of the idea. She suspects she would have liked it. A lot. Her mom loved dogs, and she loved to hike. What's not to love?

"Well?"

"Well, okay. There's no harm in trying."

They spend the rest of the afternoon and evening creating a flyer and then printing out copies. They place an ad on Craigslist. Ryan stays for dinner again and eats twice as much mac and cheese as the rest of them. They walk around the neighborhood in the evening, tacking flyers to poles.

"Now we wait for the calls to come in," Ryan says. They're standing at his car. He's getting ready to leave.

"If they come in."

"Oh, they will," he says. He glances at the house, wondering if they're being observed. He gives her a quick kiss and a longer hug. "Keep me posted."

Oct. 6
If Ryan were a dog, his tail would be constantly wagging.

Brenna takes her phone out of her purse at the lunch break on Monday. She's hoping to find a message from Ryan but is startled to see she's missed six calls. She listens to the first one. It's a dog-hiking request. So is the second. And the third. The fourth is a message from her driving teacher confirming her lesson, but the remaining two are more dog-hiking requests.

She texts Ryan:

I'm in business! 5 phone requests and I haven't even checked my email yet.

His response is immediate.

☺ ☺ ☺

Brenna slips into an empty classroom, plunks herself down at a desk and pulls her planner out of her bag. She starts returning calls and sets up appointments to meet the dogs and their owners.

thirteen

Grief doesn't change you...it reveals you.
(JOHN GREEN, *THE FAULT IN OUR STARS*)

Brenna towels Charlie off before letting him into his house. His owners have trusted her with a key to their home. Other owners simply hide a key outside for her on the days she takes their dogs. She gives the black Lab another back rub and then collects her money from the table by the door. After locking up, she unties Barkley and Winston from the railing where they wait patiently. By hiking with three dogs at a time, she can make sixty dollars a day. She's been in business for less than three weeks, but she has all the dogs she can handle for now, and the wait list is growing.

At home, she leaves her muddy hiking boots at the door and peels off her wet rain gear. She pulls the money out of her pocket and adds it to the envelope on her desk, which is already getting thick. She flops down on her bed and makes eye contact with the baby orangutan in the Borneo poster. If she keeps this up, she will have more money than she ever expected by the time she graduates. The trip to Borneo and the orangutan sanctuary could easily become a reality, even without her mom. Maybe she could spread some of her mother's ashes there.

Her parents had always encouraged her and Naysa to divide their money three ways: one third they keep, one third goes to charity, and one third goes into savings. Soon, she realizes, she will have a significant amount to donate somewhere.

She rolls onto her side and closes her eyes. Maybe she should ask Justin how to donate it to Aid-A-Child anonymously. She smiles, but then a twinge of guilt makes her squirm. Is this being disloyal to her mom? She thinks about it. She could donate half of her charity money to the Seek the Peak relay and the other half to Aid-A-Child.

There's a knock on her door. Her father is there, jangling car keys. "Ready to drive?" he asks.

"I thought we were going out after dinner to practice."

"I phoned Pizza Palace and placed an order. We can pick it up on our way home."

"Perfect." Brenna climbs off her bed and takes the keys from her father. "Let's hit the road."

⌒

Brenna flips the page in her school planner. A pumpkin sticker grins out at her. Halloween is less than a week away. Where has the month gone?

Ryan has been working long hours on the mountain, preparing it for the ski season, and she's been busy hiking every afternoon with the dogs and practicing driving in the evening. She picks up her phone and sends a text to Ryan.

Miss you! ☹

The response comes quickly.

Same! ☹ **Working late 2nite. First flakes of snow today! See you tomorrow! And the next day!**

Feeling restless, Brenna wanders down the hall and looks into Naysa's room. It's empty. She's rarely home anymore, especially not on a Friday night. Brenna and her dad ate the whole large pizza themselves.

She steps into the room and scans the pile of stuff heaped on Naysa's desk. Textbooks, scraps of paper, old school newsletters, makeup, jewelry, dirty plates and half-empty cups are all jumbled together. Only six months ago Naysa had prided herself on how organized and tidy she kept her desk and bedroom. Her school planner lies open on the edge of the mess. Brenna picks it up and turns the page. A pumpkin identical to Brenna's grins out at her, one of the stickers that came with the school-issued planners. She flips the page back and looks more closely at the notes that are scribbled on the page. *HALLOWEEN PARTY!!!* is noted for the next night, Saturday. That's the first Brenna has heard of it.

She returns the book to the desk and pulls open the top drawer. Matches and a corkscrew are tucked in between pens, sticky notes and highlighters. Alarmed, she quickly closes the drawer and glances around the room. The bed is unmade, and the laundry hamper sits in a corner, empty, while a week's worth of clothes sits in small mounds around it. She kicks at a pile and then reaches down and pulls out a bright-pink, lacy bra. This is new, she thinks, and then notices the matching panties, also half buried. Her foot kicks at another heap of clothes and she uncovers two sets of lacy thongs and matching camisoles. She opens the closet and starts rifling through the mess. Her toe hits something hard. She lifts up a crumpled jacket and finds a half-empty bottle of vodka.

She closes the closet and returns to her own room, her heart pounding. She's suspected Naysa was getting into trouble, but seeing the evidence makes it much more real. What should she do? She needs to share this with someone.

She grabs her phone and calls Georgialee but only gets her voice mail. She doesn't leave a message. Who else can she talk to about Naysa? She can't dump this on her father. He's got enough to deal with, as do her aunts, her mother's sisters. She needs someone who cares but also has some distance.

The answer comes to her. She sits in her desk chair, lifts the lid on her laptop and starts to type.

To: angiehazelnut@hotmail.com
From: brennayoko@gmail.com

Hey, Angie,

I'm sorry I haven't contacted you since we met and especially sorry if I seemed grouchy when you asked me not to connect with Kia through Aid-A-Child. I withdrew the project from the SJ Club's list of projects and will donate anonymously if I decide to do that.

I'm wondering if you can help me out with something else. I don't know who to talk to. I don't want to upset my dad or my mom's sisters—they've been through enough already—but I think my little sister is getting into some serious trouble. This is really, really sudden, since Mom died. She's always been a sweet kid, but she started high school and wham! She changed overnight. I think she's drinking and probably smoking too. She's always grouchy when she's home, but she's out who-knows-where more and more often. I know you said you are going to be a teacher, so I thought you might have some advice for me.

Thanks!

There is a skiff of snow on the ground as Brenna heads across the mountain. Even from a distance she can see one of the bears rolling in it. Snow always turns them into playful cubs again.

She's sweeping the light snow off the bridge between the ponds when Ryan appears. He looks around, assuring himself that they are alone, and then he gives her a hug and a quick but delicious kiss.

"No staff fraternizing allowed," he says.

Brenna wishes they could go somewhere and "fraternize" in private.

"What should we do tonight?" he asks.

It's been three weeks since they tried watching a movie together. Ryan knows better than to watch TV after a mountain shift now, so they'd played video games at his uncle's house one Saturday night, and Georgialee had invited them over to play board games with some other friends last week.

"I'm up for anything," Brenna says, "though I wouldn't mind being home until Naysa leaves. Apparently she's going to a Halloween party, and I'd like to see her costume."

"Your friends aren't having Halloween parties?" he asks.

"No." None that she wanted to go to anyway.

"Hey!" His face lights up. "Why don't we carve pumpkins? That's such a cool tradition. We don't have Halloween back home."

"No? Okay. And we can roast pumpkin seeds. You'll love 'em."

"Tell you what. I'll pick some pumpkins up after work," he says, "and bring them to your house."

"Perfect."

He gives her another furtive kiss and starts to walk away, then turns back to her. "About tomorrow," he says.

"Yeah?"

"Let's not hike." He hangs his head and gives her a sideways look. "I'm tired, and you've been hiking all week."

Brenna laughs. "Are you kidding me? You dragged me hiking when I didn't want to go. Now it's my turn to drag you."

"Be nice."

"Not a chance."

"What if I come up with a plan B, something so much fun you won't be able to resist?"

"Well, maybe. But I can't imagine what that would be."

"Then trust me. I know exactly what we're gong to do instead." He turns and begins to run. "See you tonight!" he calls over his shoulder.

From: angiehazelnut@hotmail.com

To: brennayoko@gmail.com

Hi, Brenna,

I, too, am sorry if I overreacted when we met. I REALLY want to stay connected with you, yet I don't want to mess up things with my sister. I guess this is kind of dishonest, but I don't know how else to handle things. I've been struggling with it.

Anyway, I'm sorry to hear about your sister. This is another tough one. You are too young, and too fragile yourself right now, to take this on. Like your dad and your aunts, you've gone through a lot. Is there a counselor at school you could ask to get involved? Let me know.

Love,

Angie

Brenna has to swallow a lump in her throat.

From: brennayoko@gmail.com
To: angiehazelnut@hotmail.com

Thanks, Angie, but I'm afraid that if I get a counselor involved, Naysa will find out that I was the one who squealed on her. It's kind of like what's happening with you and Kia. I don't want to wreck my relationship (what's left of it) with my sister either.

B.

PS. I'm glad you want to stay connected. Me too.

The doorbell rings. When Brenna answers it she finds an enormous pumpkin sitting on the doormat. Ryan has run back down the steps and is hoisting another one out of his trunk.

"Leave it!" he calls to her. "It's super heavy. I'll carry it up the stairs."

She squats and wraps both arms around it. "You're the one who's so tired."

He follows her up the stairs and they place the pump-kins on the table. Ryan turns to head back outside.

"Where are you going?"

"There's more."

She follows him out to the car and sees three more pumpkins in the trunk. "Five pumpkins?"

"Yeah, you know, a family of pumpkins."

"Oh my god!" she says, reaching for another one. "We'll be carving all night."

"Well, unless we're alone," he says quietly, glancing at the house, "in which case we might get distracted."

She smiles and feels her skin burning. "I'm not sure we'll be so lucky."

In the kitchen Brenna begins wiping the mud off the biggest pumpkin while Ryan brings up the remaining one. He also takes a cloth and begins wiping them down.

Naysa comes into the kitchen as they work. "Five pumpkins?" she asks.

"Yeah, there's one for you if you want to skip the party and carve with us," Ryan says.

"What party?"

Brenna feels the sharp look her sister gives her, but she doesn't meet Naysa's eyes. She forgot to tell Ryan how she found out about the party. She feels him looking at her too, waiting for an explanation, but only an awkward silence fills the room.

"I guess I just assumed there'd be a party," he says, returning to the pumpkins. "Halloween is next

Thursday, right? So this is the Saturday night before Halloween. Of course there's a party."

Naysa glares at her sister for another moment, then turns and leaves the kitchen.

"I saw *Halloween party* written in her planner," Brenna whispers. "I was snooping. She didn't know that I knew." She runs her hand over the smooth surface of the pumpkin. "I'm sorry—I should have mentioned that part."

They line the pumpkins up in order of size on the table. "I took the liberty of downloading these," Ryan says, pulling a wad of folded papers out of his back pocket. As he flattens them on the table, Brenna can see that he's printed multiple designs for pumpkin carving.

"Whoa! These look complicated," Brenna says, picking up a sheet that shows a Mickey Mouse face carved into it. Round ears have somehow been affixed to the top. "Whatever happened to plain old scary faces?"

"Those are for amateurs," Ryan says. "Look at this one!" He holds up a page showing a pumpkin with a ghost carved into it. The word *BOO* runs down the side. Ryan grins.

"You're as excited as a little kid," Brenna says.

"I told you. We don't have Halloween at home. I carved my first pumpkin last year. It was awesome."

Brenna's dad comes into the kitchen. "Whoa! Pumpkins! Makes my mouth water for pumpkin pie."

"Pumpkin pie!" Ryan says. "That's something else I never had till last year." He makes a face. "But I don't think I was missing much there."

"You don't like pumpkin pie?" Brenna's dad says, astonished. "The girls' mom made the world's best pumpkin pie." He sighs. "I bet you would have liked hers."

"I bet I would have," Ryan agrees.

"I'm driving Naysa over to her friend's," Brenna's dad says, shaking the car keys. "I thought you might want to drive, but I see you're busy."

"Another sleepover?" Brenna asks.

Her dad nods.

Brenna is about to say something, but Naysa appears in the doorway behind him, carrying a duffel bag. "Let's go, Dad," she says. There's an edge in her voice, and she doesn't look at Brenna or Ryan.

Brenna knows she should tell her dad to search that duffel bag and forbid Naysa to sleep over, but she's torn. She doesn't want to create a scene with Ryan there.

"You two be careful with the knives," her father says. "They're really sharp."

Brenna rolls her eyes. Once he's out of earshot, she says, "Sharp knives should be the least of his worries."

"We didn't get to see her costume," Ryan says.

"It's probably X-rated," she says, thinking of the underwear she saw lying around Naysa's bedroom. "I'm really worried about her."

"How 'bout we take your mind off Naysa," Ryan says, taking her into his arms. He kisses her eyes, and his hands run down the length of her body. She melts into him and savors the lingering kisses. She does, for the moment, forget all about Naysa.

~

When Brenna's dad returns from dropping off Naysa, they take a break to warm up some leftovers for dinner. Then they get back to work. They've each found their pumpkin-carving roles. Brenna likes reaching into the pumpkin's cavity, pulling out the guts and then separating the seeds from the innards. Ryan designs and carves. The aroma of freshly cut pumpkin fills the kitchen.

When they're finished, Brenna rinses the seeds and spreads them out on paper towels to dry. The guts have been added to the compost bin. Brenna places a tea light inside each pumpkin, and when the candles are lit, she calls her dad into the kitchen and turns out the lights. Two ghoulish faces stare back at them, and intricate designs glow from the remaining pumpkins. Ryan snaps photos of them on his phone and immediately texts them to his "mates" in Australia.

"Now that was fun," he says, unlocking his car a few minutes later. "I can't believe Halloween hasn't caught on back home." He yawns, gives her a hug and promises to be back in the morning.

Before she turns out her light for the night, Brenna checks her email.

To: brennayoko@gmail.com
From: angiehazelnut@hotmail.com

I can see your problem, Brenna. Tell me, what does Naysa like to do? Does she have any hobbies? Interests? I thought maybe the 3 of us could get together and do something...and we could talk. Maybe she needs a good listener in her life right now, an adult who is not quite family. What do you think?

⌒

Brenna is mixing tuna with mayonnaise when Ryan returns on Sunday morning.

"Are you sure I'm going to like this mystery trip better than hiking?" Brenna asks.

"I know for sure. What can I do to help?" he asks.

"You can butter the bread. There's a loaf in the freezer."

When she sees him buttering eight slices, she opens another can of tuna and adds more mayonnaise, diced celery and red pepper. He lays lettuce on the bread and puts slices of cucumber on top of the lettuce.

When the sandwiches have been placed into containers, they pack them into a cloth grocery bag and put water bottles and baggies of the freshly toasted pumpkin seeds on top. Ryan has told Brenna's dad where they are going, and he watches as they climb into Ryan's car.

"Drive safe!" he calls and waves as they pull out of the driveway.

Ryan drives west, passing Horseshoe Bay. Brenna can see a ferry pulling into its berth far below as they continue along the Sea to Sky Highway. The sun sparkles on the water, and Brenna sits back, relaxing. "Don't tell me we're hiking the Chief," she says. The Chief is a towering granite dome near Squamish that's popular with experienced hikers.

"No, not this week. But that's a good idea for another Sunday."

Brenna rifles through Ryan's case of CDs. She selects Mumford and Sons and pushes it into the slot. They both sing along. Brenna feels the cares of the week fall away as Ryan turns north, leaving Howe Sound behind. She expects him to stop in Squamish, but he drives straight through. "Are we going to Whistler?"

"Nope, not Whistler."

A few kilometers past Squamish, Ryan turns off the highway and Brenna sees the sign for Brackendale Eagles Provincial Park. "Dad gave you permission to take me camping?" she teases.

"I wish!" He laughs. "No, silly, we're going to see the eagles. This is the time of year they return to the area, because the chum salmon are spawning. There could be three thousand or more eagles in this valley by the end of December."

"You'd think you were the local Vancouverite and I was the newcomer."

Ryan pulls into a gravel parking lot alongside a river. "Look!" Brenna says, pointing to the other side. "There are three eagles on that one tree! And four more on that one down there!"

Orange and yellow leaves still cling to the trees, giving the birds partial shelter, but Ryan and Brenna have no trouble spotting them. They scramble out of the car and stand on the riverbank. "Your mouth is hanging open," Ryan teases, looking down at her.

"Oh my god! I can't believe it. There are so many, and they're so beautiful!" They watch as an eagle swoops low over the river. Its wingspan is easily two meters.

"Thank you, Ryan! This is amazing!"

"I thought you'd like it," he says. "Wait here. I'll be right back."

Ryan jogs back to the car, and when he returns he's carrying two sets of binoculars and the grocery bag with their packed lunch. He hands her a set of binoculars.

"Ha! Now we're bird-watchers! I thought you had to be at least sixty to qualify."

"Not here," he says.

Brenna puts the binoculars to her eyes and looks across the river. "You're right—this is way better than hiking."

Ryan rests his arm around her shoulder and they stroll down the riverside path, stopping often to look through the binoculars. Eventually he leads her over to a bench at the side of the path. "Lunchtime," he says and pulls a sandwich out of the bag.

Brenna checks her phone. "It's only eleven o'clock," she says.

"My stomach tells me it's lunchtime. I don't care what your phone says."

Brenna smiles and takes a sandwich too. She leans back and soaks up the whole wilderness setting. "Mom would have liked it here. I'm surprised she never brought us out."

"Who explores their own backyard?" Ryan says. "Before they have out-of-town guests, anyway."

Ryan has eaten two sandwiches before Brenna finishes her first. "Maybe you should try the whiskey-jack trick with the eagles," he suggests. "But instead of peanuts, we'll offer them the last tuna sandwich."

"Are you kidding me?" she asks. "Have you seen the talons on these guys? They'd take my arm with the sandwich."

"You're probably right. I saw one grab a huge salmon out of the river when I came here last winter," he says. "Too bad. I guess I'll have to eat it then." He reaches into the bag.

They sit in silence, watching the eagles and snacking on pumpkin seeds, but after a while Brenna senses a shift in Ryan's mellow mood. His foot begins to shake erratically, and he keeps running his hand through his hair. She glances at him and is about to ask what he's thinking about when she feels a drop of rain on her head. She looks up, surprised to see that heavy black clouds have moved in. "I think we're about to get very wet," she says and quickly starts putting the remains of their lunch back into the bag.

The drops turn into a full-on downpour as they walk back toward the car, and after a few minutes they begin to jog, but they're both soaked by the time they reach the parking lot. They scramble into the car. "Put the heat on," Brenna says, feeling a chill run through her.

"Sorry, ma'am," he says, firing up the engine of the old car. "There's no heat in Big Red." He looks over at her. "But I know a better way to warm you up," he says as he pulls her close.

The windshield wipers slap loudly as they drive back down the Sea to Sky Highway. The scenery looks entirely different now, with no more sunlight sparkling on the water. Instead the clouds hang heavy and ominous. Everything is a flat shade of gray—the sky, the water, the mountains in the distance.

They stop in a coffee shop to warm up and dry off. Not wanting the carefree mood from the morning to end, Brenna continues to sing along with the music when they get back in the car, but she notices she is singing alone, and when she glances at Ryan she sees an uncharacteristically serious expression on his face. "You okay?" she asks.

"Yeah. Sort of." His thumb taps the steering wheel. He takes a deep breath and sighs loudly. "But there is something I need to tell you."

Dread sweeps through her. She knows that when someone says *there's something I need to tell you*, the news is never good.

"Don't tell me right now. I don't want to spoil a perfectly perfect day." She slides lower in her seat, realizing the futility of it. The day has already been ruined just by knowing he has some bad news to share.

Ahead of them, the sheer rock surface of the Chief towers above the road. Ryan pulls off the highway again, into the gravel area where the hikers park before making the climb. He shuts off the ignition and turns to take one of her hands in his.

He's breaking it off, Brenna thinks. He's decided I'm too young.

"My uncle and I are going to see my mom," he says. "We're going at the start of December and will stay at least through Christmas."

Brenna stares at him, a mixture of relief and alarm transforming her face. "But you are coming back?"

Ryan's eyes flicker away. "That's undecided. We're going to see how she is. She's being discharged from the long-term-care facility, and someone needs to be with her."

She studies his face. "So you might not come back."

He doesn't respond or meet her eyes.

"How long have you known this?" The disbelief is turning to anger.

"Only a couple of days. When I got home last night my uncle was still up, and we had a long talk, ironing out the details. He feels he should come with me, but he can't stay longer than a month."

"Why didn't you tell me this earlier?"

"I didn't want to ruin today. I was looking forward to bringing you out here."

Brenna slouches down farther as the truth of his words washes through her. Someone has to stay with his mother, and it won't be her brother, Ryan's uncle, because his home is now in Canada. That leaves Ryan. She brushes a lone tear off her cheek. "Can you bring your mom here?"

Ryan releases his seat belt so he can lean over to hold her. He sighs again. "I always knew I'd be going home eventually. I just didn't think it would be this soon."

Brenna allows him to hold her, but she has nothing to say and she doesn't return the hug. She's too numb.

"We have a whole month left," he says. "We'll spend as much time as we can together and make all kinds of great memories."

Brenna takes a deep, ragged breath. "I have enough memories." She pushes him away. "I want to go home."

"Oh, Brenna. It's going to be okay."

"Nothing is okay anymore. Take me home."

Ryan hesitates, but when she folds her arms across her chest, he turns the key and reluctantly pulls the car back out onto the highway.

Oct. 27

I hate him I hate him I hate him I hate him I hate him.

fourteen

Love is like the wind. You can't see it, but you can feel it.

(NICHOLAS SPARKS, *A WALK TO REMEMBER*)

"Are you okay?" Naysa asks. They're in the kitchen, packing lunches for school.

Brenna glances at her, surprised. Naysa hasn't shown any interest in her in weeks. Her red and swollen eyes must have given her away. Or maybe the persistent sniffling. Neither Naysa or her dad had noticed her mood when she returned from Brackendale the previous day, but then she'd hardly left her room all evening.

"Not really," she admits.

"What's the matter?"

Brenna can hear the alarm in Naysa's voice and realizes that her sister is prone to expecting the worst these days too. She's reluctant to share her news, but she doesn't want Naysa to worry that she has some life-threatening disease.

"Ryan's going back to Australia in December. Maybe for good."

"Oh no! I'm sorry. I like him."

She sounds genuine, but Brenna thinks she also hears a hint of relief in her voice. It's not something life-threatening. Her eyes begin to well up again. She smacks the sandwich container onto the counter. "You know, I don't think I can face school today."

"Then don't go."

Brenna stares at her sister. A year ago she'd never have suggested skipping school. She'd never shown even a hint of rebelliousness.

"Do you want me to stay home with you?"

"Thanks, Nayse. I think I'm having one of those days, you know?"

Naysa nods. "Text me if you change your mind."

"I will." They look at each other, and for a moment it's almost the way it was before school started. It seems the old Naysa is back, at least temporarily. Brenna sees nothing but compassion in her face.

In her darkened bedroom she pulls out Kia's journal and flips through it, rereading some of the entries. Then she rereads Angie's last email and considers a response, but she can't think of anything to suggest the three of them do together, especially because she doesn't know which

Naysa will show up on any given day. She pulls out her own journal.

Oct. 28

It's dark at the bottom of this pit. Every time I get a foothold, every time I think I'm going to climb out, I slip to the bottom again. What's the point in trying?

Yet...it feels like Nayse and I have reached an unspoken truce. Who'd have guessed?

Her phone pings with a text from Georgialee.

Bren! R U sick? Bentley & I were going to hook up with you and the hiking dogs this afternoon. Will you be going?

She texts back.

Yep. Meet at the base of Quarry Rock, 3:30.

Her phone pings again and she expects to see something else from Georgialee, but this one's from Ryan.

Pls don't be mad, Bren. It's not like I have a choice.

She closes her eyes, sighs deeply and texts back.

Not mad. Just sad.

She sits back and waits for his response. It comes quickly.

Me too. And I'm kinda scared.

He's scared? What of? His mom? His future? She'd been so busy feeling sorry for herself that she hadn't even considered how he must be feeling.

Eventually she opens her computer and composes an email to Angie.

To: angiehazelnut@hotmail.com
From: brennayoko@gmail.com

Hi, Angie,

I can't really think of anything Naysa would do with us. The things she used to do, like playing the piano and reading, she's not doing anymore.

She sits back in her chair and stares at the computer. An idea begins to percolate, but she hesitates. Is it a stupid idea?

She continues to type.

We had Ryan over for dinner the other night, and he sat in Mom's chair. It was nice to have it filled with someone I like, so I was thinking...would you come for dinner and meet my dad and sister? It would be nice to have someone sitting there again, someone I like. You could get to know Naysa and then, hopefully, we can come up with a plan.

B.

PS. I'll totally understand if that feels creepy to you. Sitting in my mom's chair, that is.

Brenna rereads the letter, takes a deep breath and presses *Send*. The response is almost immediate.

To: brennayoko@gmail.com
From: angiehazelnut@hotmail.com

Brenna—I would be honored to have dinner with your family and sit in your mother's chair. Just name the day.
Love,
A.

Despite her mood, Brenna smiles when she reads Angie's note. Now she'll just have to find a way to explain to her dad how Angie came to be in her life.

"Were you sick or just skipping school today?" Georgialee asks. Bentley has quickly befriended Brenna's hikers, as she calls the dogs, and the four of them are leading the way up the off-leash trail.

Brenna really doesn't feel up to talking about it yet. She still needs to process it herself, but she knows it's inevitable. "I found out yesterday that Ryan's going home in December, and he probably won't be coming back."

Georgialee stops so she can look directly at Brenna. "Are you serious? That's awful!"

"I know." Despite her best effort, she can't hold the tears back. Georgialee puts her arms around her friend and lets her cry. The four dogs circle around them, watching anxiously.

"It's okay, guys," Georgialee says. She points up the trail. "Go!"

They follow the dogs. "I really like him," Brenna says. "He makes me forget everything else, you know?"

"He's a pretty cool guy."

"Exactly." She uses her sleeve to wipe her nose. "This weekend we carved pumpkins and then we drove up to Brackendale to see the eagles. He's always got good ideas for things to do."

Georgialee nods.

"Moving back to Australia…he might as well be dead, like my mom."

"No, Bren," Georgialee says. "You'll be able to Skype and email and maybe go and see him."

"We won't be able to do stuff together."

The girls grow quiet as they cross one of the wooden bridges that span the myriad streams trickling down Mount Seymour.

"Do you want to hear something weird?" Georgialee asks.

"What?"

"I've been kind of jealous of him."

"Jealous?"

"Yeah. He was able to get close to you. You were doing things again. I felt like I'd let you down somehow. I always said the wrong thing. Because no one close to me has died, it's like…like I can't understand… you know?"

Brenna looks at her friend, but she doesn't know how to respond. It's true, Ryan has filled a void that Georgialee hadn't been able to. She wonders if she herself is partly to blame. She was never able to tell Georgialee what she needed. "Do you wanna know what else is going on?"

"Yeah, what?"

Brenna fills her in on meeting Angie and Justin and then shares her ongoing concern about Naysa. By the time she's finished, they have arrived at the lookout. They begin snapping leashes on the dogs, but instead of going out to the ledge that overlooks Indian Arm, they sit on a mossy log in the forest. The dogs lie down around them, panting.

"You've got a lot going on," Georgialee says.

Brenna nods.

"So that Aid-A-Child idea. What was that all about?"

Brenna tells her the truth, that she was hoping to find a way to contact Kia.

"God, Brenna, I don't know what to say."

"There's nothing to say." She shrugs. "Thanks for listening."

They sit quietly, soaking up the stillness of the forest. Georgialee presses her shoulder into Brenna. Brenna leans into her. They sit like this for a long time.

Eventually they pull away, unclip the dogs and head back down the trail.

"So," Georgialee says, "have you and Ryan..." She doesn't finish the sentence.

"Done it?" Brenna says, smiling.

"Yeah. Done it."

"No, but we've talked about it. Sort of."

"Well," Georgialee says, picking up the pace, "you've got a month." She breaks into a jog, and the dogs yap at her heels, happy to play a new game.

⌒

"More snow fell today," Ryan says, breaking the uneasy quiet. He's come over to Brenna's to work on the puzzle, and he's trying to fit a piece into a hole. "At this rate, the mountain might open early for the ski season. They're scrambling to get enough lift operators and rental people trained in time." He looks up. "Do you need a winter job?"

"Thanks, but I've got my own company, remember?"

"Oh yeah. Right."

There's a gulf between them tonight, a clumsiness. Conversations started but not finished, the problem not addressed but hanging heavily in the air between them. Brenna's relieved he's found a topic that's easy.

Her dad had raised his eyebrows when Brenna told him Ryan was coming over, had mumbled something about it being a school night, but Brenna had ignored him. They only had a month.

"Yeah," he says, thinking out loud, "but the days are getting so short. You won't be able to hike in the afternoons much longer. Maybe you'll have to take a hiatus until spring, you know, like seasonal work. Lift operator in winter and dog hiker in summer."

Brenna nods. She's been thinking that too. "The dogs still need to get out, so maybe I'll just give them neighborhood walks until spring. I can adjust my rates."

"Spoken like a true businesswoman." He smiles, but silence quickly settles over them again. A smattering of firecrackers can be heard out on the street.

"I'm hoping we'll get a chance to showshoe," he says. He doesn't add *before I leave*, but they both know what he means.

Brenna nods and swallows a huge lump. They focus on the puzzle.

"Dad, there's something I haven't told you." Brenna has spent the whole meal trying to figure out how to broach the subject, but finally she just blurts it out.

Her dad and Naysa both look up with matching worried expressions.

"My birth mom's sister, Angie, contacted me a few weeks ago. She'd run into Justin, the minister, and he told her about Mom. She messaged me to say how sorry she was."

"That was nice of her," her dad says. "I'd forgotten that Kia has a sister." He returns to his meal, but Naysa is still studying her face.

She clears her throat. "So we met for coffee, and Justin came too. He said to say hi," she adds.

Brenna's dad regards her, sensing there's more.

"I was wondering if we could invite her over for dinner one night. You'd really like her. She's studying to be a high school teacher."

Her father takes a long drink from his glass of water. He removes his glasses, rubs his eyes and puts the glasses back on. "You know your friends are always welcome here, honey, but I'm not sure if the timing is right to revisit that part of your life."

"What do you mean?" Brenna feels a tightening in her stomach. "You're the one who gave me Kia's journal." She puts her fork down.

"That was your mom's idea." Her father sighs. "I expect this means Kia will come back into your life too."

"Actually, no."

Her dad tilts his head, expecting her to continue, but she doesn't offer anything else.

"Brenna, we're all a bit…a bit vulnerable right now, trying to adjust to our new family situation. I'm afraid you're going to open a whole new can of worms…and maybe for the wrong reasons."

Brenna cuts him off. "My birth family is not a can of worms. Why do people keep saying that? You and Mom always encouraged us to seek out good role models. I think Angie is one. She cared enough to contact me. She has no hidden agenda."

Her dad raises his hands, palms out. "Fine, Brenna. Invite her over."

They eat in silence. Finally her dad speaks again. "Why didn't you mention you were meeting her?"

Brenna shrugs. "It was kind of awkward. I didn't know how you'd feel about it, and I didn't even know if I'd like her. But I do. A lot."

Her dad wipes his mouth with his napkin and pushes his chair back. He changes the subject. "Naysa tells me she's going out on Thursday night, Halloween. Will you be here to hand out candy? I've got a meeting that night."

Brenna nods. She glances at Naysa, who shoots her a look that speaks volumes: *Don't ask where I'm going*—and Brenna's pretty sure it won't be trick-or-treating.

Her dad knocks on Brenna's door before entering her room. "Have you got a second?" he asks.

"Yep." She drags her focus from the math problem she's been trying to solve and meets his tired-looking eyes.

He remains in her doorway but leans against the jamb. "I'm going to be honest with you, honey," he says. "Your mom and I encouraged Kia to stay connected with you. We didn't feel at all threatened by that. We were too grateful to her for giving you to us. But at dinner, when you brought this up about her sister, well, my knee-jerk reaction was...it was a sense of alarm. Like somehow I might lose you too if you reconnect with your birth family. I know that's stupid, but that's how I felt for a moment. Your mom would definitely have encouraged this. I just wanted to say that."

"Thanks, Dad."

He stands there with his hands deep in his pockets, looking uneasy. She wants to tell him that it's for Naysa that she really wants to invite Angie over, but she doesn't dare, not with Naysa in the house. "I probably opened that whole can of worms by inviting Justin to officiate at your mom's service, but that was what she requested."

He starts to leave her doorway but turns back to face her. "Naysa told me that Ryan's going back to Australia. I'm really sorry to hear that."

Brenna only nods, not trusting her voice to remain strong.

Her dad wanders away, but a moment later Naysa comes into her room and plunks herself down on Brenna's bed. Brenna swivels around in her chair to look at her.

"So technically," Naysa says, "you still have a living mother."

"Technically," Brenna agrees.

"I'm jealous." It's spoken like a challenge.

"Don't be. She doesn't want to see me."

Naysa's eyes widen. "Why not?"

"I guess it's that can-of-worms thing Dad was talking about."

"What do you mean?"

Brenna slumps in her chair. "From what I understand, putting me up for adoption was hard for her. She struggled afterward. Now she's found *meaningful work*," she says, putting air quotes around the words, "on the other side of the world. She's working with kids who have AIDS. Reconnecting with me would, apparently, be a setback for her."

Naysa mulls this over. "I guess that's kind of hard for you."

"Yeah. Kind of."

"Well, then, I guess I'm not jealous anymore." Naysa climbs off the bed and stomps out of the room.

Brenna shakes her head. Just when she thought the old Naysa was returning, her evil twin sister has reappeared.

⌒⌒

November arrives, bringing shorter days, longer nights. The uneasiness between Brenna and Ryan persists.

The Grouse Grind has closed for the season, but there's not yet enough snow for snowshoeing. A few days after Halloween the bears go into their hibernation den, and Brenna's volunteer work ends for the season.

"How about a movie?" Ryan asks. It's the first Saturday they've had off together, and they've spent the late morning and early afternoon lounging in Brenna's family room. The rain is coming down in gray sheets outside. Ryan's long legs are spread wide, and Brenna sits between them, scrolling through Facebook while Ryan looks over her shoulder.

"What's playing?"

He pulls his phone out of his pocket. "I'll check the movie listings."

Now Brenna looks on as he scrolls through the options.

"What do you like?" he asks, tilting his head so their faces are pressed together as they look at the choices.

"No thrillers or shoot-'em-ups."

"Oh. Well, that narrows the field."

"And no aliens or vampires."

"I don't think *Bambi's* playing this week."

She elbows him in the ribs.

"But there is this." They watch the trailer together. It's a movie about survival, where the character has to face the elements as well as his own emotions.

"That'll do," she says. "What do you think?"

He glances toward the door, then kisses her gently on the lips. "I don't care what we watch as long as we're watching it together."

"Oh, Ryan," she says, her tone mocking. "You say the sweetest things."

He doesn't respond but takes her hand and kisses the back of it. She glances at him and notices a shimmer in his eyes. Tears?

Before she can figure out what he's feeling, Naysa comes into the room, flops onto the couch and flicks on the TV.

"How was Halloween, Naysa?" Ryan asks, pulling himself up on the couch. He clears his throat, and Brenna studies his face.

"Good," she says, staring at the screen.

"Do you have any loot to share with me?"

She gives him a quick glance, then also glances at Brenna. "I didn't go trick-or-treating, but there are leftovers in a bowl in the kitchen," she tells him.

"There are?" he says, jumping up and heading toward the kitchen.

"Save some for me," she calls after him.

Halfway through the movie Ryan reaches for Brenna's hand. Until then they'd been sharing a large soft drink and popcorn, but the empty containers have been placed on the floor. Ryan doesn't hold her hand but rubs his palm across hers, ever so softly. Brenna has never felt her nerve endings spring to life so intensely. She leans her shoulder into his as the character on the screen prepares his sailboat for the approaching storm. The music builds, and a wave of energy flows between them. She leans closer and their fingers clasp. The adventures on the big screen seem small compared to the swell of sensations rushing through her body. All the awkwardness of the past week evaporates as the current between them grows. Words were the stumbling block, she realizes. The pull between them is beyond words.

Brenna resists returning to the present when the final credits roll and the movie character has conquered all his battles, external as well as internal. She knows that her demons are all still waiting for her outside the theater. For the duration of the movie, she was safe to revel in the flow of feelings between her and Ryan.

They step outside as the afternoon is turning into evening. The rain has not let up. Ryan pauses on the sidewalk, looking down at her. He looks like he is about to say something, but then he simply takes her hand again and leads her to his car. She doesn't ask where they are going, just holds his right hand while he steers with his left. She draws patterns on his palm with her fingers. She feels if she says anything she'll break the spell that still lingers from the movie.

He pulls his car into his uncle's driveway, and they go into the house together. As soon as the front door is closed behind them, Ryan pulls her into him. She breaks away just long enough to ask about his uncle.

"Out for the evening," he says and leads her down to his bedroom. She doesn't resist. Every fiber in her body knows that she's ready.

~

Hours later they climb back into Ryan's car. "You're sure you're okay?" he asks.

"Way more than okay." She smiles, and they gaze at each other for another moment.

"I wish you could stay all night."

"I wish I could too."

He leans over and gives her a soft kiss before putting the key in the ignition. She leans back, melting into the seat. "Is that what you meant when you said we would create memories?" she asks.

"Well, maybe in some hopeful place in my mind. But I really didn't know if we would go there—or whether we should."

They drive in comfortable silence. As they turn the corner onto her street, Brenna's about to ask what he'd like to do on Sunday, but then her mouth and brain freeze. A police car and ambulance are sitting at the curb in front of her house.

fifteen

Tears are the silent language of grief.
(VOLTAIRE, *PHILOSOPHICAL DICTIONARY*)

Ryan has barely come to a full stop when Brenna jumps out and races over to her father's car, which is parked in the driveway. The paramedics are attending to someone in the backseat.

"Brenna!" her father says. He's standing close to the open car door. "Where have you been? I've been trying to reach you! Naysa's in a bad way."

Brenna barely hears him. "Is she going to be okay?" she asks the paramedics as they pull Naysa out of the car and place her on a stretcher. Her eyes are closed, and Brenna can see how pale her face is.

"We're going to take good care of her," one of them says.

She knows that's a polite way of saying they don't know. "What happened?" she asks her dad. His face is also ashen.

"I'll tell you on the way to the hospital."

As Brenna turns to follow the paramedics who are carrying Naysa to the ambulance, she sees Ryan hunched over beside his car, hands shoved in his pockets. Brenna simply shrugs when he meets her eyes, looking for answers. "We're going to the hospital."

"I'll meet you there."

The paramedics load the stretcher into the back of the ambulance. Then, with lights flashing and the siren screaming, the ambulance pulls away from the curb. Brenna jumps into her dad's car, and he backs out of the driveway and follows. His hands grip the wheel tightly. Brenna feels like she might throw up. She checks the side mirror and sees that Ryan is behind them.

"One of her friends called the home phone about forty-five minutes ago," her dad explains, glancing at the clock on the dashboard. "They said Naysa seemed to be having some kind of seizure and that I should come and get her." He swallows, and Brenna waits, her heart pounding so hard she feels deafened by it.

"I got there and found her lying on the floor. Her eyes were open and she was trying to talk, but she was incoherent. I managed to get her to the car, though I was practically carrying her." He pauses. "I should have called the paramedics there, at that house, but all I knew was that I wanted to get her out of there and away from those kids as fast as I could. I was hoping she was just drunk and could sleep it off.

"By the time we got home she was no longer even responsive. I couldn't get her out of the car, so I called the ambulance. It only took them a few minutes to get to our place, thank God. We need to find out what she took tonight. The police are at that house now; they'll call me if they learn anything."

Brenna forces herself to take a deep breath. She had known her sister was headed for trouble and yet she'd done nothing to stop it. If Naysa doesn't pull through, it will be all her fault.

"Do me a favor, Brenna, and call Laura and Tamara. Tell them to meet us in the ER."

Brenna pulls out her phone and searches through her contacts for her mom's sisters.

"Where were you tonight anyway?" he asks. "I've been trying to reach you."

Brenna thinks back to what she was doing while Naysa was getting wasted. Her face burns as she remembers. She was thinking of no one but herself and Ryan, and how blissful it was to forget everything else. That already seems like hours ago.

"We went to a movie, so my phone was on mute. I forgot to turn it back on. I'm sorry."

"That was a matinee, Brenna. It's eleven thirty now. Why didn't you check in? It's so not like you."

Brenna doesn't answer. Shame courses through her the same way pleasure had a few hours earlier. She listens to Aunt Laura's phone ring.

"How ironic that it was you I was worried about, but it was Naysa who was getting into trouble," her dad says.

He pulls into a parking stall at the hospital, jumps out of the car and begins to run toward the ER. Brenna leaves a message on her aunt's answering machine and with shaky fingers begins scrolling through the list, looking for Aunt Tamara's number.

Ryan pulls into a stall close to where her father has parked and waits while Brenna finishes leaving another message. They begin to walk across the parking lot toward the ER. Brenna quickly fills him in. "And the stupid part was, Dad was worried about me—not Naysa—because I forgot to check in."

Ryan puts his arm around Brenna's shoulders and pulls her to face him. "This has nothing to do with what you and I were doing," he tells her.

She doesn't meet his eyes but hears him sigh.

"Brenna." Now she does look up, wondering at the change in his tone. "I can't go in there," he says, glancing at the hospital. "It brings back too much...too many memories of...of that day..."

He doesn't finish, but Brenna realizes he's talking about the day his brother died.

"I'm sorry, but I just...I just can't," he says. "But I'll be waiting in the car. Keep me posted, okay? I won't go anywhere."

She nods. "It's okay. I left messages for my aunts. They'll probably come right away."

The screaming siren of another ambulance can be heard in the distance. They see the lights, and moments later it pulls up to the automatic doors. They watch as the paramedics begin to unload the stretcher.

Brenna glances at Ryan and sees that his face is stricken. "Go back to your car," she tells him. "I'll keep in touch. I promise."

Inside the ER waiting room Brenna finds her father standing in a corner, talking on his cell phone. The hand holding the phone is shaking.

"You're sure?" he's saying. "There's no doubt about that?"

He listens to the response before tucking the phone back in his pocket. "The police finally found a girl who would talk about the party. Naysa took Ecstasy and then drank shots of tequila," he tells Brenna. "I need to tell the doctors."

She watches as he speaks to the triage nurse. The nurse gets up and indicates that her father should take a seat in the waiting room. He turns, and together they find two empty plastic chairs, but as soon as he sits, her dad jumps up again and begins pacing the room. Brenna looks down at her hands and sees that they are trembling too. Bile begins to creep up her throat. She looks around for the nearest washroom, just in case.

Forty-five minutes feel like twenty-four hours. The outside doors open. Brenna's aunts have arrived. They spot her dad and rush over to him. "What's happening?" Aunt Laura asks.

Brenna can see that both women must have been asleep when she called them. Their makeup has been washed off, and Tamara is wearing an old pair of glasses instead of her contact lenses.

"Possible alcohol poisoning," he tells them. "Combined with Ecstasy. She had some kind of seizure and then passed out. They're pumping her stomach right now. They'll let us know when they're done."

Brenna joins the small group, and both aunts give her a hug. Her father rubs his face, wiping away tears.

"Let's sit down." Tamara guides them to the bank of plastic chairs.

Brenna sits and looks around the stark room. The fluorescent light is harsh, and there are clusters of distraught people talking and pacing. An old woman sits across from her, a scarf over her head, her fingers rubbing the rosary beads that lie in her lap. Brenna pulls out her cell phone and fills Ryan in.

Another hour slowly passes. More patients arrive via screaming ambulances. There's nothing to do but watch the other people who are coming and going, all of them as distressed as they are. Her father paces and her aunts sit on either side of her, each with an arm around her. She wishes she could join Ryan in his car and get away from the waiting-room drama.

"Mr. Yokoyama?" calls the triage nurse, looking around. She has stepped through the doors that lead from the patient area to the waiting room.

Her dad identifies himself.

"Come with me, please."

He glances at Brenna and her aunts but follows the nurse through the swinging doors.

Twenty minutes pass. Brenna pulls out her phone again and texts Ryan.

I am so scared.

She waits for a response, but there isn't one. She puts her phone back in her pocket.

The outside doors open again, and Brenna meets Ryan's gaze. She stands up and hurries over to him.

"You don't need to come in," she says. "My aunts are here."

He shakes his head. "I want to be with you. I can do this." He swallows hard.

Brenna leads him over to where her aunts are waiting and introduces them. Then she and Ryan sit in chairs across from them. He takes her hand in both of his. The last time he did that, Brenna remembers, was in the movie theater, before this nightmare began, when the nerve endings in her palm nearly exploded. If only she had gone home after the movie and forbidden Naysa to go to another party...

The swinging doors open again and her dad strides over to where they are sitting. "They've pumped her stomach and they're giving her fluids through an IV," he says in a quiet voice. "There's some concern about the seizure she had, whether it could leave any brain damage.

I'm going to wait beside her bed. I want to be there...
when she wakes up."

Brenna notes he said *when*, not *if*, although he
hesitated.

"Are they keeping her in the ER?" Laura asks.

He nods. "So why don't all of you go home and get
some sleep. I will call the minute there's any more news."
He looks at Brenna's aunts. "Maybe one of you could go
back to my place with Brenna?"

"We'll sort it out," Tamara says. "You get back in there
with Naysa."

"Okay, thanks." He leans down, clasps Brenna's
shoulders and looks directly into her eyes. She wants him
to say that it's going to be okay, but he doesn't. He never
said that when her mom was sick either. After a moment
he turns and heads back through the swinging doors.

Outside the hospital, Brenna turns to Ryan. "I'll call
you when we hear from Dad."

He nods. "You know I can be there—with you—in a
flash, right?"

She nods.

He hugs her, then leaves her to get home with her
aunts, who have both decided to go back to Brenna's house.

"I take it that Naysa was at some kind of party tonight?"
Laura asks. She's sitting at the kitchen table. Tamara is

stretched out on the family-room couch and has closed her eyes.

Brenna realizes she hasn't eaten anything since the popcorn she shared with Ryan hours ago at the movie. She puts some bread into the toaster.

"I guess so. I wasn't home tonight." She takes a knife out of a drawer.

"Do you think this is the first time she's done drugs and had alcohol?"

Brenna shakes her head. Her toast springs up, and she spreads peanut butter over it. "I don't know about the drugs, but there have been a few parties this fall," she says. "I tried to talk to Dad, but I didn't want to worry him too much."

"Why didn't you come to Tamara or me?" Laura asks.

Brenna takes the chair across the table from her. "Same reason."

"Oh, honey."

Brenna stares at her toast through tear-filled eyes. "I was hoping it was just a little phase she was going through. I figured that any day she'd get over it and start hanging out with her old friends again."

The kettle whistles, and Laura gets up and drops a tea bag into a mug. She pours the hot water over it and returns to where Brenna sits with her elbows on the table, her face in her hands. She places her mug on the table but steps behind Brenna in order to rub her back.

Brenna's hand shakes as she picks up her toast.

"Ryan seems like a nice young man," Laura says, massaging Brenna's shoulders.

Brenna nods.

"How long have you two been seeing each other?"

"He's the guy I've been hiking with."

"Oh, right! You did tell me about your hikes."

"But he's moving back to Australia at the beginning of December."

"Oh. That's not good."

Not good, Brenna thinks. An interesting way to put it.

Aunt Laura lies down on her parents' bed, and Brenna goes to her own room but doesn't shut the door. If her dad calls the house phone, she wants to hear it.

She lies on top of her bed. There's no point putting on pajamas and getting under the blankets, as she won't be sleeping anyway.

She scrolls through the email messages on her phone. There's one from Angie. They have yet to find a night for dinner that works for all of them. She has suggested the following Thursday night. Brenna shuts off her phone and gets out her journal. It's too late for Angie to help now.

Nov. 10
I am SO pathetic.
I saw this coming.

I did nothing.
Did I really think Angie could help Naysa?
No, I just wanted an excuse to have her in my life.
Fuck.

The night drags on. Brenna dozes off but wakes with a start when a motorcycle buzzes past on the street outside. She gets up and paces around the house. Aunt Tamara, on the couch, has rolled onto her side and is snoring softly. Brenna unfolds a soft blanket and carefully lays it over her. The snoring stops for a moment, but her aunt doesn't stir.

She looks in on Aunt Laura, who has also rolled onto her side. She has pulled a blanket over herself. Brenna watches her sleep, noticing how much she looks like her mom when her eyes are closed. If her mom were still alive…Naysa wouldn't be in the hospital, and her aunts wouldn't be here.

Brenna goes back to her room, pulls a light blanket off her bed and returns to her father's room. Trying not to disturb her aunt, she lies down beside her. She breathes in the comforting scent of her father on the pillow before noticing the less-familiar scent of her sleeping aunt. Climbing off the bed, she quietly steps over to the closet and pulls a sweater off a hanger. She holds it to her nose and breathes in the faint smell of her mother. Taking it with her, she lies down beside her aunt again and holds the sweater close to her face.

~

Brenna's eyes spring open when the house phone rings. She leaps off the bed and races to the kitchen, beating both of her aunts to the phone. She's surprised to see that it's already beginning to get light outside.

"Hello?"

"Brenna, it's me." Her dad's voice croaks, and Brenna's heart sinks.

"Naysa's awake," he says.

"Oh my god! That's great!" She collapses into a kitchen chair. Her aunts are both staring at her from the doorway, and Laura's hand flies to her chest when she hears the word *great*.

"Yeah, it is. She feels like hell, of course, but it doesn't appear that there's any brain damage—not obvious brain damage anyway."

"That's great," Brenna repeats.

"Yeah."

"What's the matter, Dad? You don't sound relieved."

"I'm just...just...." His voice cracks. "I just didn't take good enough care of her. She needed help and I wasn't there."

Brenna can hear his sobs. "Oh, Dad." Her own eyes fill with tears. "That's not true."

Her aunt Laura takes the phone from her, and Brenna goes to her room, shuts the door and collapses onto her bed.

sixteen

The emotion that can break your heart is
sometimes the very one that heals it.
(NICHOLAS SPARKS, *AT FIRST SIGHT*)

Monday is Remembrance Day, so there is no school and her dad doesn't have to work. He had brought a wretched-looking Naysa home on Sunday afternoon. She'd gone straight to bed. When Brenna went into her room with a glass of water, she'd noticed that the room was tidy and the dirty clothes and hamper were missing. Her aunts must have cleaned up. She wondered what they thought of Naysa's new underwear.

What do you want? Naysa had growled before Brenna could even ask how she was feeling.

Just checking on you. She'd placed the water beside Naysa's bed. *Dad's napping, but I warmed up some food. Do you want some?*

Naysa had shaken her head, squeezed her eyes shut and rolled over so her back was to Brenna.

Today they have hardly spoken, and Brenna has given up even trying to make conversation. They are slouched on the couch, watching talk shows on TV. Her dad has gone to meet with the parents of the girl who had the party. Her phone pings with a text from Ryan.

How is she this afternoon?

Brenna responds. **Quiet. Grumpy.**

Oh dear. How are you?

Quiet. Grumpy. ☹

Hang in there, Brenna. You're a good sister.

Nov. 11
It feels like someone else has died.

"I'm not going back to school. Ever."

Somehow her dad has persuaded Naysa to join them at the table for dinner, but his attempts at conversation are not going well.

"You can't drop out of school in the eighth grade, honey."

"Watch me."

They eat in silence. Brenna wishes she was anywhere but at this table.

"You can stay home tomorrow," he tells Naysa, "and I'll make an appointment with the school counselor."

"Don't bother. I'm not going back. You can't make me."

"Then what are you going to do, Naysa?"

Brenna can hear the exasperation in his voice.

Naysa shrugs. She's staring at her plate but hasn't touched the food.

Eventually he gets up and puts his plate in the dishwasher. "Your aunt Laura will be coming by tomorrow morning to keep you company. I'll check and see who is available in the afternoon."

"I don't need a babysitter," Naysa says, still staring at her untouched dinner.

He ignores her. "I'll make you a follow-up doctor's appointment for Wednesday," he says. "And we'll see where we go from there."

Naysa doesn't comment. She gets up from the table and leaves the kitchen. Brenna hears the door to her bedroom close. Her dad leans back against the counter and sighs.

Nov. 11

I didn't think it was possible for my dad to look any sadder than he did after Mom died. Can it get any worse?

From: brennayoko@gmail.com
To: angiehazelnut@hotmail.com

My sister ended up in the hospital on Saturday night with alcohol poisoning. She'd also taken Ecstasy. I was too late in trying to get help for her. She's going to be okay, but things are bad around here, so I think we'll have to cancel dinner on Thursday.

    B.

From: angiehazelnut@hotmail.com
To: brennayoko@gmail.com

    Oh no! I am so sorry! How can I help?
    A.

    Brenna doesn't respond. How can anyone help?

∽

Her dad is in the family room, staring at the TV. The screen is blank. He has not turned it on.

"I'm going out for a bit, Dad. I won't be late."

It takes him a moment to register what she has said. Then he simply nods. He doesn't comment about it being a school night or ask who she's going out with. For a moment she thinks maybe she should stay with him, but then she turns, grabs a coat from the closet, runs down the steps and climbs into Ryan's car. He doesn't say anything, just puts both arms around her and pulls her in.

The tension of the day immediately begins to melt away as she breathes him in. She focuses on the beating of his heart. After a long time he pulls away, just enough to see her face.

"You okay?" His voice is soft.

She nods. His features are shadowed in the glow of the streetlight. She looks at his lips and remembers the way they felt on her skin. Was that just two nights ago?

"Where should we go?" he asks.

"I shouldn't be gone long," she says, thinking of her dad's blank expression. "But," she says, glancing at the house, "let's get away from here."

A couple of blocks away Ryan pulls into the empty gravel lot beside a park. He shuts off the car and turns so he is facing her. He reaches out for both of her hands. She's amazed at how warm his skin is. She softly strokes a new callous on his palm.

"I was shoveling snow all day," he explains.

The sound of his voice, the feel of his skin—she wants to bury herself in him, lose herself again, just as she did on Saturday night.

"Is Naysa okay?" he asks.

The question pulls her back to the present. "I don't know. She's angry. She's sad. She's…she's remote. She says she's never going back to school."

"Is she talking about what she did?"

"No…and I don't dare ask anything."

Ryan begins to gently squeeze each of Brenna's fingertips. She watches him, amazed at how something so simple can feel so good.

"How about you?" he asks.

"I'm okay."

He's now massaging her palm with his thumb. She wants to forget all about Naysa. "After the movie," he says. "I want you to know that...that I hadn't planned that."

She touches his lip with her fingertip. "I know. I felt it too. In the theater, right?"

"Yeah." He nods. "I've never felt such a...well..." He struggles to find the words.

"A connection?" she asks.

"Yeah, but more than that. It was overpowering."

"I know." She wants to add that she's feeling it again now but holds back.

They sit quietly, and he continues to massage her palm. She doesn't want him to stop. Ever.

"Ryan, what did you mean the other day when you said you were scared about going back home?"

She feels him sink away.

"You don't have to talk about it if you don't want to."

He has stopped massaging her hand, so she begins to press her thumbs into his palm. He watches her fingers. "I'm not sure what my mom's going to be like," he says. "She wasn't...she wasn't my mom that last time I saw her. She was just kind of...a shell. Like there was nothing going on behind her eyes. She was still breathing, but she wasn't really alive. I don't think I can handle it if she's still like that."

Brenna doesn't respond, just holds his hand tightly. Her dad had been a little like that tonight.

"And leaving you, especially now..."

"Especially now?"

It's dark in the car, but Brenna can see the troubled expression on his face.

"After Saturday night…it's like…like we've moved to a whole new level. Maybe it was a mistake."

Brenna shakes her head. "How can that have been a mistake? It was…" She can't finish the sentence.

"I know," he says. "But now it's going to be so much harder to leave." Ryan's eyes are shiny with tears.

Brenna lets go of his hand and pulls him to her. They sit there until they are both chilled, and then, without a word, Ryan drives her home.

"How's Naysa?" Georgialee asks. They're standing in the school cafeteria, looking around for a place to sit. Brenna had called her on Monday and filled her in on what had happened.

"She says she's never coming back to school."

"I don't blame her."

Brenna looks at her friend. "Really?"

Georgialee leads the way to a free table. "Those little bitches she was hanging with? It's all over Facebook. They're not saying very nice things."

"Are you kidding me? She could have died!"

"Seriously, Brenna." Georgialee pulls a sandwich out of her bag. "You should get your dad to enroll her in another school. I wouldn't come back here either if I were her."

Brenna unwraps her own sandwich, but she doesn't take a bite—her appetite is gone. "What's the matter with those girls?"

"Well, I guess they were a little choked when the police showed up at their party and escorted them all home. They're blaming Naysa for getting them busted."

Nov. 12
I promised Mom I'd take care of her.

Reluctantly Brenna shares with her father what Georgialee told her, and his anger propels him out of his stupor. He agrees to look for other schooling options for Naysa, provided Naysa shuts down her social-media accounts and changes her email address. She agrees, without much fuss. She refuses to attend her appointment with the school counselor, but she agrees to see the family doctor.

For the first time in a while, Brenna pulls out Kia's journal and rereads the passage that describes the night she was conceived. Kia's experience was different than Brenna's with Ryan, yet there were similarities.

It was right before he was leaving to go on holidays with his family. I couldn't bear the thought of being apart. It was a physical pain.

And Kia only had to deal with Derek being gone for a couple of weeks, Brenna thinks. She has to accept that Ryan might be gone for good.

It was like he had ignited a fire in me and I couldn't (wouldn't?) put it out. What could go wrong when it felt so good?
Only everything.

Brenna closes the journal and feels a cold sensation spreading through each of her limbs. What if she, too, had gotten pregnant the other night? They'd used condoms, but still…

❧

Angie emails Brenna, asking her out for lunch, and they decide to meet at the Daily Grind after Brenna's driving lesson on Saturday. Just seeing her face through the coffee shop's window cheers Brenna. Angie stands as soon as Brenna steps through the door and welcomes her with a hug.

"So good to see you," Angie says.

Unlike the first time they met, when she'd been so nervous, Brenna takes the time to study Angie while she's reading the menu. She realizes that anyone seeing them together would guess they're related, possibly sisters. It is really only her own blue eyes that set them apart. They are about the same height and build, their dark hair color matches, and they both wear it long and straight. Brenna notices that Angie has a dimple in her right cheek, just as she does.

They select soup and sandwiches, and then Angie leans toward Brenna. "How was your driving lesson?"

"Pretty good. Except for parallel parking. I hate that."

"Everyone does. And how's your sister?"

Brenna sighs. "Not so good. Physically she'll be okay. The seizure she had doesn't seem to have caused any permanent damage, but she's really upset and embarrassed about the whole thing and won't go back to school. Dad's looking for another school for her."

"Oh dear." Angie looks sincerely troubled.

"She was being bullied on Facebook, which really didn't help."

"Sometimes I wonder if I'm up for the challenge of teaching high school," Angie admits. "Kids can be so hard on each other."

"Just some kids."

"Yeah, I know."

Their lunch arrives and they begin to eat.

"What else is going on?" Angie asks. "How's Ryan?"

Brenna can feel herself sink down in the booth. "He's fine, except that he's moving back to Australia." She fills Angie in on the situation with Ryan's mom.

"Wow," Angie says. "Life sucks for you right now."

"Yep."

They eat in silence for a minute. "I'd still like to meet your sister," Angie says. "Maybe I can find a way to help."

"I'm not sure how."

"Well, maybe I could homeschool her until she finds another school."

"Aren't you in university?"

"I am. But not all day every day."

Brenna thinks about it. "That's a really nice offer. I could run it by my dad. Maybe he could even pay you, like a tutor."

"Well, let's not get ahead of ourselves. We should all meet first."

Brenna nods.

"I might even be able to incorporate homeschooling into one of my class projects, on setting up lesson plans or something."

"I should warn you. My dad was worried about me reconnecting with you right now."

Angie nods. "Yeah, I haven't told my parents about meeting you yet. I will though."

"But not Kia."

Their eyes meet. "No, not Kia. Not yet anyway."

Not yet, Brenna thinks. At least she didn't say *not ever*.

As arranged, Ryan picks Brenna up from outside the coffee shop and they drive to Georgialee's house. The plan is to order in pizza and play games that evening. It turns out that Ryan's competitive streak runs as deep as Georgialee's, so he encouraged them to plan a games night. But first they're going to take Bentley for a hike, before it gets dark.

"Remember what we were doing this time last week?" Ryan says. They are sitting on Quarry Rock, which, for a change, is deserted. The clouds have lifted, and streaks of sunshine slash the water. Mist hangs over Indian Arm. A lone paddleboarder in a black wet suit glides by far below.

Brenna glances at her phone. "Actually, we were still at the movie." She smiles.

"Do you have any regrets about…about the rest of the evening?"

She leans her shoulder into his. "No. Unless, of course, I got pregnant. Then I'd have regrets."

"You didn't get pregnant."

"Nothing's foolproof. Especially not condoms. Maybe I should have taken one of those morning-after pills."

"Don't be silly."

"Kia didn't think she was going to get pregnant with me. She sounds like a smart person. She would have used something."

Ryan twirls her hair with his finger.

"Did your parents plan you?" she asks.

"I don't actually know, but not likely, given my father's disappearing act."

"I always wished I'd been planned and not just an accident."

Ryan doesn't comment but twirls Brenna's strand of hair in the other direction.

"Mind you," she continues, "if I did get pregnant and had the baby, you'd have a Canadian child. That would be one way to get you back here."

"Shh, Brenna," he whispers in her ear. "Don't talk like that." He kisses her temple.

"Seriously, Ryan. Some girls might even do that on purpose."

"Brenna."

"I wouldn't give my baby up like Kia did. I'd make it work. She might have been better off if she'd kept me. She wouldn't have gotten so depressed."

"Brenna," Ryan says again. Now he kisses her on the lips, but she turns her head away.

"Seriously," she says again. "I know I had great parents, but you can't know what it feels like to be given away as a baby."

"Brenna, I've never heard you talk like this." He's studying her now, his head tilted. "What's going on?"

"Nothing's going on. It's the truth."

Ryan scuttles over so he's sitting behind her. He lifts her hair and begins to massage her shoulders. She stiffens. "Maybe seeing Angie isn't such a good idea after all," he says.

She jerks away from him. "Of course it's a good idea." She scrambles to her feet and pulls on Bentley's leash. "We'd better go. It's going to get dark soon." She heads toward the trail, leaving a bewildered Ryan staring at her back.

⌒〜

"Hey, you two," Georgialee scolds. They're in Georgialee's rec room with a bunch of her friends. "Get in the game or no one's going to pick you to be on their team next time."

Next time. Will there even be a next time? Ryan is only here for two more weekends, unless, by some stroke of luck, he ends up coming back after Christmas. But even he's not holding out much hope of that.

Despite Georgialee's threats, Brenna finds she can't muster up any enthusiasm for the game.

"Wanna go home?" Ryan asks quietly.

She nods.

There are lewd comments about where they're really going and what they're actually going to do, but Brenna can't even find the energy to respond.

"Thanks, Georgialee," she says at the door. "I'm just not into it tonight."

Georgialee hugs them both. "No worries. You've got lots going on. I'll call you tomorrow."

~

Ryan pulls his car up to the curb outside her house and turns off the ignition. "I only have two more weeks," he says. "We have to make the most of them."

Brenna knows that this is his tactful way of suggesting she shouldn't launch into senseless rants or be a party-pooper. She's too empty to respond.

"On Quarry Rock," he says, "I just wanted us to remember how nice it was...being together. I didn't want to upset you."

"I know."

"We don't have to...to be together like that again if you're too worried." He cocks his head, looking at her sideways. "There are other things we can do...or not," he adds.

Brenna doesn't respond.

"I'll call you tomorrow," he says. "How 'bout I come up with a new adventure?"

She tries to smile. "Okay."

They hug for a long, long time.

Nov. 16
A can of worms.
Maybe they were right.
Now that it's been opened, can I shove them back in the can?
I don't think so.

✦

Bright sunlight wakes Brenna on Sunday morning. Looking out her window, she notices the thick layer of frost on the cars parked on the street.

Her phone rings. Ryan. She takes a deep breath and wills herself to sound cheery.

"A ton of snow fell on the mountains last night," Ryan says.

"Hi to you too."

"Sorry. I'm just so excited. We're going snowshoeing for our big adventure today! Put on your snow clothes!"

"Are you sure you don't want to go back out and see the eagles? I bet there's already a lot more." She yawns loudly.

"I'm giving you one hour, Brenna. And I'll pack the lunch this time, and you can borrow my uncle's snowshoes. You just get your beautiful self ready."

Brenna finds her father in his office, staring at the computer screen.

"Hey, Dad."

"Morning, Brenna."

She sits in the plush chair beside the window. "Any luck finding another school for Naysa?" she asks.

He swivels around in his chair to face her. The circles under his eyes are darker than ever. "Not yet. But Dr. Price, the psychologist the doctor recommended, seems to be a good fit. We both like her, and Naysa's willing to talk to her. She's not convinced that changing schools is the answer, though she hasn't told Naysa that. She just feels it would teach her to run away from her problems."

Brenna nods, but she thinks about what Georgialee said, how she wouldn't return to their school under the circumstances.

"She says the drugs and alcohol were just a way of lashing out, kind of a breakdown. Losing Mom and starting a new school so soon after that was too much for her. She's always been a sensitive kid, and with all this... well, she's struggling." He rubs his face. "I should have realized, but I've been too caught up in my own stuff." His eyes snag hers. He frowns. "Maybe you'd like to talk with Dr. Price too?"

She shakes her head.

"Okay, but promise you'll let me know if you change your mind."

Brenna promises, but she knows that no amount of counseling could help her stop missing her mom.

"I hope Naysa can find a way back to her old group of friends. In the meantime she'll keep on meeting with Dr. Price."

Brenna nods, thinking about it, and then remembers why she came to see her father. "I saw Angie again yesterday. We met for lunch after my driving lesson."

"Angie? Oh. Kia's sister." He regards his daughter.

"She suggested that, if you wanted and if Naysa agrees, she might be able to tutor Naysa or homeschool her until you have something arranged or until she's ready to go back."

"You shared our family problems with her?"

Brenna stiffens. "They're my problems too, and she really wants to help."

Her dad takes a deep breath and lets it out slowly. "It just seems that she's...she's an odd person to turn to right now."

"Why? I think she's just the right person. She didn't know Mom, so she's not sad like Aunt Laura and Aunt Tamara. Her own sister is far away, and she seems to genuinely care and want to help. You could at least meet her."

Her dad doesn't say anything for a moment. He stares out the window. Finally he turns and meets Brenna's eyes. "How about dinner on Tuesday? I'll let you cook."

"Thanks, Dad. I know you'll like her."

He nods, but not convincingly.

"And I'm going snowshoeing today with Ryan."

"Snowshoeing? That will be a good workout." He watches as Brenna gets up and walks across the room.

"He's been good for you."

Brenna spins around.

"Ryan. I can see how strong you're getting, how fit."

"Really?"

"Yeah."

"Ryan has a theory that if you get strong on the outside, it helps you get strong on the inside."

He nods thoughtfully.

"You want to come?"

Her dad smiles. "Not today. But I like the way he thinks."

Ryan shows Brenna how to strap the snowshoes onto her hiking boots. He takes Bentley's leash and leads the way across the parking lot toward the Dog Mountain Trail. Bentley can barely contain his excitement. He's prancing and tugging on the leash. Brenna smiles at him, glad that Georgialee agreed to let them take her dog out again.

When they reach the trail Ryan unclips the dog, and they watch as he gallops ahead. He finds a flat area under some snow-laden trees, drops to his back and wriggles in the powdery snow. When he gets up, he turns to look at them. His tongue is hanging out the side of his mouth, and snow clings to his coat.

"I swear he's smiling," Brenna says.

"He's in heaven," Ryan agrees.

"Dogs really get it. How to live in the moment."

"Yeah." Ryan turns to Brenna. "Let's see if we can be like that today too."

She tries to smile, and he leans in to kiss her before turning to follow the dog, who is racing ahead.

Brenna finds it easier than she expected to walk in the snowshoes, and she feels her mood lifting as she stomps along behind Ryan. The air is crisp, clean. The tree branches are rimmed with snow, and the sunlight sparkles off the forest floor. The world feels completely still, with only the squeaking of their snowshoes to disturb the peace. Reality and all its problems seem a million miles away.

I am the diamond glint upon the snow. This line from the poem read at her mother's memorial service bubbles to the surface of her mind. Is her mother really here?

"I want us to do something special on our last night together," Ryan says. They've reached the lookout after snowshoeing for an hour. Ryan has brushed the snow off a log, and they've removed their snowshoes. He passes her a sandwich.

"Do you have any ideas?" Brenna asks. She doesn't want to think about his last night yet.

"I'm not sure, but I think we should be on Grouse Mountain, because that's where we met."

Brenna leans into him. The enormous sadness in the pit of her stomach stirs. "I guess we could have dinner in the chalet restaurant."

"I was thinking that too, as long as we go for a snow-shoe first."

Brenna takes a bite of her sandwich, then separates the slices of bread to look inside. "What *is* this?"

"Vegemite. With lettuce, cheese and tomato." He takes one big bite, and the remaining half of his sandwich disappears. He reaches in the bag for another one before looking down at her watching him. "Everyone eats it back home. Don't you like it?"

"Not sure yet." She takes another nibble, then reaches for her water bottle to wash down the bitter taste. She rewraps the sandwich in its paper. "I'm not really hungry."

Ryan pulls a granola bar out of the backpack. "Here, I'll trade you my granola bar for your sandwich."

As she eats the granola bar, she looks into the sky. Tiny flakes of snow have started to fall again. She sticks out her tongue to catch one.

"And between now and then…" he says.

"Yeah?"

He doesn't answer but puts his arm around her shoulders and pulls her back. They fall onto the snow, and he straddles her. She smiles up at him.

"You've got way too many layers of clothes on," he says, scanning her body.

"Same as you," she says, laughing.

He lets his weight press into her as he puts his mouth on hers, but after a short time she squirms to get up. "The snow is cold," she complains. "I think it's soaking through my jacket."

He rolls off her and onto his back, pulling her on top of him. "You won't hear me complaining about a little snow," he says.

She laughs and lets her weight sink into him. She runs her tongue across his lips. "You taste like Vegemite."

"And you taste like granola bar." He draws her lower lip into his mouth.

"And by the way," she says between kisses, "I'm not pregnant. Sorry about yesterday. Must have been a little PMS going on."

Ryan docsn't respond; he just keeps kissing her.

Bentley begins to bark from where he's tied to a low tree branch. Brenna looks up and sees a group of snow-shoers arriving at the lookout. It's their dog that has caught Bentley's attention. "We've got company," Brenna says, scrambling to get up.

"Damn," Ryan says, brushing snow off his pants and reaching for their snowshoes. "I was just getting comfortable."

Brenna laughs and repacks their lunch items. "You never finished your sentence," she reminds him. "Between now and then…"

"I'm not letting you out of my sight."

She pulls on her mitts and unties Bentley. They nod to the people who are now marveling at the view and start their stomp back across the mountain.

Ryan drains the lasagna noodles in the sink. He has come over to Brenna's house on Monday night to help her prepare for Tuesday night's dinner with Angie. She won't have time to make anything after school and dog walking, so she's preparing ahead.

"I'm a little nervous about having Angie over," she says. "What if Dad's right? What if opening a can of worms turns out to be a bad thing?"

"Some worms turn into beautiful butterflies."

Brenna hip-checks him. "You know that's not what they mean."

"Who is *they*?"

"I don't know. Whoever made up that saying."

He grabs a wooden spoon that is lying on the counter and lightly smacks her on the butt.

"Hey!"

"Hey what! Have you looked at your butt lately?"

"Don't be rude."

"I'm not. Hiking becomes you."

He holds the wooden spoon to his face as if it's a microphone. He begins to sing to the tune of a Brad Paisley song they both like. "Bren's everything I ever wanted. She's so beautiful to me. She teaches me Canadiana, she's my hiking queen…" He pauses and looks directly into her eyes before finishing very softly, "And I want to take her home with me."

"Brad Paisley you're not," she says, but she's smiling. Her eyes shine as she gazes back at him.

"Maybe I don't sound like him," he says, "but the words come straight from my heart."

Brenna turns back to the frying pan, not trusting herself to speak.

Nov. 18
Maybe those worms really will turn into butterflies. It's just a matter of perspective. And what beautiful butterflies they could be!

seventeen

Grief softens…
(JOEL ROTHSCHILD, *SIGNALS*)

"Nice to meet you, Angie. You look a lot like your sister."

Angie reaches out to shake Brenna's dad's hand before sinking into a chair in the family room.

"*And* you look like Brenna," Naysa comments after being introduced.

"Well, that's a compliment to me," Angie says, smiling at Naysa, who is slumped on the couch, arms folded across her chest.

"So how is Kia?" Brenna's dad asks. "We lost track of her some time ago."

"She's fine now," Angie answers. "She's working in Uganda for an organization that cares for children born with AIDS."

"Uganda? In Africa?"

Angie nods.

Her dad glances sharply at Brenna but, to her relief, doesn't say anything.

The room grows quiet. Angie stands to study the family photos that hang on every wall. "I hear she was really lovely. I'm so sorry." She doesn't need to say who *she* is. They all know.

Naysa stares at her feet, and their dad shifts in his chair. A timer chimes in the kitchen.

"Dinner is ready," Brenna says. "Let's eat."

They move to the table and Brenna directs Angie to Joanna's chair. While her dad and Naysa get seated, she places a green salad on the table. "Help yourselves," she says. "I'm going to put out the rest of the food."

"So I hear you're in teacher training," Brenna's dad says, passing the salad bowl to Angie.

"I am. I'll be fully qualified by June, and then I'll be looking for a position, which is another huge challenge."

"Would you be willing to go north, to a smaller community?"

"Yeah, I think so. For a few years."

Yet another person who will leave me, Brenna thinks, serving up plates of cheesy spinach-and-mushroom lasagna.

"I hear you play piano," Angie says to Naysa.

Naysa shrugs. "I used to." The scowl doesn't leave her face.

"Kia played the piano," Angie continues cheerfully, ignoring Naysa's sullenness. "My parents tried to get me to take it up too, but I hated practicing. Now I regret not learning it, because I think it would be such a stress buster to pour yourself into music. Just belting it out in the shower or even in my car can change my mood," she says.

Brenna notices a flicker of a smile cross Naysa's face, and her eyes linger on Angie for a moment.

"And you like to read? Any favorite authors?" Angie asks Naysa.

Between bites of lasagna Naysa quietly rattles off the names of authors and their books.

Angie smiles. "Wow, you're well-read! Those are some of my favorites too."

Although Naysa tries to hide it, Brenna can see that she is pleased.

"Naysa's a really good writer herself," their dad says. "She used to share some of her short stories with me."

"Do you like to write too, Brenna?"

Brenna thinks of her journal and her short entries. "Sometimes, but not when it's a school assignment. I always draw a blank when I have to write an opinion piece or something."

"Kia likes to write."

"I know. I have the journal she wrote when she was pregnant with me."

"That's right. You mentioned it. I'd love to read it someday." She looks up from her food. "If you want to share it, of course. And if it's okay with Kia."

"Would you like some more lasagna?" Brenna asks, panicked. She gets up and reaches for the pan. "Or garlic bread?" She definitely doesn't want to share it, her only connection with her birth mom and the one that was just between the two of them.

"I'll have more," Naysa says.

Brenna catches her dad's eye. It's the first time they have seen Naysa really eat, not just nibble, since her night in the hospital ten days ago.

The conversation begins to flow more easily as they tuck into second helpings and then the brownies that Brenna pulled out of the freezer earlier. Eventually her dad asks Angie if she'd like some tea. Brenna can see that he is relaxing, enjoying Angie's company.

As they drink their tea, Naysa excuses herself to use the bathroom. Her dad pounces on the opportunity. "Brenna said you might consider doing some tutoring or homeschooling with Naysa," he says to Angie. "Short-term, of course."

"I would," she says.

"Obviously, Brenna has your contact info," he says. "Could I call you later, when I've talked to Naysa?"

"Sounds good." She smiles.

He nods and changes the subject. Brenna loads the dishwasher, and, to her surprise, Naysa begins washing the pans when she returns to the kitchen.

The final days leading up to Ryan's departure take on a surreal quality. Brenna's dad quits reminding her that school nights are for studying. Ryan picks her up and they usually drive over to the park, where they mostly just sit and hold each other, saying very little. Only once do they go back to his house when his uncle is out for the evening.

Nov. 25

How can it feel so good when I'm so miserable?

There's a total disconnect between mind and body.

Naysa is surprisingly receptive to having Angie tutor her—anything not to return to school, Brenna figures—and she finds Angie in their home after school on Tuesdays and Thursdays, guiding Naysa through her schoolwork. Angie has contacted each of Naysa's teachers to determine what she's missing. One night Brenna is startled to hear piano music coming from the living room. Naysa's mood is improving after only a couple of sessions with Angie, while Brenna's is plummeting with the approach of Ryan's departure date.

When Brenna wakes on Saturday morning, the familiar ache in her chest has intensified tenfold. It is Ryan's last day in Canada. The night before, some of his coworkers had taken him out for pizza, and she'd been invited along. The boys and a few of their girlfriends had kept the mood light, teasing Ryan about some of his moments on the mountain, remembering the practical jokes they'd played on each other. They mimicked his accent and exaggerated his mistakes. There was lots of laughter, and Brenna had struggled to shake her deep sadness, but she'd wished she wasn't there. It was too hard to play along. She'd gone back to Ryan's and helped him finish his packing. His uncle was also home, doing his own packing. Ryan had eventually driven her home and promised to be back first thing in the morning so they could spend the entire day together.

Brenna had suggested they return to Brackendale to view the eagles again, so they leave early and head west, stopping at a little diner at Sunset Marina for breakfast. The silence between them is heavy, as are the clouds that hang over the water, obstructing their view of the Sunshine Coast and the islands. They hold hands for the remainder of the trip, listening to music but not singing along. In Brackendale they walk along the river path, Ryan's arm draped across Brenna's shoulders and her arm wrapped around his waist. They watch the eagles perched on branches across the river. Occasionally one swoops low over the water and rises back up with a wriggling salmon clutched in its talons. The number of eagles has increased considerably since their first visit. When they arrive at the bench where they had their picnic the time before, they sit down and wrap their bodies together while absorbing the beauty of the river valley. Brenna inhales deeply and closes her eyes.

On their way back they stop for lunch at a small diner on the Squamish River, and they arrive at Grouse Mountain in midafternoon. Brenna hasn't been on the mountain for several weeks, and the clientele has changed. People carrying skis, snowboards and snowshoes crush Brenna into Ryan as the tram fills. She lays her head on his chest, and he wraps his arms around her. As the tram begins its ascent, it quickly becomes engulfed in a thick mist that swirls around it. Brenna remembers the bright blue sky and the fresh breeze on that day late in the summer when she'd returned to "her mother's mountain" and Ryan had welcomed her back. So much has changed since then, but the ache in her heart feels every bit as heavy.

They jostle their way through the throng to a bench where they can put on their snowshoes. "This is where the Snowshoe Grind starts," Ryan tells her. "Serious snow-shoers swipe their passes on this post and then try to beat their own personal bests, just like the regular Grinders do. Maybe you'll want to sign on."

Brenna shakes her head. "If I keep snowshoeing, it won't be about speed. It'll be about enjoying the experience."

"*If* you keep snowshoeing?"

They stand up and begin to head toward Dam Mountain, where the snowshoe trails are. "It won't be the same without you."

"Maybe you can find someone else to snowshoe with."

"Still won't be the same."

As the climb gets steeper, the snow begins to fall in large wet flakes.

"Just think," Brenna says, pausing to catch her breath. She tilts her head back to let the snow fall on her face. "In two days you'll be welcoming in the spring."

"Does that mean I get to miss a whole winter, or will next winter be my *this* winter?" he asks.

Brenna shakes her head and smiles at the question. It's so Ryan. Once again she wonders if she would have been better off if she'd never met him. Then she wouldn't have to miss him and all his goofy remarks.

When they reach the summit Ryan removes his snowshoes and falls onto his back in a bank of deep, unblemished snow. He slides his arms up and down and drags his legs back and forth.

"A snow angel!" Brenna says.

"Yep." He gets up carefully to look at the figure he's left in the snow. Then, using a stick he's broken off a nearby tree, he prints *JOANNA* beneath it.

Swallowing hard, Brenna lowers herself to the snow beside the angel and makes another one. Getting up, she takes the stick from Ryan and prints *NICK*, the name of

Ryan's brother. Ryan takes the stick from Brenna and draws halos above the angels' heads. Then, with arms around each other, they watch as the falling snow slowly blankets the angels; within minutes they've disappeared.

∽

"Did you notice that you kept up with me for the whole climb?" Ryan asks when they are seated in the chalet bistro.

Brenna tips her head. "Yeah…"

"When we first started doing the Grind, I had to slow my pace so you could keep up."

"But you didn't today?"

"Not at all. I had to work to keep up with you."

She thinks about it. "It has gotten easier."

"You're a whole lot stronger than you were just three months ago."

Brenna takes a sip of her hot chocolate. "Do you think I'm stronger on the inside too?" She watches his face for his answer.

He smiles. "That's harder to measure, but I bet you are. You held up well when Naysa had her…her crisis. And you're resourceful. You called on Angie for help when you needed it. I'd say that's showing strength of character."

"Do you hike in Australia?"

"A little bit, in the Blue Mountains, but my mates are more into surfing."

They order dinner and then sit quietly, their features soft in the glow of the candlelight. The snow has stopped falling, the clouds have lifted, and the lights of the city twinkle far below them.

Ryan clears his throat. "The past three months have been really special for me," he says, breaking the long silence. "I was so nervous about asking you to do the Grind with me that first time."

"You were?" Brenna's eyebrows arch.

"Oh my god. I almost chickened out. I had to muster up all my courage to cross that mountain and ask you."

"I'd never have guessed."

"And each time we hiked, I did everything in my power to make you smile or laugh. Your face…it really…changes when you're happy. You had me from the first smile."

"Are you serious? I'm surprised you even noticed me."

"Oh, I noticed you. And I can also say I wasn't too surprised when I found out who your mom was. You're equally lovely."

Steaming cups of clam chowder are placed in front of them. Brenna picks up her spoon. "I thought I was your service project," she admits, blowing on the soup.

Ryan looks up from the crusty roll he's slathering with butter. "My service project? That's a joke." He takes a bite and regards her. "Though one thing I have learned is that when you help other people, you tend to help yourself too. So actually, you were helping me." He nods, affirming what he's said.

They eat in silence for a few moments, and then Ryan tackles the topic they've avoided for the past month. "It's hard to know where we go from here, Bren. Hopefully I'll be back, but it's really hard to say. We'll keep in touch— Skype, email…"

"It won't be the same."

"No. It won't."

Ryan puts his spoon down and leans into the table. "Brenna, I'm crazy about you. Maybe we'll be together again sometime in the future, but even if it doesn't happen, at least we've had this much time together."

Brenna struggles to remain composed. When the server arrives to take their soup bowls, she excuses herself and goes to the washroom. She sits on a toilet, drops her head between her knees and takes in deep, shuddering breaths. She leans her head back, struggling not to wail at the injustice. She sighs deeply instead. Leaving the stall, she stares at herself in the mirror. The reflection shows a tired, pale face. She forces herself to smile. It's true her face is transformed, even if it's a fake smile.

Pulling herself together, she returns to the table. "When I graduate from high school, I'm going to Borneo," she tells him. "My mom and I planned to go together, but I'm going to go anyway and sprinkle some of her ashes in the jungle."

"Borneo?"

She tells him about the orangutan sanctuary. "And once I'm in Borneo, maybe I'll carry on down to Sydney to see you—unless you have a new girlfriend, of course."

He shakes his head and closes his eyes. "It drives me insane to think of you with another guy."

Plates of fish and chips arrive, and they drip vinegar and ketchup onto their food.

Brenna ignores his comment. "Depending on how much money I've saved up from my *business*," she continues, putting air quotes around the word, "I may continue on to Uganda—with Angie's permission, of course. And Kia's."

"Maybe I'll go with you. After we volunteer at the orphanage, we can go on a safari."

"And then a mountain gorilla trek," Brenna adds.

"A what?"

Brenna smiles. "I've been doing some research on Uganda. It's one of the few places in the world where mountain gorillas still live, and there's fewer than a thousand of them left on the planet." Brenna's voice grows stronger as she warms to her subject. "Guides take tourists into the jungle, and you get to hang out with a group of gorillas for an hour. Can you imagine? How cool would that be!"

Brenna sits back and then notices the way Ryan is looking at her. "What?"

He doesn't say anything for a moment, and they simply gaze at each other.

"Listen to you, Brenna. You *have* grown strong on the inside."

She tilts her head.

"You're looking ahead. Planning your future. That's huge."

Brenna thinks about it, remembering the months of inertia when it was almost impossible to climb out of bed each day. "Mom would have wanted me to go to Borneo," she says. "And now I have an ulterior motive. Borneo's in the same hemisphere that you live in. Maybe I'm not getting strong so much as I'm figuring out how to see you again."

"Call it what you want." Using his fork, Ryan stabs a French fry from Brenna's plate. His plate is already polished clean. "I'm hoping my mom has grown strong on the inside too. After Nick died, she couldn't look forward. Couldn't make plans. She couldn't function at all. I hope that has changed."

Brenna remembers that Ryan has a lot of apprehension about going home and seeing his mom. She has been so wrapped up in her own stuff that she hasn't given it much thought. She passes him her plate, and he passes her his empty one. "This is really hard for you," she says quietly. "Going home, I mean."

He sighs and stabs another French fry. "It's weird. I keep thinking Nick is going to be there, and then I remember that he's not. Even though it's been a couple of years, it still hasn't really sunk in."

Brenna nods, understanding completely. She often catches herself thinking she should tell her mom something, or do something for her, before remembering that she's gone.

When their dishes have been cleared away, Ryan rummages in his pack and pulls out a small box. "This is so you'll remember me and our connection to this mountain," he says, passing it across the table to her.

Brenna opens it and pulls out a key chain with a heavy silver bear paw dangling from it.

"I know you're going to get your license soon," he says. "And I figured you could think of me every time you reach for your keys."

"Thank you," she whispers, stroking the smooth paw. "It's beautiful."

"And I'm also leaving you my snowshoes. Just to keep for me until I come back."

Their eyes meet and hold for a long time.

It's dark and cold in the tram as it begins its descent. They stand in a corner, arms wrapped around each other. Ryan leans down to whisper in her ear. "I love you."

She simply holds him tighter, finding it impossible to speak.

At noon on Sunday there's a knock on Brenna's door.

"C'mon in," she mumbles.

Naysa comes in and sits on the end of her bed. "Want to do something today?" she asks.

Brenna wants to say no and just lie there thinking of Ryan, who is already thousands of miles away, but she knows Naysa is only trying to help. "What are you thinking of?"

"How 'bout a yoga class?" Naysa asks.

"You don't do yoga."

"I'm thinking of starting. My counselor, Dr. Price, recommends it, and Angie says she loves it. I thought maybe you could take me to the studio where you and Mom used to go. Hopefully they have a beginner's class."

"Dr. Price recommends it?"

"Yeah, she says it's good for reducing stress."

Brenna regards her little sister. "How are you anyway?"

Naysa shrugs. "Good days and bad ones. Probably better than you today anyway."

"Oh, Naysa, I'm really going to miss him." Tears stream down Brenna's face, and she flops back onto her bed and hugs a pillow to her face.

She feels Naysa's body nestling in beside her. She reaches for her sister's hand and squeezes it and then allows herself to cry until there are no more tears. They lie together in silence. Finally Brenna stirs. "Let's go check the yoga schedule."

The days drag by. Christmas lights begin to appear on houses, and seasonal music can't be avoided.

Stepping out of the shower one morning, Brenna studies herself in the full-length mirror. She cranes her neck to look at her butt. Simply walking the dogs every day is not going to help her keep her newfound muscle tone, she realizes.

Naysa and Angie have found a couple of yoga classes that the three of them can take together. There are moments when Brenna feels a stab of jealousy at the bond that is clearly growing between her sister and Angie, but mostly she's so immersed in her own misery that she doesn't care. Her mood is elevated following each yoga session, but it plummets before they get back to the yoga studio for their next class.

The one thing that keeps getting her out of bed each day is the anticipation of a text from Ryan, and he never disappoints. There's one waiting for her each morning. They've connected on Skype twice, but it was a bittersweet experience. At first it was wonderful to see his face and hear his voice, but when they finally had to disconnect, neither one of them wanted to hit *End call*. The realization of the distance between them sent her plummeting all over again. She's decided it's just as well that the seventeen-hour time difference makes it difficult to find a convenient time to Skype regularly. It's too hard.

In an email, he's told her about his tearful reunion with his mom and how they've moved back into her apartment. He says she is fragile but no longer numb and distant. He's applying his get-strong-through-exercise theory and has her out walking and swimming every day, and his uncle has hired a life coach to, as Ryan puts it, *help navigate her into her future.* Every text and email ends with *I love you and miss you.*

For the week following Ryan's departure, Georgialee was willing to listen while she talked about all the things that were so special about him and how much she was missing him, but then she started hinting that Brenna should think about *moving on*, and Brenna knew Georgialee had reached her limit. How could she possibly understand?

Dec. 12

Mom would understand. I could tell her how much I miss him. I could tell her about all the funny things he says and the kind things he does. She would understand about the snow angels. (How stupid. She was one of them!!) She would listen. She would not tell me to get over him. She wouldn't suggest I date someone else. She would just get it. Fuck Fuck Fuck

Brenna and her family force themselves to go through the motions of Christmas, but nothing is the same. On Christmas morning, after exchanging gifts with each other, Naysa hands Brenna the last wrapped box under the tree.

"What's this?" she asks. The package, shaped like a flattened shoe box, is very light, and nothing rattles when she shakes it.

"Ryan sent it for you," Naysa says. "He messaged me and asked me to watch for it and then hide it until Christmas."

Brenna holds the box, staring at it.

"Did you send him anything?"

"Yeah, a framed photo of us hiking the Grind. Lame, I know."

Brenna rips away the gift wrap and lifts the top off the box. "Oh my god!" Two stuffies lie on a cushion of green tissue paper. She grins at the fuzzy faces smiling back at her. One is a baby orangutan and the other is a small gorilla. She lifts them out and finds a couple of folded sheets of paper beneath them. She scans the information. The first is the adoption certificate for a baby orangutan named Cinta who lives in Borneo. Apparently Ryan has adopted a real orangutan in her name and will send small monthly donations for the orangutan's care. The other sheet is a receipt for a donation made to Gorilla Doctors, an organization that cares for the orphans of gorillas who have been killed by poachers. She hands the sheets to Naysa and her dad, who have been watching her. Then she opens the enclosed Christmas card. There is a letter folded up inside.

Merry Christmas, Brenna!

I chose these two little rascals to remind you of your big trip. I hope they help to keep you focused on making it a reality. (And that way I get to see you too!) Fingers crossed that you'll get to meet the real Cinta in about a year and a half. (Her name means "love," which is why I chose her

from the bunch.) I also hope they are good company for you
until we meet again.

I love you and miss you!

Ryan

Brenna presses the two stuffies to her cheeks and closes her eyes. Deep inside she feels an elusive shift.

Dec. 25
I'm an adoptive mom now too! Of an orangutan. LOL.
Only Ryan could dream up the perfect gift.
Oh my god I adore him.

eighteen

The only cure for grief is action.

(G.H. LEWES, *THE SPANISH DRAMA*)

The silver bear claw clangs against the steering column as Brenna slides the key into the ignition of Joanna's car. It's the middle of January, and Brenna has asked Angie, Justin and Georgialee to meet her, her dad and Naysa at the Daily Grind. She wouldn't tell any of them the reason for the meeting, just asked them all to be there. She is driving her dad and Naysa because she's still accumulating the driving hours she needs before she can take her test.

They choose a round table, and when the others arrive Brenna introduces Georgialee to Angie and Justin. They order and Brenna insists on picking up the tab. When they're all sipping their drinks, Brenna looks around the circle and then pulls a thick envelope out of her purse. She lays it on the table.

"When Naysa and I were younger," she says, "Mom and Dad encouraged us to give one-third of our allowance to charity. I have a small business now, and I'd like to stick to that guideline. In this envelope is a third of what I've earned so far." She pauses and looks at Angie and then Justin. "I'm giving it to you guys," she says, pushing the envelope across the table to them. "And I hope you'll send it on to Aid-A-Child—from an anonymous donor, of course."

The group sits in startled silence. Justin finds his voice first. "Are you sure, Brenna? That's a big chunk of what you've earned."

"I don't have many other expenses," she says, "though as soon as I get my driver's license I'll have gas and car insurance." She smiles at her dad. "But until then…"

"I'm overwhelmed," Angie says, reaching for the envelope. "This is so generous of you, Brenna." She comes around the table to give Brenna a hug.

"And there's something else I want to talk to you all about," Brenna continues after accepting a hug from Justin too. "On a Sunday in May each year Grouse Mountain hosts the Seek the Peak charity relay, which donates all proceeds to breast cancer research." She explains how the race can be run as a team, with four members each taking on one leg of the route. "I'm going to donate my charity money from the next few months to this race, in memory of Mom. I'd also like to participate in it." She pauses, letting the information sink in. "I was hoping Ryan would be back, but as you know," she says quietly, "that's not going to happen. So I'm looking for three teammates."

"I'm in!" Georgialee says without hesitation.

Brenna high-fives her before looking around the table.

"I don't think my knees could handle it, honey," her dad says, "but I'll certainly sponsor you."

"Thanks, Dad."

"I can't commit either," Justin says. "I'm in the pulpit on Sundays."

Brenna turns to Angie and cocks her head.

"I'm not much of a runner," Angie says. "And I'm not sure I'd have enough time to get in shape for a race like that."

"We have a few months," Brenna tells her. "And Ryan taught me how a couple of hikes a week can make a huge difference."

"Yeah, but it's winter. Hiking's not so great right now."

"Maybe not, but snowshoeing is awesome, and you use the same muscles."

Angie looks doubtful, but after a moment Naysa gently elbows her in the ribs. "I'll do it if you do it."

"Really?" Her face is skeptical.

"I'm in lousier shape than you, but what's the worst that can happen? We probably won't win the race, but I don't think that's the point anyway."

Brenna smiles at her sister across the table.

"I don't know, Naysa," Angie says. "Have you ever done the Grind? It's frickin' hard."

Brenna sees the doubt that flashes across her sister's face.

"Just come snowshoeing with me, Naysa," Brenna says. "You'll be in shape in no time."

Naysa nods at her sister, but she looks unconvinced.

"And you too, Angie. It will be fun."

Angie shakes her head. "I'm sorry, Brenna, but my schedule's pretty full with school and work and tutoring."

"I'm going back to school next week," Naysa says. "So you won't have to tutor me anymore."

They all turn to look at Naysa.

"What?" she asks, as if she doesn't know why they're all surprised.

"When did you decide that?" her dad asks.

"Right now," she says, and they all laugh. "I hope that's okay, Angie. Sorry, I should have told you first."

Her dad puts his arm around Naysa's shoulders and pulls her in close.

Angie is smiling. "I think that's great! That means my job is complete. You can always call me if you need some support. But," she says, "I still don't know if I'm up for the Seek the Peak, though I'll be on the sidelines cheering for you guys. And maybe they'll need volunteers on race day."

"That's a great idea, Angie," Justin says. He turns to Brenna. "And if it's okay with you, I'd like to join you for the snowshoeing sometimes, and for sure you'll be able to find a fourth person to be on your relay team by then."

⌒〜

Brenna notices that Naysa is panting after only a couple of minutes of snowshoeing. The conditions are lousy, and she regrets her decision to bring Naysa up the mountain today. If she were by herself, she'd climb to the top and get it over with as quickly as she could, but she knows she needs to dig deep and find the patience for her sister.

"You're doing great, Nayse," she says.

Naysa nods and stomps along behind.

"We'll take a rest when we get to that fallen tree up there," Brenna says, pointing to the landmark.

Naysa's jaw is clamped tight. It's unseasonably warm, and there's a light rain falling. Brenna's jacket and pants are waterproof, but Naysa bought hers secondhand. If Naysa gets wet she'll be miserable, and she might lose her resolve.

When they reach the tree, Brenna stops so Naysa can rest. "The conditions really suck today, Naysa. Do you want to go back and we'll try again another day, when it's better?"

"Nope. Let's keep going."

Brenna smiles. "Good for you, sis. This is hard work."

They continue on. Brenna finds it hard to go so slowly, but she remembers that Ryan had to go slowly for her too when they started doing the Grind. She smiles inwardly thinking about him, and it helps her find the patience for Naysa. She's glad Naysa discouraged her from inviting

Justin along on her first snowshoe trek. She was afraid his presence might make Naysa self-conscious, especially if she was holding them back. It was a good call.

"I was kinda disappointed in Angie," Brenna confides. "I thought she'd take up the challenge of Seek the Peak. For us, you know?"

"She didn't even know Mom," Naysa says between huffs.

"That's true." But Kia did, Brenna thinks and then wonders if she would have joined them on the team if circumstances were different.

When they reach the halfway point of the trail, Brenna insists they turn around. "You've done amazing for your first time," she tells her sister. "And just wait. It doesn't take long before it gets way easier."

Their dad has offered to pick them up, and he lets Brenna drive. "How did you like it, Naysa?" he asks.

Brenna looks at her sister in the rearview mirror. She's pulled off her tuque, and her hair is plastered to her scalp, wet with sweat. Her cheeks are rosy, but her eyes are flat as she stares out the window. She simply shrugs.

Jan. 25

PLEASE PLEASE PLEASE let Ryan's exercise-to-get-strong program work for Naysa. I had the added incentive of wanting to be with Ryan to motivate me. If only Angie had signed on—that might have been a great incentive for Naysa. She really likes her.

Brenna notices the crocus heads nudging through the soil as she walks the dogs. She looks west and realizes there's probably an extra hour of daylight now too. She decides to send an email out to her dog-hiking clients that evening, letting them know she will be resuming the hikes the following week and that her fee will reflect the longer sessions.

The weeks of winter have passed slowly, but Naysa has persevered with the snowshoeing, and Brenna can see her fitness level improving. Her return to school was bumpy—there were more than a few bouts of tears—but a couple of her old friends have started hanging out with her again. She has weekly visits with Dr. Price, and Angie still joins them at yoga classes. Brenna likes the sound of the piano music floating through their home again, though she notices that it's often somber music. Anything is better than the silence that filled their home in the months following their mother's death.

Brenna and Justin snowshoe past the bear den where Coola and Grinder are sleeping. Naysa had begged off the day's hike at the last minute when she woke up with another sore throat and runny nose. She'd been hit with one virus after another all fall and winter. Their family doctor said that stress can play havoc with the immune system, but that exercise can help build it back up. Brenna decided to let Naysa off the hook anyway. She liked being able to talk openly with Justin.

"Not much longer before the bears wake up again," Brenna tells him.

"Will you resume your volunteer work then?"

"Yep, though it's not the same on the mountain without Mom and now without Ryan too."

"How's he doing?"

"Pretty good, I think. His mom's making really good progress, and he's finishing up his last year of school online. I wish he'd bring her here for a holiday in May," she adds. "I'm still short one person for the Seek the Peak relay, and he'd love to do it. It was his idea in the first place."

Justin changes the subject. "I received an email from Kia this week. It sounds like she's doing well too."

"How long will she stay in Uganda?"

"I don't know, but she's in a relationship with a British doctor who is also working there. It sounds pretty serious."

Brenna doesn't respond.

"Do you still feel sad that Angie asked you not to contact her?"

"Yeah, but I get it."

"I expect Kia will be home sooner rather than later, to introduce the doctor to her family. Maybe they'll ask me to marry them. Now that would make me happy." Justin grins.

"I keep rereading the journal she left for me. I'm a bit obsessed with it, actually."

Justin pauses to take a sip of water. He waits for her to continue.

"I've been thinking that someday she might be interested in reading it again."

"You could give it to Angie for safekeeping," Justin says over his shoulder. "Then she could give it back to Kia if she ever felt the timing was right."

Brenna nods, though the thought of giving away the journal is painful. It's all she has of Kia, except for an envelope full of old greeting cards. "I'd also like to write her a letter, tell her that I'm okay and that Mom and Dad were—are—awesome parents, and I even got a sister in the deal. Maybe it would bring her some peace."

"Write the letter," Justin encourages. "It might make you feel better. Just don't send it. Give it to Angie too, to hold on to, you know, in case."

No wonder Kia liked Justin so much, Brenna thinks. As much as she loves her parents, she realizes that if he'd adopted her, as he'd once considered doing, it wouldn't have been so bad.

Brenna has her phone camera pointed at the closed door to the bear den as Mark begins to yank on the pulley system that draws it open.

As in past years, Grinder is the first bear to poke his nose out of the den. He blinks in the sunlight and looks around at the crowd that has come to witness the end of another hibernation. Then he digs a path through the snow, away from the den. A moment later Coola's head emerges before he too steps through the open door. Both bears are much skinnier versions of their pre-hibernation selves. Moving deeper into the enclosure, Coola begins to dig in the snow with his long claws. Grinder has trundled over to a bank and is rubbing his body vigorously against the snow.

After snapping a few pictures, Brenna immediately emails them to Ryan. *Spring has sprung,* she writes. *The bears have emerged.*

It is April 15, exactly two years to the day since her mother was first diagnosed with breast cancer. So much has happened in those two years, but here on the mountain the reemergence of the grizzly bears has the same feel as it does every year. The crowd cheers, but the bears ignore them and begin sliding down banks and digging tunnels. She smiles as she watches them. Her mother never missed this moment each spring. Just as Justin mentioned at her memorial service, she will have to carry on in her mother's place.

From: ryanfromdownunder@hotmail.com
To: brennayoko@gmail.com

I have found a fourth person for the relay. He'll be there at the start. Don't worry...he'll recognize you and

will do the last leg of the relay—the really steep one!
Have fun!

I love you and miss you!

Ryan

May 24

Is Ryan the 4th person? Would he surprise me like this?
It would be just like him...OMG!! Do I dare hope?

nineteen

Often it is the deepest pain which empowers
you to grow into your highest self.
(KAREN SALMANSOHN, *THE BOUNCE BACK BOOK*)

Brenna gets up before her alarm sounds on the day of the relay. The sun is cresting the horizon while the moon still hovers in the western sky. There are no clouds, but the forecast predicts it won't be too hot. The entire race should be over by noon anyway, so she's not concerned about the heat. It's her stamina she's worried about. She's hardly slept all night. Has Ryan really returned for the relay? Why else wouldn't he have told her who it was that was taking his place? She's afraid to get her hopes up, and yet…

There's a tap on the front door and Brenna lets Georgialee in, then checks to be sure that Naysa is up. She pulls their breakfast out of the fridge, a concoction she made up the night before with oatmeal, milk, yogurt, chia seeds and fruit. Energy food, she tells them.

"I can't believe you talked me into this," Naysa grumbles when she comes into the kitchen. "I am so not a runner."

"You're going to be fine. Walk as much as you need to." Brenna and Naysa have walked and jogged Naysa's leg of the route numerous times in the past month, so she knows her sister can do it. "All that matters is that we finish the race, and Georgialee will probably make up for any lost time anyway."

Georgialee puts her arm around Naysa's shoulders. "You're doing it for your mom, right? Remember that. Oh, and that reminds me." She opens her small backpack and pulls out a bag. "I had these made up, one for each of us."

She reaches into the bag and pulls out four round discs, each about the circumference of a hockey puck, but thinner, with a pin on the back. She hands a disc to each of the girls.

"Oh, Georgia!" Brenna says when she sees the picture of her mom smiling out at her. "Thank you!"

"It's your mom we're doing this for, so I thought it was important that she be with us every step of the way."

Brenna's dad drives them to the start of the race. Naysa will take the first leg, the least steep one, and her dad will drop Brenna off at Cleveland Dam to start the second leg. Georgialee will do the Grind portion, and the mystery person will do the last stretch.

"Are you sure Ryan didn't let either of you know who the mystery teammate is?" Brenna asks the other two yet again as her dad drives through the early-morning light.

She sees them glance at each other and shrug. Their faces don't give anything away.

At Ambleside Park a huge crowd is gathering to cheer on the runners. The girls collect their race numbers and listen to the instructions being announced over a loud-speaker. Brenna scans the crowd, hoping beyond reason to see Ryan but knowing how dumb it is to do that. Georgialee keeps an arm around Naysa.

"Brenna!"

A young man slips through the crowd and stands in front of her. His smile is huge. She recognizes him from the mountain. It's Cole, one of the guys Ryan worked with on maintenance. Her heart plummets.

"You're our fourth teammate?" she asks, the truth sinking in. She can't believe she really thought Ryan would travel to Canada for the event.

"I am," he says. "And don't look so disappointed. You can call me Ryan."

"Huh?"

He tugs on his T-shirt, and that's when Brenna notices the enlarged photo of Ryan printed on the front of it. He's grinning out at her. Cole turns around. On the back of the shirt is the back of Ryan's head. Brenna would know it anywhere.

Cole is clearly delighted with himself. He puts his hands on her shoulders and looks into her eyes. "Ryan told me to tell you that he really wanted to be here, but, obviously, he couldn't be. So he did up this T-shirt to make it look like he's here, because, as he said, he is here in spirit."

Despite her deep disappointment, Brenna smiles back. Only Ryan would go to such trouble. She introduces him to the rest of the team. Georgialee still has her arm around Naysa.

"And he made these T-shirts for you," Cole says, pulling them out of a bag. He holds one up. The front of the T-shirt has a picture of Coola's handsome face, with *Team Bear* printed below it. Cole flips it so they can see the back, which sports a closeup photo of Grinder yawning. His fangs are huge, and if you didn't know better, you'd think he was about to chomp someone's head off. *Bears BITE Breast Cancer* is written across the bottom of the shirt.

"Awesome!" Georgialee quickly pulls hers over her running singlet. Naysa is less impressed, but she takes off her jacket and slips the shirt over her tank top. Brenna does the same.

The race marshal blows on a horn, a five-minute warning until race time. The girls quickly pin their numbers and the picture of Joanna onto the front of the new shirts.

"This is for you," Georgialee says, handing Cole his pin.

"Awesome!" He fastens it to his shirt, over Ryan's left ear. "I'll see you all at the top!" He turns and disappears into the crowd.

"Not bad," Georgialee says under her breath.

Brenna gives her a look. Her disappointment is a dead weight in the pit of her stomach. "Remember, go at your own pace," she tells Naysa one more time.

By noon the entire race is complete. Team Bear gathers in the Grouse Mountain parking lot, where a celebration is taking place. Brenna's dad, who has been handing out water at a checkpoint, joins them. He pulls his daughters into a hug. "I am so proud of you girls."

Naysa, face flushed, eyes shining, smiles up at him. "I'm proud of me too!"

Brenna scans the crowd, looking for Angie, who she knows was also volunteering somewhere along the race course. Georgialee and Cole are sharing a joke, and Brenna can see that her friend is in full-on flirt mode. Catching her eye, Cole approaches her. He pulls off his T-shirt, holds it to his nose and then hands it to her. "For you," he says. "Though you may want to wash it before you wear it."

Brenna takes it, holds it up to study the photo and then brings it to her face and kisses the photo of Ryan right on the mouth. "Oh you," she says.

"Oh, I almost forgot." Cole pulls Brenna into a tight hug. His skin is damp, his body hard. She suddenly longs for Ryan's body. Cole holds her for a moment and then releases her. "That was from Ryan too."

"Thanks," she whispers.

The mood at the celebration is exuberant. A small band is playing in one corner of the parking lot, and smoke from a barbecue wafts over the crowd. Cole grabs Georgialee's hand and pulls her over to join a bunch of participants who are dancing to the music. Naysa, who has consumed a lot of water, heads to the washroom.

Scanning the crowd again, Brenna spots Angie close to where the Skyride docks. She waves to her. Angie smiles and waves back. She begins to weave her way through the mob toward Brenna. An older couple follows her, at a short distance behind.

"Congratulations, Brenna, you did it!" Angie wraps her arms around her.

Even while she is being hugged, Brenna can see that the older people, who are standing back a short ways, are studying her closely. Could it be? The man is Caucasian, and the woman is Asian.

"My parents are here," Angie whispers in Brenna's ear. "They'd like to meet you if you're okay with that."

Brenna nods, and Angie steps aside so that there is now no one between Brenna and the couple. The sound of the crowd and the music fade away, and Brenna looks from one to the other. The woman's eyes are glistening. The man has his arm around her.

"Brenna," Angie says softly, "these are my parents."

Brenna doesn't respond, but continues to look from one to the other. They, too, seem beyond words.

After a few moments Brenna's dad, who had moved away to speak to friends, returns to Brenna's side. He looks at his daughter and then at the couple she is staring at.

Angie is the first to speak. "Brett, these are my parents, Anthony and Marcia Hazelwood."

"Oh. Right." Brenna's dad also takes a moment to comprehend. Eventually he extends his hand, first to the woman and then to the man. "We met once in the hospital. Sixteen years ago. Nice to see you again. I'm sorry. I'm just completely surprised." He turns to Angie. "You didn't mention you were bringing your parents."

"I didn't know until this morning."

"We didn't know Angie had connected with Brenna," Angie's father says. "And then it all came out last night when we met her for dinner. We were kind of…kind of shocked to hear what Angie has been doing, but by this morning we'd gotten used to the idea, and, well…"

"We wanted to come and cheer Brenna on," Angie's mom says, helping her husband out. "And we made a donation online to your team," she adds.

"Thank you," Brenna says, still numb with shock.

Through the loudspeaker the event MC's voice booms. "Could I have everyone's attention for a few minutes?

There are a few people we need to thank and recognize. People who made this fantastic event possible."

Georgialee and Cole join the group again, and they all turn to face the stage, but Brenna's mind is elsewhere. She has just met Kia's parents, her biological grandparents, her flesh and blood. She struggles to wrap her head around that.

The MC thanks the sponsors and recognizes the teams who have raised the most money in donations. Brenna's mind eventually returns to the event.

"Seek the Peak is a grueling race, yet it is a walk in the park compared with the battle that those with breast cancer face. And it has been brought to my attention," he says, "in an email from a former Grouse Mountain employee—" he checks his notes "—Ryan Kirkwood, that Team Bear has raised money for a very special woman who had to fight that battle and who also once worked on this mountain. Team Bear, can you raise your hands and make some noise so we can see you?"

Cole and Georgialee already have their hands in the air and are cheering madly. Naysa looks at Brenna, and they raise theirs as well.

"Ah, there you are!" the MC says. "And not only did Team Bear raise a lot of money in memory of Joanna Yokoyama, but on their team is the youngest participant in today's event. Naysa Yokoyama, we have a special medal of achievement for you. Will you come up to the stage to receive this recognition, please."

Naysa glances at Brenna before Georgialee gives her a shove toward the stage. With her eyes lowered, she makes her way through the crowd and up to the platform. The MC puts the medal around her neck and turns her so she is facing the crowd. "Your mother would be very proud of you today, Naysa," he says. "And with the help of the money we have raised, we expect that a cure will soon be found for breast cancer, so that no one else has to pay the ultimate price as your mother did. Maybe this will be the first of many fundraisers you'll participate in. As you know, your own life becomes richer when you work to make a difference."

A huge cheer goes up as the MC shakes Naysa's hand. Smiling, she returns to the place where the rest of the team is waiting. Angie hugs her, and her dad puts his arm around her shoulders while wiping his eyes with his other hand.

Brenna takes a deep breath and looks at the faces of the people assembled at the large round table at Wo's Chinese Restaurant. Team Bear is there, as are her father, Angie, Angie's parents and Justin, who joined them after his Sunday service. The server is dropping off plate after plate of food at the table. Everyone is chatting. Georgialee and Cole are oblivious to anyone else at the table, Angie and Naysa are deep in conversation, and her father and

Angie's parents are listening carefully to something Justin is telling them.

Once again Brenna is feeling her mother's absence, but, unlike at her sixteenth-birthday party, she's also keenly aware that they are assembled here because of her mother and what her life meant to them. She is also aware of Ryan's absence, especially because it was Ryan who had talked her into participating in this event in the first place. She hands her phone to the server and asks him to take a candid photo of the group that she can send to Ryan later.

Justin catches Brenna's eyes across the table. He smiles at her, then stands up and gently taps his water glass with his knife to get the attention of everyone at the table.

"I have a bad habit of turning almost every occasion into a small ceremony," he says once everyone is listening, "but I think today's gathering truly warrants one. Please bear with me for just a few moments."

One by one, he looks at each person sitting at the table.

"The word that comes to me today," he says, "as I look at each of you, is *connection*. Each of us is connecting in a different way, but at the root of all these old and new connections today is Joanna, who is the reason for us gathering and connecting like this. She is no longer with us in the physical world, but her spirit is truly alive and well, as we can feel from the energy around this table."

"A toast to Joanna," Cole says, raising his water glass. Everyone joins him, and they all clink glasses with each other.

"Joanna would be so proud of her daughters," Justin continues once everyone is quiet again. "Grief often steals all our energy, making it difficult to even function day to day, but her daughters have worked hard to get in shape for this grueling race and have raised a lot of money for breast cancer research. Joanna's untimely death has not ended the contribution she continues to make in life, but now it comes in the form of her daughters' actions."

Justin sits back down. "Does anyone else want to say anything?"

After a moment Brenna clears her throat. "I just want to say that one of the things I'll always remember about my mom is that she fought her cancer without ever complaining, and she even kept smiling to the very end. She also shared her beautiful self with so many people, and it was one of those people, Ryan, who encouraged me to pull this team together. I now know exactly what you meant, Justin, when you said at her service that her spirit is indomitable and that it would live on." Her voice cracks. "It really has."

Her dad places his arm around his daughter while she wipes her eyes.

Angie's father stands up next. "Marcia and I feel like we've crashed your party today. After all, we didn't know most of you before this morning, but I really appreciate that you've welcomed us to this event and to this lunch. It is great to see firsthand that Brenna's family has been so loving, and she's been well taken care of." He looks directly at Brenna. "We have always wondered how your life was turning out," he says, "and although we're terribly sorry that your mother passed away, we can see that you are a remarkable young lady. Joanna, and Brett, of course, have raised you well. This brings us great peace of mind." He looks at Angie and then Justin. "Thank you for helping us reconnect with this lovely young woman, her family and her friends."

Cole stands up next. He's found another T-shirt, and Brenna notices he's fastened the pin of Joanna to the front. He holds up his water glass. "And this is a toast to my buddy Ryan. Thanks to him, I was able to race with you today and meet some really cool people." He smiles at Georgialee. "To Ryan!" he says and guzzles his glass of water.

Yes, Brenna thinks to herself. To Ryan. She also gulps down her entire glass of water.

Brenna's dad clears his throat. "Thanks, Justin, for reminding us of how we remain connected, even after death." He turns and looks directly at Cole. "And if Ryan were here," he says, "I can assure you that there'd be no food left on this table. But there is. So unless anyone else has anything to say…in honor of Ryan, let's eat."

Brenna checks her personal page on the Seek the Peak website. The total amount that Team Bear raised has far exceeded her goal. Her mom's friends all donated gener-ously, and Kia's parents, the last to donate, matched what she had already raised.

All the hikes. All that pain. It was worth it.

From: brennayoko@gmail.com
To: ryanfromdownunder@hotmail.com

Dear Ryan,

You really were with us in spirit today. We all felt it. Cole was great too, and, of course, I LOVED his T-shirt. He gave it to me, and I think it will now be my go-to pajama top. That way I can sleep with you every night.

Love you and miss you.

May 26

I used to worry it was inappropriate that Ryan and I got together BECAUSE MY MOM DIED, but today Justin made me think about it differently when he talked about connections. Maybe I can see this as Mom's parting gift to me. It sounds like she really liked Ryan, and, obviously, she loved me. Her death connected us. I think she would have approved.

Thank you, Mom.

twenty

When you come out of the storm you won't be the same person
who walked in. That's what this storm's all about.
(HARUKI MURAKAMI, *KAFKA ON THE SHORE*)

It's the first anniversary of Joanna's death. Her sisters, Laura and Tamara, are in the master bedroom, packing her clothes into boxes. Naysa is with them, pulling the items back out as fast as they go in. She's making her own pile of Joanna's things that she intends to keep. Brenna watches, heavyhearted, from the doorway. Her dad has gone for a walk, not able to take part in the packing up.

Laura sighs. She sits on the edge of the bed and pats the space beside her. "Come here, Naysa," she says.

Naysa drops a sweater onto the pile and then sits beside her aunt. Tamara leans against the chest of drawers, her arms crossed.

"You know you're not going to wear all those things, Naysa."

Naysa shrugs. Brenna hasn't seen her look so miserable in weeks. She's having trouble holding it together herself. The weeks leading up to this day have been extra painful.

Laura looks from Naysa to Brenna and then to Tamara. "I have an idea. Why don't each of us choose one of Joanna's scarves to keep forever. Each time we wrap the scarf around our shoulders we can think of it as Joanna wrapping her arms around us. Everything else we'll pack up and give away. Someone who really needs clothes will be so happy to get them." She puts an arm around Naysa and squeezes her in. "Your mom would like that."

Brenna crosses the room and joins them on the bed, sitting cross-legged. Tamara follows suit. "I think it's a good plan," Brenna says. "And I'm going to spray a bit of her perfume on the scarf I choose."

Laura nods. "What about you, Tamara?"

"Yeah. I agree. We have lots of pictures and memories. Keeping her stuff won't bring her back."

"Naysa?" Laura asks gently.

The tears are streaming down Naysa's cheeks. She turns and buries her face in her aunt's chest, but Brenna can see that she's nodding.

Tamara gets up and begins to lay all of Joanna's scarves out along the bed. "Girls, you choose first."

Brenna selects a long, intricately woven wool scarf with dangling tassels. "Do you want this one, Nayse?"

Naysa shakes her head.

"Okay, then I'll take it and wear it on the cold days on the mountain." She wraps it around her neck and glances at herself in the mirror.

Reluctantly Naysa climbs off the bed too. She reaches down and chooses a brightly colored silk scarf. "This one reminds me of Mom," she says. "It's so pretty."

Brenna takes it from her and shows her a new way to twist it, and then puts it around Naysa's neck. Naysa looks at herself in the mirror. She smiles sadly.

Both aunts choose scarves and wrap them around their necks, despite the heat of the day. Then together they pack the rest of Joanna's clothes into boxes and load them into the trunk of Laura's car. Brenna's dad arrives home just as her aunts are pulling away from the curb. Brenna, Naysa and their dad watch them drive down the street.

In the kitchen the box of pizza sits on the table. There is a stack of DVDs on the counter, all borrowed from the library.

"I found as many of your mom's favorite movies as I could," her dad says. "And it's Friday night. How about a movie-and-pizza marathon? I think your mom would have loved that."

Brenna takes plates out of the cupboard while Naysa flips through the DVDs. "This one first," Naysa says, holding up Disney Nature's *Bears*.

"A documentary?" her dad asks.

"It's the one Mom would have chosen first," she says.

Her dad takes it from her and plugs it into the player in the family room. The three of them sit shoulder to shoulder on the couch, their dad in the middle, the girls wearing their scarves. Plates of pizza sit on their laps.

As the movie begins Brenna remembers how her cousin Danika had said that it would be the first occasions after her mom's death that would be the hardest. Although she resented the remarks at the time, she suspects that Danika was right. Today is the last of the firsts. They have made it through Christmas, Mother's Day, Easter, birthdays. With her newfound circle of support, and her mom's indomitable spirit to keep them all going, she knows they will get through the second year too.

Dear Kia,

On my 16th birthday my mom (who has now passed away) gave me the journal you kept when you were pregnant with me. You wrote me a letter at the end of your journal, and now I feel I want to write you a letter in return, almost seventeen years later, so you can see how the choices you made ended up being good ones—for me, anyway.

Thank you for giving me the journal. At first it felt really weird to read about myself before I was even born, but I came to know you as a 16-year-old girl and really felt how much you loved me.

Thank you, too, for selecting Mom and Dad for me. They turned out to be great parents. Even though Mom has died, I realize how much I've come to be like her. We both love the

outdoors and animals, especially wild animals! Every day I
work to be as kind and compassionate as she was.

You are still my biological mother, though, and even if we
never meet again, I am still learning from you. I sense that you
and I are a lot alike too. Keeping a journal has helped me vent—
just like you did in yours. And from your sister and Justin I've
learned that you are passionate about working with children.
Being in nature and around animals is what makes me happy.

The pain of losing my mom still feels fresh in many ways.
I'm planning to keep her spirit alive by continuing to raise
funds for breast cancer research. Maybe that will mean her
life didn't end too soon for nothing. I might even go into medicine someday and continue the work to find a cure. If not that,
I'll work at preserving the planet so that the wild animals we
both loved will be able to thrive. In this way you and I are the
same. We want to do work that matters to us.

Anyway, thanks again for giving me the journal. I imagine
it will bring back some memories for you. But knowing that it all
turned out well for me will, I hope, bring you some happiness.

Love,

Brenna

Brenna puts down her pen and reads what she has
written. It will have to do. She picks up Kia's journal and
runs her hand over its rough surface one last time. She
folds the letter, tucks it into the journal and puts that into
a large envelope. She prints *Kia* on the front. Angie has
promised to keep it until she feels Kia is ready for it.

From: brennayoko@gmail.com
To: ryanfromdownunder@hotmail.com

I did it! Got my driver's license! I'm a big girl now! LOL.

And guess what. The countdown has started. In less than one year I will be winging my way to Borneo to meet Cinta. When I get sick and tired of the dog hikes, I remind myself of why I'm doing them and it helps. You won't recognize me, I'll be in such great shape. ☺ Which reminds me— you already wouldn't recognize Naysa. She's grown about a foot—she's taller than me—and the yoga has been really good for her. I don't think I made a hiker out of her, but she's talking about taking some dance classes to stay in shape. I think that would be good—dancing is such a joyful thing to do. Who couldn't use a little more joy in their lives? Despite some rough patches, she seems to be doing okay.

Big news! Justin is getting what he wished for. Kia has announced that she is marrying her British doctor, and Justin will conduct a service when they come home at Christmas. I don't know if Angie will give her my letter or even tell her about how we connected. Anyway, it doesn't really matter. Justin was right—I felt better just writing a letter to her.

Love you and miss you.

Brenna

PS. The bears miss you too.

PPS. Can't wait to meet the koala bears.

acknowledgments

Heartfelt appreciation to my first readers and cheer-leaders: Kim Denman, Diane Tullson, Beryl Young and Linda Irvine. Thanks also to Shannon Kirkwood for her Aussie-isms, friendship and for wielding the shovel while I held the bag. To the wildlife team of Grouse Mountain— thank you for including me in the fold. Your knowledge and passion for the animals in your care are inspiring.

Orca Book Publishers is a collection of true professionals and the nicest, most approachable people in the business. I know how blessed I am to have another book published by them.

Finally, a huge thank-you to all those readers of *Dancing Naked* who begged for more. This is for you.

The memorial service in chapter 1 was inspired by the Unitarian Church. The poem on page 2 was written by Mary Elizabeth Frye, and the reading on page 3 was written by Christine Robinson (Reading #454, from *Singing the Living Tradition*, Unitarian Universalist Association hymn book).

SHELLEY HRDLITSCHKA discovered her love for children's literature when she was teaching school and is the author of numerous novels for teens, all published by Orca Book Publishers. She lives in North Vancouver, British Columbia. When she's not writing, she can be found hiking, snowshoeing, practicing yoga, Zumba dancing or volunteering at the Grouse Mountain Refuge for Endangered Wildlife. For more information, visit www.shelleyhrdlitschka.wordpress.com.